Oblivion

Barry Grills

Books by Barry Grills

Non Fiction:
Snowbird (Quarry Press)
Ironic (Quarry Press)
Falling Into You (Quarry Press)
A New Day Dawns (with Jim Brown) (Quarry Press)
Every Wolf's Howl (Freehand Books)

Fiction:
Roadkill (Fluid Grouse Enterprises)
I And You, And Me And Her (Fluid Grouse Enterprises)
Oblivion (Fluid Grouse Enterprises)

Oblivion

Barry Grills

FLUID
GROUSE
enterprises

Library and Archives Canada Cataloguing in Publication

Grills, Barry, 1948-, author   Oblivion / Barry Grills

Cover Design: Jennifer Rouse Barbeau

Author photo: Liz Lott

ISBN:
978-1-7751389-2-1

For my sons, David and Richard

CHAPTERS

ACKNOWLEDGMENTS

Oblivion owes a great deal of its completion to peers, organizations and people with helpful opinions. First of all, I gratefully acknowledge the Ontario Arts Council and the Canada Council for subsistence grants permitting me to write this novel. I want to thank Samantha Haywood and Stephanie Sinclair for their helpful observations about earlier drafts of this story. Finally, I wish to thank my partner, Jennifer Rouse Barbeau, for so many fine things, including this enterprise and our marriage, but also for her fine and sensitive editing. I thank her too for the fine artwork on the cover.

ONTARIO ARTS COUNCIL
CONSEIL DES ARTS DE L'ONTARIO
an Ontario government agency
un organisme du gouvernement de l'Ontario

Canada Council   Conseil des arts
for the Arts   du Canada

We acknowledge funding support from the Ontario Arts Council, an agency of the Government of Ontario.

We acknowledge the support of the Canada Council for the Arts. Nous remercions le Conseil des arts du Canada de son soutien.

Bees build societies, ants wage wars, hamsters amass riches
—Hermann Hesse

True triumph is triumph without glory—Derek Cavanaugh, just sayin', one February day while panhandling a few hundred feet from a Starbucks on a street corner in a major city

THEN

IN THE *REAL* WORLD, as Richard Braddock would much later recall it, spring came early that year. The city's palette turned from white, to sooty gray, then brown in a mere couple of days. Soiled wrappers, napkins, and cartons emerged rotting in the gutters. Mud, sand and salt griped under newly sandaled feet. People sniffed at that curious stench of tainted soil that characterizes a Canadian spring, regardless of how early it arrives. No one minded the odor much—spring showing up ahead of schedule in mid-March was too much cause for celebration. Young women and young men shed clothing and donned a curious swagger, different from one another but the same, demonstrating their chop, their mojo. Some took selfies of their new freedom, to capture images of this early spring and the roles they were playing inside it.

That March too, in the *real* world, Venus and Jupiter shared the same immediate sector of night-time sky. Some Sagittarians—Richard was a Sagittarian—viewed the sight ambivalently, as if these two planets appearing side by side in their astrological house would doom any new initiative to failure. Others were hopeful about success. Ambivalence remained the usual either/or that we know to be astrology.

Sometimes during this period of extraordinary heat the early morning hours filled up with rain. There was even a rare mid-March thunderstorm one night, lightning flickering like rocket fire against the layered cloud banks forming to the south beyond the city's tallest buildings.

Richard Braddock's slumber the night of the thunderstorm included a dream about his failed attempt to save three of his children—all of them very young and small again in the dream—from a powerful undertow along an unfamiliar stretch of ocean shore. Richard's dilemma was this: he could save any two of his children from drowning but the third eluded his grasp. In the end, wrestling futilely with tiny childlike bodies, he felt punished by the dream's apparent preoccupation with choice. Some cold, nagging, omnipresent voice, not quite godlike, but large, deep and reverberatory, kept asking him to make up his mind. The voice, as tired in tone as it was tiresome, addressed him by name. "Stop dithering, Richard," it demanded. But Richard was too frantic to save *all* of his children. How could he select which child to give up to the violent surf? He hadn't read *Sophie's Choice* but he'd seen the movie. Sophie's dilemma was old news now, right? What was he doing dreaming a version of it tonight? Then, just before Richard's dream woke him up with a pounding heart, the waves receded and the powerful undertow dissipated, allowing him to wrap his arms around all three of his progeny and pull them to safety. Released from the dream's clutches, he drifted gradually back into comfortable slumber, although, in the distance, he was aware of a trickle of sweat on the back of his neck that soiled his pillowcase.

MARCH CONTINUED BUT ITS UNUSUAL WARMTH did not. On the last Monday in the month, the temperature dipped below freezing point again and a malicious wind came up. People now shivered on the same streets that had warmed them only days before. Richard buttoned his topcoat on his way out the revolving door of his building—Cascade Enterprises—headed for the Starbucks located a hundred yards away at the corner of the street. It was brilliantly sunny despite the cold and Richard squinted because it was early in the morning and the sun, low in the sky and newly abetted by Daylight Savings Time, angled blindingly down the avenue towards him like some cosmic flashlight beam.

As he approached Starbucks he noticed a panhandler on the corner, backlit by the sun. The panhandler's cap was positioned upside down on the sidewalk in front of him, soliciting donations, yet nearly invisible in the wash of the sun's glare. Vaguely Richard was aware he'd seen and ignored this panhandler on other mornings when he walked this particular section of sidewalk, but today it was disquieting for him to suddenly realize—out of the blue—that he knew this man by name. Richard's astonishment grew as he realized the panhandler sitting on a piece of cardboard, his back against the black and gold-flecked marble wall of Cascade Enterprises, his hat soliciting favors in front of him, had once been a close friend. Recognizing this fact, Richard felt a deep shame in the area around his heart, the sensation so sharp and hot, it was like being startled when someone unexpectedly leaps out at you from behind a door, trying to frighten you.

Richard was briefly tempted to hurry by—afraid or embarrassed or some combination of the two—the heat around his heart, the rush of surprise, gradually beginning to evaporate. But instead he circled the panhandler to get a better view of the man's face, wanting to be sure he was the former friend he thought he was.

"Derek?" he said. "Derek Cavanaugh? My god, can it be you?"

Derek seemed at first to not want to acknowledge him. He looked rough—scraggly beard, a smudge on his cheek. While he had always been half a foot taller than Richard, today he looked diminished somehow, bent

3

over, even misshapen. Richard could only conclude he was shrunken by the way he sat cross-legged on the sidewalk. Or maybe Derek too felt a significant embarrassment that they were meeting this way after such a long time apart.

"Richard Braddock," Derek said at last, in a flat monotone, as if he'd been expecting Richard to show up all along and was almost disappointed he finally had.

Crazy, Richard thought. Just crazy. It had been years and years!

For a long, awkward moment, the two men gazed at one another in silence. On the fringes of their mutual scrutiny, a passing woman bent down in front of Derek, her fingers releasing coins. Out of reflex, Richard moved away a little as if he didn't belong this close to the primal intimacy of someone else's financial exchange. There was a muffled clink of metal against the fabric of Derek's hat. Derek said thank you and told her to have a nice day.

"Jesus, Derek," Richard said, "how long have you been in trouble?"

Yet he could see for himself that it had been a reasonably long time. Derek's clothes were tattered and grubby, his gloves had holes in them. His coat leaked stuffing from a split seam at the shoulder. More tellingly, he looked comfortable in this location on his weathered piece of cardboard, like he knew what he was doing here and had been aware of it for a very long time.

"I'm okay," said Derek. "I'm a lot more okay than I look."

While his friend sounded certain of this, Richard didn't believe him. Richard earned nearly four hundred thousand dollars a year at Cascade Enterprises, including bonuses and options. He was not going to believe a street corner panhandler—even a former friend—when the panhandler tried to persuade him that he was okay.

"It's been a long time," Derek was saying, his voice rising to carry over the hubbub of the street.

"I make it around twenty years, a little less maybe," Richard admitted.

"Do you want to go inside? I'm headed for Starbucks. We could have coffee. I could buy you something to eat."

But Derek shook his head and raised a hand, warding Richard off. "I'm having a decent morning. I don't want to move right now."

As if to bear him out, another woman donated to his hat, then a man not far behind her did so too. Richard heard the clinking of the coins, even over the traffic noise. The sound of the coins only added to how ethereal this moment in time felt to him. Derek Cavanaugh panhandling on the street— how could this be?

"How long has this been going on?" Richard asked shortly.

"Long enough, I guess," replied Derek.

"Are you homeless? Do you have a place to stay?"

Derek didn't answer.

Richard felt stupid for asking. *Of course* he was homeless. You didn't sit out here on the street if you weren't, did you? "You could stay with me and my family," he suggested. "You know, until you get back on your feet." It was cold here on the street corner. There was a wind. The cold and the wind injected urgency into Richard's need to rescue his friend.

"Not necessary," Derek said. "Everything's okay."

"How can it be okay? I mean, here you are. You're on the street."

"That's quite true. I'm on the street. It could be that the street is where I belong."

"How long?" asked Richard, repeating the question.

"A long time now."

"But you're a lawyer, aren't you? Last time I heard, you'd become a lawyer."

Derek smiled ever so slightly. "Guilty as charged," he said.

Richard stood there looking at his friend, resisting an ill-defined, yet powerful temptation to reach down, grab him by the scruff of the neck, and drag him down the sidewalk in the general direction of good sense, better judgment, and improved circumstances. Because enough was enough. Like Derek's act of being here was stubborn and willful, motivated by some ill-advised principle no one else in the world would ever have understood. Like this act of begging and homelessness was malicious and betrayed not just the beggar, but former friends as well, who were unprepared for it and clearly knew what was wrong with it.

"What happened, Derek?" Richard asked after a moment.

"A long story."

"Look," said Richard in annoyance. "I want to help. We used to be good friends. I had no idea that this had happened to you. We can work together to get you back on your feet. This can end right now, man."

Derek ignored his words. "How's Alex?" he asked instead.

"She's fine," Richard replied impatiently. "Jesus." He was going to tell Derek something to the effect that Alex would want him to stay with them too, but in the end he kept silent: he felt suddenly cautious now that his wife had been brought into the conversation. In truth, he wasn't sure what Alex would or wouldn't want in a situation such as this. Her image hovered over them here on the street; a homeless former friend wasn't something for which he and his wife had planned, although sometimes it seemed they planned endlessly for everything else.

"Kids?" asked Derek.

"Fine. They're fine."

"Grown up, right?"

"Nearly," said Richard. "Teenagers. I don't suppose you . . ."

". . . Gone," offered Derek without dismay.

"Whaddyuh mean, gone?"

"Gone. Just gone."

"You mean, passed away or something?"

"Not dead. Gone."

"Your whole family?"

"Yes. It's what happens sometimes."

"Well, where are they?"

"Safe and happy, I hope, their choices made. That's the way I imagined—imagine—them."

"Imagined them? You mean they left you?" Richard said, frustrated by his former friend's obtuseness.

Derek didn't respond.

Having reached the end of the blind alley about Derek's family, Richard sighed, nodding vaguely. "But what happened to you?"

Derek thought about this a moment. "Different choices, I guess," he said at last.

"You mean booze? Drugs? Jail?" Here, Richard hesitated. "Mental illness?" he added after a moment, wishing he could come up with a more euphemistic phrase.

"None of the above," said Derek. "Can we stop with the interrogation now? I'm not a drug addict, I'm not a drunk, I don't have a criminal record, and I don't feel particularly crazy."

"I just want to help."

"I know. But all of these questions sound aggressive to me, judgmental. You know?"

"You don't want to talk about it, right?"

"Not right now."

"I just want to help," Richard said, needing to stress the point, feeling defeated by Derek's intransigence. Richard felt inept, inadequate. What to do? What to suggest? Only nine o'clock and his morning was going for a shit already. "Stop dithering, Richard," he suddenly remembered the voice saying in his recent dream where he'd saved his children from drowning.

"I could use a large Colombian, black, on your way back to the office," Derek said then, gazing up at him, squinting in the sunshine, rescuing Richard from his helplessness.

"You want some food with that?"

"No thanks."

"You sure?"

"I'm sure. Heavy breakfast." And Derek rubbed his belly with his right hand in a parody of gastronomic satisfaction.

"Okay," said Richard. "I'll be right back."

When he returned, he was surprised to see that Derek was still in the same place on the street. While lined up in Starbucks for Derek's coffee and a cappuccino for himself, he'd become convinced to a certain extent that Derek had been an apparition of some kind, that when he went back to the spot on the corner where they'd met a few minutes ago, his former friend would be gone, replaced by someone else, someone he didn't know after all. It would all be clearly some kind of mistake. Because now that he thought about it, he'd been passing the same man for several months without knowing it was Derek. Why he could recognize his old high school friend today—and had not those other times—was a disconcerting mystery to him. No confusion there; Derek was very tall. Derek was the man he'd been seeing—not seeing?—for months. Derek had always been noticeable. So why now, why *today*?

"You're here most days," Richard said almost accusingly, as he leaned down to hand Derek his coffee.

"Most days," Derek admitted.

"And you didn't acknowledge me, didn't try to get my attention?"

"You're usually in quite a hurry," Derek said. "You're often not alone. You've never looked at me before today—too much on your mind, I guess. It seemed better to wait until you recognized *me*."

Richard nodded, supposing Derek was right. "Still . . ." he said.

"Choices," said Derek. "It's all about choosing."

"Choosing?"

"What we do, what we want, what we look at, what we actually see. That's life, isn't it?"

Richard said nothing. His friend's words felt irritatingly esoteric to him. He imagined Derek and a group of homeless friends chanting a mantra together about choice and freedom, the mission statement of a cult of disenfranchised victims who believed there was nobility in associating together as drop-outs. Would he be able to help Derek if Derek turned out to be proud of being a drop-out? He frankly didn't know.

"You look prosperous. What do you do?" Derek asked. "What's your job title?"

"Vice-president of . . ." And Richard hesitated. To his chagrin, the nature of the work he did all day chose this moment to elude him. Like he was thinking too much and, in thinking too much, couldn't come up with what he normally revealed by rote.

". . . Marketing, I'd say," Derek answered for him, plainly amused by his friend's hesitation.

"Yes. Marketing." It was true, Richard knew. "And communications. I'm sorry. You being here and not wanting my help is mind-boggling. My brain is mush. Just for a second there . . . Yes, I'm VP of communications marketing."

"Glad to hear it," Derek said. "As long as you're happy."

Richard shrugged. Happy? The word sounded strange to him. No one talked about being happy anymore; it never came up in conversation, not even with intimates. It was a quaint, but complicated concept—there was too much else in life to worry about. Happy? No one had a definition for happiness unless they were trying to sell it to you in the form of some kind of product or service. Richard knew this better than anyone—he was in the business of defining what happiness should be. In his mind's eye, he imagined a TV commercial, the sugary voice of a narrator: "Happiness, crafted with Joy Technology," the narrator promised.

"Thanks for the coffee, Richie," Derek said, dismissing him as the awkward silence dragged on.

Richie? No one had called him that in years. But Richard nodded in acknowledgment. He'd found a ten-dollar bill in his pocket. He picked this moment to bend and put it in Derek's ball cap.

"Thank you," Derek said.

"I don't carry much cash," Richard told him.

"It's the way of the world," said Derek. "People like me should accept e-transfers."

Both men smiled grimly at the absurdity of this notion.

Richard glanced at his watch. "You gonna be here tomorrow? I have a meeting a few minutes from now. Busy day. Squash game too." Suddenly everything Richard said sounded banal to him. What would Derek make of the vacuity in his words, considering the contrast they represented with his own harsh circumstances?

"I'll be here," Derek was saying. "Tomorrow and the next day and the next."

"This isn't the end of it, Derek."

"I know."

"We've been good friends."

"I know."

"I guess I'll see you then."

"I guess you will."

"I'm sorry about all of this, Derek," Richard said.

"It's okay. Really. Life is about rolling with the punches and making decisions. Choices. You know?"

"Choices," Richard said, finding the word and Derek's continued use of it nebulous and irritating.

"Choices," Derek echoed, making it even worse.

Richard reached down and gently squeezed his friend's shoulder. Derek, he was pleased to see, didn't flinch. Tomorrow, Richard decided, he would bring another ten dollars to show Derek he meant business about getting him off the street. And the day *after* tomorrow. And the day after *that*. And some day soon, he'd have Derek back on his feet again. Ten dollars a day until Derek got used to having money again. Then they'd take it from there. They'd work out what particular self, which particular demon, Derek needed rescuing from.

THE MEETING ROOM AT CASCADE ENTERPRISES bedazzled itself in the sun, on a corner on the nineteenth floor of the firm's tall building. Gathering here was like meeting on Mount Olympus. Sometimes people wore dark glasses, the sun was so powerful here, despite the tinted windows. Amanda Drew, the CEO here, *always* wore sunglasses for meetings in this room, even when the sky was overcast. She'd told Richard she felt more powerful in sunglasses, because people weren't able to see what she was thinking. Although he tried to prevent it, each time she said so, he thought of her as a character in *The Matrix*. Or playing poker on the sports channel. Or standing around some fat guy's pool in an extremely skimpy bikini.

"And they make me pretty fucking sexy. Right?" she said.

At the time, knowing it was expected of him, he admitted this was so. She *was* sexy, *everyone* thought so, he told her. Especially for her age, although he didn't add *that* part. The woman was over forty. No question she looked good with that chronological milestone behind her. But you didn't mention Amanda's age or aging, not even in a general sense, not even as a compliment.

No way.

Besides, today Richard was preoccupied with the memory of finding Derek Cavanaugh on the street. Dutiful declarations to Amanda about how sexy she was—an expectation begun three years ago, or four, or five, whenever the hell it had been—paled in significance to the shock of finding Derek homeless, begging for change. Richard's architectural sense of direction wasn't any good either. If it had been, he would have known at this moment that Derek Cavanaugh's location on the corner of the street was several hundred feet directly below this meeting room. But . . .

. . . *Everything just lives here*, Richard thought suddenly, for no apparent reason.

Everything just lives here.

He sighed, aware his mind had conjured something the rest of his brain didn't understand. He didn't like it when he couldn't explain to himself what he was thinking or why he was thinking it.

The meeting this morning was about—Richard surreptitiously checked his notes—digital wallets. Jesus, what was the matter with him? Couldn't he remember the topic of a meeting anymore? Digital wallets, a product still many months away, at least in North America. He wondered if he was having a stroke, or if his confusion today was the early onset of senility. No, it was finding Derek on the street. He was angry about Derek and many other things at this moment. Why didn't they buy drapes for this supernova of a meeting room, for instance? Sitting here behind dark glasses like some bloody movie gangster . . .

Leonard Chan, Vice-president of Consumer Relations, had the floor. He was talking about how the older demographic, the baby boomers, would resist digital wallets as a product. "They still like cash. They even miss the penny . . ." Here, there was the hint of what passed for a Leonard Chan smile. "They've been writing cheques for decades. They don't want another device you tap on the counter or wave in front of a scanner. They fear loss of privacy. Some even fear conspiracy, you know, the bank is out to get them and rigs their digital wallet not to work. They even worry that most technology is designed to spy on them. They'll resist. They see cash as a fundamental component of basic freedom. The baby boomers are a hard sell. The first cohort, at least."

"The first cohort?" someone asked.

"Yeah," said Leonard. "The hippies."

"I thought all baby boomers were hippies."

"No, just the first cohort. The second cohort were yuppies."

Silence. No one really cared about Leonard's sociological research. Yuppies, hippies, old farts. A baby boomer was a baby boomer, namely a strangely confident flake who was traditionally a difficult market to reach. Richard knew their resistance to digital wallets would be minimal compared to their outrage over facial recognition software. What would they do then, when they knew cameras everywhere took their picture to dig into their private database, financial and otherwise? And someday it would come out even more flagrantly than it had already that the government was spying on them electronically. The boomers would scream blue murder, wouldn't they? Richard thought so, privately anyway. Then again, didn't anyone know how to complain about ill treatment in the new millennium? To Richard, it didn't seem like it.

"A dying demographic," said Amanda pragmatically, apparently not realizing that she'd only missed by half a generation being a baby boomer herself. "Someday soon we won't have to talk about what baby boomers think, *whatever* cohort they belong to." She turned to Richard. "Can we deal with this baby boomer thing and the concept of a digital wallet?"

"We can head it off," said Richard. "An ad campaign showing boomers *loving* the digital wallet. As long as we anticipate their reaction ahead of time, we can control it. The strategy with baby boomers is to simply wear them down or make them feel alienated by their resistance to change. And, of course, we'll make them look young, you know, well-preserved for their age, the ones who approve of the product. The usual, I guess. Younger looks, a younger appearance, through compliant acquiescence."

"Excellent," said Amanda.

Richard remembered Derek again. When he had asked Richard his title, prompting him with vice-president, Richard should have said: Vice-president of Head-It-Off. That's what he did these days—he headed things off. The Derek of old would have laughed at his words. In the old days, they would have laughed *together* at an admission like that. VP of Spin, he supposed. These days, as long as you could invent reality, there was a good living to be made in communications marketing.

Richard glanced at his watch. There was a great deal of Monday still remaining and, at this moment, he wasn't exactly sure what he was required to do with it, beyond his game of squash and a meeting this afternoon with his financial planner. This business with Derek on the street had put him off his stroke. He felt like he was someone else at the moment, possessed by another version of his being. Like he was dreaming. Like he was only imagining himself here in this room in what should have been merely a typical day.

LATER, AS THE MEETING WAS BREAKING UP, Amanda asked Richard to remain behind. Almost on principle, her request caused him to feel mildly apprehensive. Conditioned reflex. Apprehension was now so prevalent in Richard's working life, he felt it had become part of his DNA. And sometimes apprehension sweated from the pores of the building's walls. It was like a virus; everyone came down with it. Everyone endured its frequent relapses. There were some who maintained that apprehension was stress and stress was motivational, and motivation was a good thing. As a commercial communicator, though, Richard knew changing the names of things didn't change what they were, even if it increased how many of them you could sell or spin in a different way. Apprehension was relentless fear, no matter what you called it. Alex worried about their financial future endlessly. As the main breadwinner, sometimes Richard did too. He felt more responsibility now than he had in the days before he became a success. Everything that could be taken from him was bigger or more numerous, now that he had done so well.

Richard approached Amanda's throne, then sat down in the chair to the left of the head of the table. His boss turned in her seat, crossing her fabulous legs. She watched him watch her do this. She wore her pin-striped blue suit. Its skirt was short, two or three inches above the knee. They'd done this dance a hundred times, him and Amanda, her showing off, him pretending to appreciate it. Sometimes Alex, his wife and high school sweetheart, was difficult to live with but Richard would never have considered cheating on her. Amanda didn't tempt him—not really. Amanda just liked to know he thought she was sexy, in the way that virtually *everyone* did, or that he probably wanted her during moments when his will was weak, that she had power and maybe he wanted *that*, in moments when his professional prospects seemed bleak. Richard had already capitulated to what Amanda liked to know—and he pretended it did no real harm. He was glad when he didn't have to think about it much.

"So where were *you* today?" Amanda wanted to know. "Your body was at the meeting, but your mind was somewhere else."

"I ran into an old friend on the street," explained Richard. "Earlier this morning. It looks like he's homeless."

"You mean *really* homeless?"

"Yeah. On the corner, in tatters, the ball cap on the sidewalk, the whole nine yards."

"Oh," said Amanda. Then, bored with this piece of news already, she waved her hand in the air in an *is-that-all?* flourish. "So he's decided. He's given up. Was he a close friend?"

"Yeah. Way back." Decided *what?* Richard wondered. What the hell was she talking about? Had Derek *decided* to be homeless? He didn't think so.

"Tough times," Amanda said. "People stop fighting back."

"Yeah."

"It's a choice," Amanda pronounced, reaching out to touch Richard's arm.

"That's what *he* said. Sort of, anyway. The word, choice, came up a lot."

"See? Homeless people are homeless because they *want to be*. Ultimately it's because they prefer homelessness to the hard work we put into being successful." She pulled her hand away, her pronouncement complete.

Richard nodded, although he found Amanda's view simplistic and harsh—she'd voiced it many times in the past in exactly the same way—an opinion that made no logical sense to him. Who in their right mind would opt to be homeless, especially during a Canadian winter? Who would opt to sleep over a grate or live in a cardboard box? Who would willingly give up like that? Who would actually have that *preference* to holding down a job and having money? No one, Richard believed. Not until everything was gone. Not until there wasn't anyone left. Not until you couldn't stand society any longer because it had given up on you so completely. Then you might give in to homelessness. Bad things happened to people that made them homeless, things outside their control, mental illness, for instance; it wasn't necessarily because the homeless aspired to be losers.

Abruptly Amanda stood up and Richard followed suit. She was tall, five ten, the same height as Richard, in her heels. Their eyes would have met evenly, had she not been wearing shades. "Well, I don't know about you,

Richard, but I've got work to do. An important lunch too."

"Yes," said Richard, annoyed that she'd dismissed him this way. Hadn't *she* asked *him* to stay behind to have this conversation?

She leaned forward, coming in close, lifting the shades, staring at his collar. Green eyes, he remembered, now that the sunglasses were perched on her forehead, nestling in her auburn hair. "Wow, that's quite the zit you've got there.

Richard pulled back. "Zit? Where?"

"Right at the edge of your collar. You'll want to do something about that before you go out in public. It's got that getting-ready-to-ooze look about it."

"Thanks," Richard mumbled, embarrassed.

"Pus is not in our vocabulary," Amanda said with a raised eyebrow. Seeing him blush, she kissed two fingertips on her right hand and placed the psuedo endearment on his cheek. Then she left the room.

RICHARD CHECKED HIMSELF OUT in the mirror in the washroom closest to his office a couple of floors below. It *was* a nasty-looking blemish, but it didn't seem to hurt. When he was a child, his mother would have burst it with her fingers, letting it drain into a tissue. Richard remembered wondering then if she *enjoyed* squeezing pimples. As a child, he feared that she did. It was one of the many tortures he had catalogued during his childhood and occasionally revisited when he needed to feel sorry for himself. To his relief, both Richard's parents were dead. He felt honest acknowledging he was relieved. Everyone blindly liking their parents was another empty proposition designed to sell a wide variety of products and special occasions.

To be honest with himself, Richard didn't remember his parents well. It wasn't clearly a case of whether or not he liked them. Nine-Eleven. The plane that crashed in Pennsylvania, the passengers fighting back against the terrorists that had hijacked them. The plane where people phoned in their goodbyes. Richard hadn't received a phone call. He didn't blame anyone for this. He knew about cell phones, batteries always flat, reception too often lost in some dead zone or other. Now he only remembered his parents in the context in which they had died. They weren't even Americans—he couldn't remember why they had been on the flight or where they were going. The infamy of their death had somehow devoured the normalcy of the lives they had been living before that day. Crazy. Even old photos didn't say anything to him about events or feelings. "Your parents?" someone would ask him now and then. "Killed on Nine-Eleven," he would reply. The whole story of their lives, his parents' and his own with them, reduced to one day concluded by one terrible event.

He went to Corey Mackenzie, his administrative assistant, to ask her if she had a bandage. Corey's desk had a section for everything and a bandage wasn't all that improbable a request. She pulled open a drawer, reached in and then handed him one.

"Do you mind helping me with this?" He pointed at the blemish with one accusing finger.

"Hold your collar down," she said, standing up and coming towards him, leaning in close, gazing at the blemish over the ridge of a stylish pair of spectacles.

He held the collar out of the way.

"Oooh, that's an ugly one," she said as she deftly affixed the bandage. "Does it hurt?"

"Not really. Probably an allergy."

"Laundry detergent maybe. Soap powder."

"Maybe," said Richard. "Thanks for the help." He angled his head. "How's it look?"

"Like you've got a bandage on your neck."

"Could I tell people it's a shaving accident maybe? People will wonder. Better than a zit, right?"

"Sure. Why not? I'd believe it."

"Okay.

Corey sat down behind her desk, nearly grandmotherly in aspect, Richard thought, although she was less than a decade older than he was. But pushing fifty-five, she was extremely helpful about problems like this.

Gently, Richard stroked the bandage with one finger. "Thanks again," he said. Then, as an afterthought, he mentioned, "It kind of itches."

"I'll bet it does," said Corey.

RICHARD TOLD HIS SQUASH OPPONENT, Jason Leadbetter, about discovering Derek Cavanaugh on the street. Jason was an assistant comptroller at Cascade Enterprises and the two men had played squash together for nearly five years now. Jason was more competitive than Richard and nearly always won. On the rare occasion he lost to Richard at squash, it was because he had "a lot on his mind." He'd drubbed Richard today; it was Richard who had a lot on his mind and some of it—just about *all* of it, in fact—was Derek Cavanaugh.

They were showering now, scrupulously ignoring each other's penises, but so used to not looking at one another, the scrupulousness in their furtiveness almost seemed without artifice. The two men had realized some time ago that they resembled one another and were amused by this. Similar weight, similar height, similar sandy hair. As far as they knew—and they didn't intend to find out—they sported similar penises.

"So what are you gonna do?" asked Jason, lathering himself with body wash.

"About Derek?" responded Richard, scrubbing with a traditional bar of soap.

"Yeah."

"I'm working on that," said Richard.

Jason rinsed, turned his shower off, reached for his towel. "Could be more of us out there soon," he said, drying himself. "On the street, I mean."

"More rumours?"

Jason nodded "Big downsizing on the horizon."

Richard sighed. "They're always saying that."

He felt a smidge of apprehension again, the comfortable familiarity of it. In philosophical moments, Richard wondered whether apprehension still existed as apprehension, or if it was now so completely a normal feeling that technically it didn't qualify as apprehension at all. If it storms every day is it still a storm? Good question.

"And they always do it."

"Huh?"

"They warn us, drop hints, and then they do it."

Richard was drying himself too. "What's the problem this time?"

"Market volatility, I'm told. European debt. Greece. Spain."

"Christ!" muttered Richard. "I'm sick of hearing about the European Union."

"Yeah, but Cascade is over there. We have companies that buy and sell with the Euro. And I haven't even mentioned China yet."

The two men wrapped their towels around their waists and headed for their lockers.

"Cut yourself?" Jason asked, gesturing towards the bandage on Richard's neck.

"No. Zit. Allergy of some kind, I think."

"I saw one on your back in the shower."

"Where?"

"Turn around."

Richard turned.

"Middle of the neck. High up, just below the hairline."

Gently Richard located the blemish with his fingers.

"Does it hurt?"

"No. But it itches a bit, now that I've touched it."

"Well, it's an ugly little bastard," said Jason, pulling on his pants.

"Must be an allergy. What else could it be?"

Jason sat down on a bench to tie up his shoes. "You should see the doctor. Allergies can be a pain in the ass."

"Alex may have something in the medicine chest when I get home."

WALKING TO THEIR RESPECTIVE CARS in the parking garage—they both drove Audis—Jason wanted to know when Richard and his homeless friend had actually been friends. And he wasn't just being polite this time, he really seemed to want to know. Briefly Richard told him the story. He told Jason about Grade Eight. About high school. About university. About he and Alex getting married, about Derek being in the wedding party, his best man.

"So you went to school together." Jason now stood with the door of his car open and his foot on the frame by the seat.

"Yeah."

"When did you lose touch?"

Richard stopped to consider this, finding it difficult to remember. "I guess when he went to law school. Derek went to UBC. He had a yen for the mountains. It was pretty far away from here. We didn't see each other for a few years, not until he came back east. It wasn't the same by then. Alex was pregnant, Derek was still single. We didn't have much in common. I didn't even know he was married until a few years after his wedding.

"Shit happens."

Richard nodded. "After a while, you put off reconnecting for so long, it gets embarrassing. You forget how to go back and close the gap between you because it's just too uncomfortable. You know what I mean? You keep procrastinating."

"Yeah. Been there."

Richard wanted to go now. He felt a measure of sadness that he and Derek had lost touch the way they had and he no longer wanted to be standing here with Jason Leadbetter, discussing the matter. And it was cold down here in the bowels of the parking garage. Doors were slamming in the distance as other commuters prepared to depart for home, and the sound reverberated loudly against the concrete. Richard felt lonely at this moment, although he would have been hard-pressed to explain why. He felt loss, he supposed, not a specific loss, but something larger than just Derek, something more abstract. His life maybe. He felt lonely for his life somehow, which wasn't a feeling he could explain. His knuckles, he noticed, were white with cold on the handle of his briefcase. In some vague way he didn't want to be here, in this garage, in this kind of life. Or so it seemed, anyway.

"I gotta go," he said.

"Me too. Alex and Amy are cooking up a night out for us this weekend, I hear. Some new restaurant they want to try."

"Okay," said Richard.

He listened to his heels on the concrete as he walked towards his car and he pulled his topcoat closed at the throat with his free hand, afraid he might begin to shiver at any moment. When Richard shivered these days, he shivered in convulsions—he didn't know why.

SOMETIMES, WHEN RICHARD drove his car into the driveway and parked beside Alex's Nissan SUV at the end of the work day, he would sit behind the wheel for a couple of minutes, after he turned the engine off, to overcome a subtle, yet mysteriously thorough dread that fell on his body like an anvil. They'd lived in this house—a four-bedroom ranch style bungalow at the north end of the city—for six years now, yet most days returning home here felt strangely new to him, like part of him was still at the office, some other self that hadn't come home with him. Or sometimes he contemplated checking his GPS to make certain he hadn't gotten lost in the suburbs and arrived home at the wrong house. Gradually, though, he would recognize details that made it clear this *was* his house—the gardens Alex had planted out front in kidney-shaped islands, now brown and resisting life in the Canadian spring chill, the colonial light Alex had had installed a few years ago at the end of the white stone walkway to the front door. These details would, if not alleviate his dread, at least clarify that it was dread. Eventually the house would grow familiar again. Soon he would be able to get out of his car, retrieve his briefcase, and gratefully make his way to the door in the way most normal working men and women did at this time of the day.

He'd loved this house in the first year or two that they'd owned it. He'd loved its spaciousness, the large sunken living room, the breadth of it, the width of the doorways, the relatively high ceilings. Now his children were older, they'd expanded to fill his beloved space with objects they thought important, passing phases he didn't understand, even when he *tried* to understand. So that the house felt crowded and noisy to him now. Somehow he couldn't find himself as clearly any longer within such a domestic cacophony. Although he wasn't heavy, barely one hundred and seventy pounds, he felt awkward inside his own body here, as if there wasn't much room left in the house for his frame to comfortably move. He couldn't make his way any longer through the house's high decibel levels, its dancing technologies and frequent beeps and prompts. He felt alienated as he tried to slip through the crowd of his children's endless arguments. He saw the members of his family as cyborgs, part human, part technology. They hoarded sounds from anxious devices that cried out to be acknowledged, assembled vicious sibling invectives, spat cocky, angry attitude, and collected a large assortment of peer hangers-on who barged into Richard's space in an ugly, segregated silence that he discerned as an intrusive scream, all of them plugged into something electronic he could not hear that, nonetheless, got in his way, tripping him up.

Worse yet, Richard felt guilty for these complaints. He felt guilty for wanting his space back, for not being more tolerant, for walking in his front door, trying to shake off the remnants of a state of dread he was helpless to define. He felt guilty too for being unable to embrace their technological world, the need to buy the most recent device or brand name to stay out in front of the race. He was in marketing—he should be more willing to understand, to be part of their world, the one he helped create every day, he believed. He wanted whatever was bothering him these days to simply go away. It had arrived without warning, but gradually, he supposed. Why couldn't it go away in the same way, undetected, departing a day at a time until he finally realized one day his malaise was gone?

"Hi, Dad." This was Kevin squeezing by on his way to his bedroom. Which meant the family room had been occupied by some group of somebody's friends who probably didn't want him there.

"Hey, Kev. They got you in retreat?"

"Yeah."

Kevin was seventeen, a twin. Physically identical to his brother, Drake, they were otherwise a study in contrast. Kevin. Drake. Different but the same. Like his father, Kevin remembered when there had been space in the house too. They'd talked about it one night. Him and Kevin. Last autumn, standing outside on the deck. Richard had felt unusually close to Kevin afterwards. He'd wanted to put his arm around Kevin's shoulders and squeeze him with important comfort, because they now understood diminishing space together in pretty much the same way. Because they recognized in the same way some personal space they were losing or had already lost. The others? Katie and Drake? Alex? If space was filled, it wasn't them who filled it—this was all they would say when the subject of space came up. It was another way of saying they didn't really know what Richard and Kevin were talking about. And don't blame us, they said, because *you* can't communicate what you feel is missing.

"What's up?" Richard was asking his son now.

But Kevin just rolled his eyes. "Assholes," he muttered, turning to go.

"Your brother and sister?"

"Their friends," said Kevin over his retreating shoulder.

Richard stopped at the family room door to see for himself.

"Hi, guys," he said.

But no one answered him. It was just Katie with Dougal, her boyfriend, holding hands on the couch. They were quietly quarrelling as usual, holding hands and complaining to one another about one another, falling back on the absolutes of complaint—"always" and "never"—to score their points. And Drake had set up his X-box in here, although he'd been asked repeatedly to keep it in his bedroom to free up the family television. He had his own television but the screen wasn't as big, he said. Richard sighed but didn't have the energy at this moment to remind him again about the X-box. Kevin was right, though. The family room felt like a place just about anyone would want to escape. He glanced at Katie once more. Katie was on the pill, Alex had told him recently. Although Richard wanted desperately to be liberal about this fact, Katie being on the pill seriously pissed him off. Maybe because Dougal—slightly pierced, slightly tattooed, and slightly pimpled—was exactly what Kevin said he was, an asshole, pure and simple. Kevin called him "the gruntmeister." It was a moniker Richard found apt and had warmly embraced, a little jealous he hadn't thought of it himself.

Richard, still unnoticed in the doorway, kept going, moving further into the bowels of the house until he found Alex and the kitchen.

"You're home," said Alex, glancing up from a garden salad she was assembling. Obediently her glasses slipped off her nose as she spoke and hung themselves on an embroidered cord that jutted out and over her generous breasts.

Alex was a librarian in the public library system, part-time. To Richard, the art of training your glasses to throw themselves off your face like some kind of zealous lemming seemed integral to being a librarian, although Alex was the only librarian he had ever known in any meaningful way. Richard stood there awkwardly, aware that he felt himself to be on the other side of human society's crumbling wall. *Everything just lives here*, he thought suddenly, for no apparent reason.

"You seem lost," Alex said.

"Dealing with the prospect of Dougal being here for dinner, I guess," he replied.

"Oh, Richard." It wasn't that Alex liked Dougal that much either. But the principle of tolerance, no matter to what it was applied, was important to her. It was a way to hedge your bets on the future, she believed. "What if, years from now, Katie marries Dougal and he fathers your grandchildren? Would you want there to be hard feelings from the past?" Richard was left speechless by Alex's question. If Katie married Dougal, he would shoot himself. How was *that* for hard feelings?

Theirs was an Ikea kitchen. It had an island. It had ended up being expensive. There was a place Richard had discovered for his briefcase, a hiding place at the end of the island, safely out of the way. Although the house was technically spacious, Richard had discovered there was no other place to put what he brought home from work. When it wasn't here in the kitchen, when Alex got her hands on it (usually when company was coming),

Richard would find it under the bed, directly beneath where he slept at night, as if it contained important microfilm or some illicit family shame various guests might unearth if they found his briefcase out in the open. Besides, it was an Ikea kitchen. He'd seen and appreciated the commercials—everything in its place, a place for everything. One commercial even implied you could make love on the kitchen counters, if you could get the kids to look away. Wasn't that an Ikea kitchen? Even the children put away where they weren't actually seen, let alone heard? There but not there? Wasn't that life? How had image become so huge? Richard wondered. As a marketer, was he one of the reasons empty legends of various kinds were now so pervasive?

"I ran into Derek Cavanaugh today," he told his wife at last. "He's on the street. He's homeless."

"Homeless?" Alex didn't believe him.

"He was panhandling."

Now she believed him. "You're kidding," she said at last. "I thought he was a lawyer."

"He told me everything is gone."

"So you talked to him."

"Yeah. *Of course* I talked to him."

"Right there on the street?"

"Yeah."

Alex was clearly impatient with him at this moment, like it was *his* fault that he annoyed her. "Well, what'd he say?"

"Not much," said Richard, coming closer. "He was quite vague about it." He leaned forward and kissed his wife's proffered cheek. This was their greeting nearly every day when he came home from work: they were extremely proficient at it.

"What about his family?"

"Gone, he said."

"Gone? What does *that* mean?"

Richard admitted he didn't know exactly. In the end he merely shrugged. Knowing he shouldn't, he put his briefcase in its ritual out-of-the-way spot. Alex watched him do it. She didn't say anything this time although she pulled a face.

"I've been upset about it all day," said Richard, going to the cupboard above the refrigerator, where he kept his bottle of scotch.

"Upset?" There was something challenging in her tone.

"You know," he said. "Preoccupied."

They were silent while he found a glass, while the refrigerator ice-maker coughed ice cubes into it, and he poured his Glen Livet over them.

"So what are you going to do?" Alex asked at last.

"I dunno," said Richard. "Something, I guess."

"You'll talk to me, though. Right? Before you do anything?"

"Of course," said Richard. "Whaddyuh think I'm gonna do?"

"I don't know. I just don't want it to be crazy, I guess," she said.

"You mean, like, lend him money?"

"I don't know. Something presumptuous, Richard. These are uncertain times. Everything is so precarious."

"You know I wouldn't do anything without talking to you first, Alex."

"Okay," said Alex. "Dinner in fifteen minutes."

"Okay," said Richard, glancing at his watch to synchronize the time. "I'll go and get changed."

Alex's voice behind him. "Are you going to want Derek to stay here awhile?"

"Not without talking to *you*, Alex."

For the moment he wandered over to a large bank of windows here in the kitchen that overlooked a public walkway following a nearby stream. Although it was brown and dark and moving with spring haste towards a storm sewer somewhere, the brook—and its walkway—looked appealing to Richard today. He supposed this view, his favourite in the house, had cost them an extra fifty thousand dollars when they decided to buy this house: he was relieved to be enjoying it.

"Might go for a jog tonight along the path," he said, although he wasn't entirely sure he actually would. Alex said something encouraging, but he wasn't certain about what words she'd used. "Going to get changed," he said again, steeling himself for the walk through the rest of his crowded house.

"WHAT ARE THOSE THINGS ON YOUR NECK?" Alex asked in their bedroom, as they were retiring for the night.

"Huh?"

"Those sores on your neck."

Richard moved to the full-length mirror hanging on the closet door. He contorted himself to get a view of his back. There were now three zits on the back of his neck, above his shoulder blades. "Christ," he muttered.

"How long have you had those?" Alex moved nearer to have a closer look. She approached cautiously, apparently apprehensive over whether Richard's new condition might be communicable.

He pointed to the flesh-coloured bandage on his neck. "Found this one at work this morning. Thought I'd bandage it because it's out in the open."

"I thought it was a shaving accident."

"'Fraid not."

"Well they're not very attractive," Alex said with a bit of a shudder.

"It's probably just an allergy."

"To what?"

"Laundry soap or something."

"We haven't switched laundry soap."

"I don't know then," Richard said, feeling strangely persecuted because he didn't have any answers. "Maybe it's something I ate."

"You should have gone to the drug store tonight to get something to put on them."

"I guess so. I guess I more or less forgot them."

"You'll have to get an appointment with Fred Sexsmith tomorrow."

"I suppose," said Richard.

Alex climbed into bed. She pulled the covers up to her chin as he approached the bed in his boxer shorts.

"You're going to have to wear a t-shirt, Richard."

"Oh," said Richard, slamming on the brakes.

"Those zits, they're all oozy-looking."

"They aren't oozing, though."

"They look like they could any minute. What if they ooze in the middle of the night?"

He sighed. "I suppose so," he said. Ooze. Day one of his rash and Richard was tired of the word already.

He opened a dresser drawer, grabbed the first available t-shirt, a black one, and slipped into it. At last he climbed into bed.

Alex was reading already.

Richard lifted a book from his night-table and began to read as well.

"Promise me you'll call Fred Sexsmith tomorrow," Alex said without looking up from her book.

"I promise," Richard said.

He'd read a paragraph already, but couldn't remember it. He read it again. He started to read it a third time. He gave up.

"I'm going to turn out my light," he said, closing his book. "I'm really bushed."

"Okay," said Alex. She kept reading.

Richard rolled onto his side and found himself wondering for quite a long time, what he was going to do about Derek Cavanaugh.

STILL SUNNY. STILL COLD. Richard stood at Derek's corner of the building where Richard was employed. He'd put a twenty in Derek's hat this time and Derek had positioned some coins on it to hold it in place. A corner of the twenty trembled in a cold breeze chugging relentlessly along the street. Why didn't he stuff the twenty in his pocket? Richard wondered. He felt slightly ashamed of how little he knew about panhandling. Did you allow the twenty to show, to guilt some stranger into duplicating it? Or did the twenty make you look too prosperous? Christ! Was everything complicated? Even poverty? Desperation? Was there a politics about suffering? Did even homelessness have a proper *procedure*, a complexity, a way of doing things?

Richard hadn't decided on the twenty dollars, exactly, as this morning's donation to Derek's cause. Heading out the revolving door at Cascade, he'd suddenly remembered he didn't have any cash. He'd kept on going inside the spinning door, pushing back around again into the building lobby—despite the raised eyebrows of some young prat heading out during a break from his cubicle—where he could use the ATM. Richard had taken out a hundred—it had arrived in five twenties, of course. This was at least part of the history of the twenty-dollar bill now twitching under some change in Derek Cavanaugh's ball cap.

"It's going to snow, I'm told," Richard said now. "What do you do when it snows?"

"A little better trade," Derek said drily.

"I mean how do you keep from getting soaked? The snow, it'll be that wet slop we get in March."

"I have cover."

Richard hesitated a moment. "What if I took you home with me for awhile?"

Derek had agreed to another Colombian from Starbucks when Richard had first arrived and offered it. He sipped at it before he answered Richard's question. "It'd be a terrible imposition, my friend."

"But you'd be warm and dry. You'd get your three squares," Richard countered.

"Sorry," Derek said. "While it may not look like it, I think me being here serves an important function."

"You mean like a protest."

"Sort of, I guess. A statement, anyway. It's complicated."

It was a gloomy day. No chance the sun was going to blind him today; Richard stood on Derek's left. Here, though, people stared at him as they passed. Him more than Derek. *He* was the curiosity. Shirt, tie, topcoat, tailored suit. Without even knowing it, Richard assumed, the area's passersby were used to Derek as a fixture. But Richard meeting for coffee with a homeless, tattered man, well, *he* would be the strange one from here on out.

"Does this embarrass you?" Derek asked from the pavement below, noticing Richard's frequent glances in the direction of passing pedestrians.

"I just don't know how to help you. If you'd tell me how I could help you get back on track, I'd do it."

"I know you would," said Derek. "You're a good man."

"We were good friends."

"Yes."

"I'm glad to have found you again."

Derek hesitated before he said, "me too."

"Do I drive away, uh, business?" Derek wasn't doing as well this morning, other than Richard's twenty and a few quarters and dimes. Richard was concerned for him. Did the twenty dollar bill discourage other benefactors? he fretted again. Should Derek put it in his pocket?

"Stop worrying," Derek was saying. "Stop thinking like a marketer."

FRED SEXSMITH, DOCTOR OF FAMILY MEDICINE, was into psychology more or less as a hobby. At some point a number of years ago, he'd discovered that Richard was one of his few patients willing to honestly reply to the question: "how are things going?" Since then, they almost always had their appointments together at the end of the day so that Richard—nearly a friend as much as a patient—could get things off his chest.

Today, though, it had to wait while, together, they puzzled over the blemishes located on Richard's neck.

Fred had taken a swab, then scrawled a prescription. He handed the paper to Richard, peering at him over a pair of heavy black glasses that slid frequently down the bridge of his nose.

"The prescription is for an ointment. You dab it on the padded part of the bandages. That should start the healing process. We'll get a lab report on the swab and see what that tells us. You may have to undergo allergy tests."

Richard nodded. "Alex talked about ringworm this morning." He shuddered. It was the word worm. When he was a child Richard had had a dog with worms and he'd seen the worms writhing and squirming in a pile of Roscoe's feces one day. He had remembered this sight several times recently, not wanting to remember, but helpless to resist, thanks to Alex's remarks about ringworm. The trouble with what you didn't want to think was that you ended up thinking it, over and over again, dozens of times, until you thought it would make you crazy.

"No, not ringworm," Fred said.

"Okay. It sounded awful."

"Like athlete's foot. That's all."

Richard nodded, relieved.

"But they're spreading," his doctor said.

"I know. I counted six this morning."

"Eight."

"Jeezus."

"They're spreading. But the ointment should dry them up and that'll inhibit the spread."

Richard nodded, feeling mollified—spread was such a better word than ooze.

Fred rose, went to the sink, and washed his hands. "What about everything else?" he said over his shoulder. "Everything going all right?" He was bald. His head shone in the mirror. Like he polished the mirror *and* his head.

Richard was instantly aware, now that Fred's question hung in the air between them, that no, things were not going all right. He was surprised at this. Like the question had pulled the trigger on the truth and the truth had suddenly gone off.

"Richard?"

Richard took a deep breath. The breath was a dam between everything he wanted to gush—now a surprisingly large flood of complaint—and the tranquil lowlands of what he had the ability to actually explain. Holding back the torrent, he told his doctor about Derek's state of homelessness.

"Oh my," said Fred at the end of the story.

"I don't know what to do exactly," Richard summarized.

"Because he refuses help, I gather."

"Yes."

"You can't make him accept your assistance if he doesn't want it."

"I know."

"Can't be good for you to take this on," said Fred.

"I know."

They sat in silence.

"Derek. This situation. My situation. It's like they're related in some cockeyed way. Since seeing Derek on the street, well, my own life seems rather—I hate to say this, it can't be true—but my own life seems inane."

"Inane? What's inane about it?"

Richard thought for a long moment. Now that he had started down the road he was on, he felt unable to be clear about his meaning. What could he possibly say that Fred would understand, when he barely understood it himself?

For his part, his doctor now leaned back in his wooden chair and laced his hands together behind his head. It was his most frequent position of anticipation.

"I'm not sure what I do," Richard murmured at last.

"With Derek?"

"No, no, well, yes, but I meant what I do for a living."

Fred seemed puzzled.

"I don't know what I do at work."

"I don't understand," the doctor said.

"I mean, I know what my title is. I know where my office is in the building. I know I go to meetings and say things. I know I get paid. Now and then I write things down. I give reports . . . ."

"Yes."

". . . But what the hell do I *do* exactly, Fred? What's my *job*? Derek, as a homeless person, has a clear purpose. I see it. I feel it. He focuses on survival and food and this strange sense of peace that I barely understand. Me? I spend all of my time doing things that actually have no direct relationship to anything even remotely essential. I've been thinking about this for some months now. What I do for a living isn't authentic. Which means a good part of *me* isn't authentic either."

"Oh, c'mon now," said Fred.

"You know what I do all day, every day?" Richard didn't wait for his doctor to answer. "I dance, Fred. All day, every day, I . . . dance."

The ensuing silence was long and thick this time.

"This Derek business has really got you going," Richard's doctor said at last.

"You think that's it?"

"I do. I really do. I think that's it."

Richard nodded, although some tiny voice inside his brain said, "Shit, that's only part of it." Unsatisfied with what the discussion had accomplished, he stood up and shook Fred's hand. "I guess I wait to hear from you."

Sexsmith nodded. "And use the ointment. It'll do until we get to the bottom of this."

"Thanks," Richard said as he departed.

"I'VE BEEN THINKING," Richard told Alex that night, after they were in bed, "that maybe I'm allergic to discovering that Derek is homeless."

Beside him, holding her book, as yet unopened, Alex sighed in annoyance. "You mean Derek's homelessness gave you the rash?"

"It made me think things—thinking things gave me the rash."

"Sure," said Alex bitterly. "A thinking-things rash."

"Don't make fun of me."

Husband and wife were already irritated with one another. Alex had refused to help him put ointment on his bandages and he'd had to position them on the sores himself. She'd held a mirror for him, though, complaining that he was slow and clumsy. He'd felt increasingly like a victim within her criticism, lining up ten band-aids on his dresser, squeezing ointment out of a tube on the padded part, then trying to position them over the sores. Alex's love didn't suffer rashes, he'd concluded peevishly. Alex liked everything to be blemish free.

"You know, this would be a helluva lot easier if you helped me, Alex,"

Richard said after he was done.

"I don't want to get infected."

"What about surgical gloves or something?"

"I'll look into getting some tomorrow," she said after a pause.

"These zits will be gone soon, you know."

"Is that what Fred Sexsmith said?"

Richard hesitated. "He implied it."

In bed, as they read, Richard touched Alex's leg with his leg in the area of the thigh, more or less to make amends because he'd barked at her. She moved away immediately.

"Until those blemishes go, you're right-handing it, my love," she said.

"Christ!" Richard retorted angrily, offended. "What a thing to say."

"I'm reading," his wife said.

"Alex, is this more than just the blemishes?"

"I'm reading, Richard. The blemishes are ugly. It's the blemishes. And I'm reading."

"Okay," Richard said after a long time.

He resisted sleep after this, working back in his mind to the last time he and Alex had had sex. Jesus, he concluded, three months? Really? Alex loved sex. Was she getting something on the side? He swallowed. He felt guilty about his suspicions, but he also felt uncertain. He was convinced Alex didn't love him any longer. He'd concluded at one point that this change in her feelings for him was merely the normal evolution of marriage—the emergent preponderance of its rituals and their roles as husband and wife inside marriage's relentless routines. Then again, maybe it wasn't as complicated as that. Maybe it meant she had a boyfriend, or at least there was some kind of romance going on with someone else.

She stopped reading and turned out her light. He didn't ask her if she was having an affair. Mostly he didn't think so and it wasn't worth the fight they might have if he asked her. But the last few years, he'd wondered on occasion about her fidelity. The notion of Alex being unfaithful was just another thought he usually tried not to think.

He sighed, eventually sleeping. But he tossed and turned. His marriage and his life felt like uneven ground, a bumpy bed of rocks and twigs, a vague wilderness of discomfort. He liked life better sometimes when he didn't have to think about it or lie down on it for comfort.

HE FOUND HIMSELF AMONG a number of people on a beach. His children, not young or otherwise, were not here with him this time. It was a different beach than last time. This one was not stormy or rocky. It was stunningly calm and peaceful. Gradually, as he turned, he discovered he was standing in a park. In the distance there was a gazebo, a colourful one, striped, almost gleeful in its garishness, celebratory. There were people in chairs or lying on lounges, maybe two dozen or so. There were picnic tables and several more people—singly, in duos, trios or quartets—sat at these and ate sandwiches or salads. In the distance, a couple of indeterminate age strolled hand in hand towards him, carrying a picnic basket. Food conveyed that it was sensible here—not a hotdog in sight, no sound of sizzling burgers or ostentatious steaks. Old-fashioned, he thought. The food seemed plentiful enough, but only enough for a person's needs, no more than that. Richard sensed it was a practise here that nothing would be wasted. As such, the park was astonishingly clean. There was no litter. The waste receptacles were not yet full, nothing had spilled to the ground. Although the people in the park glanced repeatedly at the ocean, they nonetheless seemed vaguely pleased to be able to take it for granted.

A woman, freckled—serene, Richard decided—ageless, he thought, not exactly knowing what made her seem so, her bearing more than anything else, he supposed, approached him and offered him half of her sandwich, her eyes calmly looking into his, as if to say she knew what hunger was and how surprisingly little was needed to satisfy it.

He was tempted to decline, more or less out of habit, more or less out of a need to reject her in some way, irked a little by her superior knowledge of what hunger was, her self-assurance.

"I have lots," she said, although he was already aware that she was not going to run out of food.

He reached to take the sandwich anyway, compelled to do so, his objections evaporating. The sandwich was delicious. The first bite made his mouth water.

He stood at the edge of his side of the bed, watching Alex snore softly a few feet away. It was morning and Richard felt gently elated, the remembered taste of the sandwich, he suspected, the memory remaining fine in his mouth. But he couldn't remember getting out of bed or where the delicious sandwich had come from.

THE DREAM REMAINED WITH HIM beyond his arrival at work, not the specifics of the dream so much, but the *sense* of it, the *feeling*, the *serenity* of it. Serenity was a difficult feeling to feel. It seemed to be at the *end* of something. *Afterwards* somehow, a feeling considered in retrospect. Quite literally, words could not describe serenity to him, although he knew he felt it. Which transformed standing near the traffic on the corner with Derek, a new twenty-dollar bill trembling in Derek's ball cap, into a collision of sound and chaos that exploded into Richard's dream-remembered perception. Horns and alarms, sirens nearby and in the distance, raucous laughter from a passerby, another one talking about how some mundane exchange with a bouncer the previous night "was so fuck-king awesome." Exhaust, chemicals, rotting food, the odour of litter and dirt in the gutter, even passing perfumes or colognes. It felt too close and overwhelming here on the street with Derek, now that he had dreamed his dream and could still feel the calm in its simplicity.

He was tempted to tell his homeless friend about his dream, but the details all vanished and Richard felt embarrassed to be so pleased about a dream he couldn't even remember, especially considering Derek's terrible circumstances here on the street. In the end he simply let the subject pass.

He and Derek often fell silent at the edge of the noise of the city's morning. This was his fifth day standing here with the homeless man; patterns were now developing. It wasn't like there was a great deal of news to impart from one man's world to the other man's world. Mostly Richard asked the occasional question. Mostly Derek only partially answered it.

Like: "Where do you go at night, Derek?"

"Home," said Derek. "Same as you."

"But where? It isn't like me going home and you know it."

"Different but the same."

"Yes," said Richard, nodding, remembering his twin sons, the way they looked the same as one another but were different in every other way and were frequently hostile with one another. Weren't twins more often extremely close? Or was that too another myth? When he was standing on the corner here with his homeless friend, Kevin and Drake were never far from Richard's mind—he worried about their ability to survive in a world with such a harsh future. What if they ended up homeless too? Derek was a clear warning of what could go wrong for his sons, if life got away from them, if bad choices were made, if they didn't pay enough attention to what was taking place around them.

"Yeah," Derek was saying. "Different but the same. You told me."

"It's like a riddle talking to you, Derek. If you'd let me find you a place to live and a job . . ."

". . . The riddle would be solved," Derek finished.

Richard sighed, annoyed.

"I have a place to live," Derek said, as if to ease the tension between them.

This was a sunny morning and Richard much preferred sunny mornings when he stood here with Derek, drinking from their Starbuck's containers, because they were rare this time of year. But it wasn't the wet when it rained. No, it was the hiss of tires on wet pavement, like they were being told to shush. Richard, who felt shushed at some point on most days of his life, hated being shushed. Rainy days were fine when there was no city traffic, when a man didn't notice the shush, the *hiss*. Strange how a man felt so shushed in the middle of his life and knew the shushing was going to get worse in future as he proceeded along the long promenade of decay that led towards his dying, the point when he was at last *permanently* shushed.

"Do you hear from your family at all, Derek?"

Richard had wanted to ask about Derek's family again for several days now. Family was more than family—family was an idea; it seemed important to ask about something that was more of a concept than what it actually was, that was more than its state of being, more than its idea of itself. Family was one of society's larger than life concepts. To Richard it had always been bigger than itself; he didn't know when or how it had grown to be that way.

"I check in with them from time to time," said Derek. "I like to know everyone is fine."

"You mean you visit them?"

"More or less."

Richard sighed once more. "When are you going to tell me what happened to your family?"

"At an appropriate time," replied Derek right away, as if he had prepared himself in advance for the question.

"I'm not going to give up on you, Derek," Richard said, wondering what wasn't appropriate about the here and now.

Derek gazed out at the noise and traffic, and nodded slightly, acknowledging Richard's promise.

RICHARD GOOGLED HIM. There was virtually nothing on the net, barely a landscape of old ruins. Derek had had no Internet presence in the past decade at all. Everything about him was ancient, revealing itself in fragments. Like a modern Menander, Richard supposed, remembering a classical literature course he had taken at university, where he learned the written works of men did not always remain extant. Derek was like Menander: his plays fragments, parts of them lost to history. Incomplete. Forgotten. Not surprising that a homeless man should appear on the Internet in bits and pieces, no longer remembered as what he'd been when he was whole. A record of his marriage was there, part of it anyway, to a woman named Susan Andracetti. The births of his children, two sons, Tyson and Ryan. Nothing else about them. Not much else about Derek, although Richard found a paper Derek had written on the need for and value of anti-SLAPP legislation in the province, written when he was a young lawyer. This article too was disintegrating in the vast confusion of the internet. It hung in cyberspace by a thread.

Did this mean Derek had been homeless for ten years? Hard to say. It did mean that he didn't Tweet. He didn't post, like or dislike on Facebook. Richard didn't either. At work, the office handled this kind of networking activity for him, the work of an employee further down the food-chain in the company's promotion department. At home Alex and their children maintained their vigorous presences on the net. Richard mowed the grass. He jogged. He watched the NHL playoffs, switching to baseball in the summer. He didn't tell people on the Internet about his life or activities: the minutiae of what he did each day didn't seem important enough. He didn't take pictures of his dinner and post them for his followers. He didn't want to read the details of everyone else's life either, only because what they lived was a life as hectically mundane as his own. Over her shoulder, at her invitation, he'd looked at Alex's Facebook page a couple of times. He'd been dismayed by its sure capture of life's immense minutiae, a strange exaggeration he found in banal events and details, embroidered by her oft-stated fear of what the future held. On the one hand postings included someone's pleasant meal, a chance sharing of a happy song or funny video. The future, though, was large and frightening, postings of economic chaos, over-taxation, failure to plan ahead, the high prices people could expect for the things they might want to purchase..

His fault maybe, him and hundreds of other marketers like him. His job was to make the future frightening. His job was to imply a potential inadequacy ahead if action wasn't taken now in the present. And the past? No lessons there beyond nostalgia. How, he wondered daily, had he ended up controlling the way history and time were perceived to sell things to worried people he made certain *stayed* worried?

Still in his office, Richard googled Susan Andracetti, Derek's wife. Susan was there in technicolour, unlike the homeless man she'd married. Richard visited Susan Andracetti and Derek's two sons for about an hour on the net. Susan was working as a nurse practitioner. She had a professional looking website and she was on Linked In. She'd taken a trip to China the previous year, accompanied by her sons. Derek wasn't mentioned anywhere, not even casually, not even as an afterthought. It was as if he'd never existed. Tyson and Ryan didn't even carry the Cavanaugh name. They were Tyson and Ryan Andracetti. Richard felt he was witnessing a crime that had taken place. He knew it was old-fashioned, but it was as if someone had murdered Derek's family tree. How could Derek have let that happen? What had he done, what had *she* done to ensure his removal from the world that just about everyone else participated in?

"YOUR SONS," RICHARD SAID the next morning on the street corner where Derek sat each day. "Your wife Susan has changed their last name to hers. Did you know about that?"

"I would have no way of knowing," Derek replied.

"Well, you know now. Whaddyuh think of that?"

"I don't know what to think," Derek replied calmly. "I guess I'd have to think about it."

"Jesus," Richard said in frustration.

Derek nodded his thanks to a woman who put some change into his hat. Richard glanced at her, vaguely recognizing her as someone's administrative assistant somewhere in the catacombs and cubicles of Cascade Enterprises. It was the administrative assistants, the janitors, who gave to the homeless, Richard knew, and not the executives who could more easily afford it. The more money a person had, generally speaking, the more a person needed to keep it, and the more someone else's poverty either embarrassed them or made them feel superior. In the larger sense of their personal family economy, Alex was like that. Richard thought her need to keep every last cent for their own use was brought on by her fear of some nasty imminent future. Every day someone lost everything when they lost their job and the bank called in their mortgage. Alex collected such stories as evidence of why she needed to worry. She hadn't been frightened like this at all two decades ago when they were starting out together, back when they were poor. The money he gave Derek each morning here on the street, a ten or, more often, a twenty that peeked out from the nickels, dimes, and quarters residing in Derek's cap—Richard now realized Alex would be angry about this; angry because the money he gave to Derek would make her more more economically vulnerable.

Richard glanced down at his friend and discovered Derek had been looking up at him while he was thinking about money and Alex. Richard didn't like people watching him think: it made him feel exposed and indecisive, especially if he was thinking about Alex.

"Never mind about the last name thing," Derek said then. "I understand it in a way you can't. You're better to never mind."

Richard nodded. He could do that. He could never mind. Never minding was something he did more often than he liked to admit.

AMANDA WAS IN A STATE of high excitement and, as usual, she wanted Richard to be in a state of high excitement along with her. They were scheduled to have lunch with John Lee Anders, last year's batting champion in the American League. Anders had signed as their spokesman for a new line of hair care products for Cascade's male cosmetic subsidiary, Torque. Torque Inc. had coughed up forty million for Anders's services in commercials, on billboards, and personal appearances over the next two years. In corporate quarters, signing Anders was considered a coup. Richard considered it mostly expensive.

Amanda drove. Amanda cursed the traffic. Amanda babbled about Anders. Amanda's perfect legs gleamed as she negotiated accelerator and brake pedal, as her skirt rode up as she drove.

Richard noticed all this only peripherally. Mostly he glanced out the window and gently feared for his life at Amanda's reckless driving. He had no enthusiasm today for Amanda's legs on the pedals of the car. He didn't know why of late, he hadn't had much enthusiasm for anything.

"God, you're a scream and a half today," Amanda said as they waited at a stoplight. "What's the matter with you?"

"Nothing," said Richard with a shrug.

"You look all pale and puffy," she said. "Are you sick?"

"I don't think so."

"Well, you look all pale and puffy. You look like shit."

"Thank you," murmured Richard.

But the light turned green. Richard was thrown back in the seat by the ferocity of Amanda's acceleration across the intersection.

"I thought you *liked* Anders."

"I do," said Richard. "I'm thrilled he's on board."

"He's the biggest star in baseball," said Amanda with startling vehemence. "Every woman I know wants to fuck his brains out."

"The price of celebrity," Richard said more wearily than he intended.

"He's a big star, Richard."

"Yes, he is."

"And he's ours," Amanda added, slapping her steering wheel in triumph.

"He certainly is."

Something in his voice, he knew. Amanda, waiting at another red light, studied him critically.

"You look pale and puffy, Richard. . ."

"So you said."

". . . Like you're not interested."

"I'm fine." It sounded lame, he knew.

"I'm not so sure," mused Amanda before she sped through the intersection, leaving Richard to wonder silently what pale and puffy had to do with perceived disinterest.

For all of that, though, the lunch went quite well. Anders was a perfect gentleman—he was dating and getting serious about a young Hollywood starlet named Rameze Roberts—and Amanda was very professional. And while his heart wasn't in it because he had attended too many similar lunches during his career, Richard was fine. They covered all the business bases and everyone left the luncheon meeting happy with the new partnership. And on the way back to the office, satisfied and exuberant, Amanda seemed to forget that Richard was pale and puffy, or that being pale and puffy was evidence he didn't care as much as he could.

FRED SEXSMITH SHARED RICHARD'S TEST RESULTS with him when they met later that afternoon in Fred's office.

"You're allergic to *something*, my friend."

"No kidding," said Richard.

The ointment Fred had prescribed last time they'd met had dried up the blemishes he had swabbed back then, but for each blemish that had healed, two more had sprouted on Richard's neck and back. New ones. Apparently he was losing the battle.

"Sometimes the source of an allergy is hard to find," Fred was telling him. "It's going to mean more tests. I'm going to have to refer you to a specialist."

"How long will it take?"

"A couple of weeks."

Richard nodded. "And in the interim?"

"Keep fighting the rash with the ointment." Fred studied the sheet of paper containing the report on the initial swab. "There are some elevations here but nothing really significant."

Elevations? Elevations in what? A few weeks ago Richard would have pounced on this report in worry. Today, strangely, he was only partially interested. At this moment he believed instinctively the rash wasn't as serious as everyone else believed, including Fred. Alex, Amanda, a few people at work all remarked that he didn't seem himself, that he looked unwell. But except for the rash, Richard felt pretty good. If there was something bothering him, it was mostly how the people in his life were treating him as if he had leprosy.

"I'll need more ointment then," Richard said.

Fred wrote the prescription, turned, gave it to him. "You seem depressed, Richard. Anything else going on I should know about?"

Richard shook his head. "Except for the allergy, everything pretty much seems normal." He forced himself to grin. "Maybe it's 'normal' that I find depressing."

But Fred merely winced when he said that, as if he didn't get the joke.

HE AND ALEX WENT TO DINNER with Jason and Sara Leadbetter at a new bistro the two women were excited about. Even though the meal had been postponed a week already, Alex had not wanted to go because of Richard's "condition."

"I mean, look at you," cried Alex after the postponement. "You have bandages on your neck. You look like Frankenstein."

Richard couldn't prevent a tiny grin from skidding across his face. Never, not in Mary Shelley's book, not in the various movie incarnations, had Frankenstein's monster worn little bandages like his. The image of it in his mind's eye was amusing. "I'll see if I can get Fred Sexsmith to screw a bolt through my neck, to finish the makeover."

Alex had seen his smothered mirth and his words didn't amuse her. "Shouldn't you be more concerned about this, Richard? I would be if I were you."

"I can't help it," said Richard. "I just don't feel like Frankenstein, that's all. Comparing me to Frankenstein seems a little over the top."

At dinner, though, the Leadbetters too where awkward with him. He had the sense that no one wanted to look at him and, when they did, they weren't really seeing him. How could a few bandages on a rash make him the odd man out in this way? How could a mere rash isolate him so much? Was

Franz Kafka back from the grave to write something new about his life as an outsider? Was he doomed to live out his own isolated Kafkaesque metamorphosis?

To Richard, the bistro, called Accolades, was anemic, Spartan. Modern-cold. He had the sense he was on a space station. Everything seemed heavily metallic, as if it was made out of titanium. After he unwrapped his cutlery from an institutional green napkin, it clattered at the edge of a place mat. He winced at the sound. Elsewhere heels clicked across a polished concrete floor. The restaurant was busy and noisy. There were no carpets or drapes to buffer sound. Even the tropical plants were as skinny and starved as supermodels, tall, single-stemmed, green-headed. The place seemed anti-tranquility, enthusiastically opposed to calm.

"You okay, Richard?" Sara Leadbetter asked at one point.

"Yeah. You okay, Richard?" Jason echoed in matrimonial harmony.

"Richard's allergy is getting him down," said Alex. "He's thinking crabby thoughts."

"Noisy place," Richard commented.

These days, in social settings, Alex answered for him, like he couldn't answer for himself. Increasingly, he had become aware that he embarrassed her somehow. When his words came out of *her* mouth, they were more *satisfactory* to her because she believed they were more *satisfactory* to everyone else. Richard wondered when she had grown faintly ashamed of him, like he was now a child who didn't behave himself in front of company.

Sara bordered on bulimic, at least in appearance. She ate salads all the time. Her hands trembled. Sometimes, when he believed none of them were noticing, Jason would take her trembling hand and squeeze it to make it still. Like her palsy—whatever its cause—was a matter he could control. Lately, Richard had been troubled somewhat by a delicate violence, a stern capture he thought he saw in Jason's grip. Sometimes—and this was a new worry for

Richard—he thought married couples had sacrificed love to a more powerful emotional need to feel less embarrassment with one another. These days Alex was like that, or so it seemed.

Then again, Richard was radically changing his views about just about everything—he didn't know why exactly. He felt himself in transition and didn't understand it a bit. His first thought was to wonder what was wrong with him. He was used to the person he thought himself to be. Change caused him to fear loss of his familiarity to himself. And these people at dinner with him, even Alex—especially Alex—were in danger of being lost to him, he thought, because they were connected intrinsically to the self he felt he was mysteriously ceasing to be. Like his panhandling friend Derek's children maybe. Just *gone*, as Derek would have put it. His friends, his family, just *gone*.

As was often the case when the four of them were out to dinner, there was much talk about their respective children. Stories about school, about broken curfews, about teenage demands for new technology, about careers and jobs and the anticipated costs of post-secondary education. Richard partook of this talk, but sparingly. The subject of children reminded him of noise, of conflict. Which filled him with guilt. He felt inadequate in the company of the Leadbetters and his wife. Was it selfish to want peace? He felt it was. He wanted to confess his guilt but there was no-one here to empathize, to understand. It was like saying you didn't like dogs. Or cats. Being unwilling to convey that your children were the single most important thing in your life was politically incorrect. Secretly Richard believed, in *this* society at least, peace itself was politically incorrect, that tranquility violated something sacrosanct in society's need for constant stimulation or distraction, for love that was ceaselessly agitated, that never grew comfortable. Even in the movies, new lovers embraced their passion for one another by crashing into furniture, walls and cupboards until, bruised with exhausted need, they collapsed, tearing off their clothing, on a nearby bed.

Didn't new lovers take each other's hand any longer and walk connected and glowing to the bedroom? Or did they see themselves as part of the spectacle of love they saw in the movies and on television?

These were new thoughts for Richard and they annoyed him. He wanted to be here with his friends in the company of his wife, not stamping out philosophical embers at the edge of some new psychological fire he didn't remember building.

They all talked shop for a while and Richard tried to concentrate. Jason discussed his fears about the rumoured downsizing at Cascade. To Richard, fretting out loud about it so much was merely a way to yell into the cacophony of so much machine. Which made him feel guilty. Was he losing his mind? Family, marriage, work. When had he become his own disagreeable island in the storm-swollen sea that had been his life until now?

"What about your friend, the homeless guy?" Jason asked midway through the first course. "You still run into him?"

"Every time I go to Starbucks in the morning."

"It bothers you," Sara Leadbetter said. She'd studied psychology in university and enough of her fascination with the field remained to inspire her remark.

"Yes it does. I don't know what to do about him."

"How to get him back on the rails," offered Jason.

"Yeah, I guess so." Richard was aware of Alex watching him as he spoke. He felt gently annoyed by this, like she was somehow twisting his arm with her glance, reminding him what his priorities should be.

"Maybe there's nothing to be done," said Jason.

Sara reached out and put her hand over his forearm. "It's normal to be worried about him. He used to be a close friend."

Richard nodded. But he felt relieved when she took her hand away; he wasn't convinced she cared as much as she pretended to. Maybe Derek was on the disagreeable island with him. They were fighting the battle over Derek's homelessness alone together, separate from everyone else he knew. Much of the concern he heard about Derek, no matter who knew about it, smacked of disingenuousness. Only *he* knew the true importance of Derek's plight.

"BOY," SAID ALEX IN THE CAR on their way home. "What the hell was the matter with you tonight?"

"Whaddyuh mean?"

"You phoned in your performance."

"Huh?"

"Wherever you were, Richard, it wasn't with us at dinner tonight."

He was tempted to argue, more or less out of habit, but he knew she was right. For the moment he said nothing.

"What's going on, Richard?"

It wasn't late; there was still traffic. Richard drove attentively. "I don't know, Alex."

"You don't know?"

"No. Derek Cavanaugh maybe. Work. The allergy, the rash. I feel funny."

Alex sighed deeply. "You feel funny? Whaddyuh mean by 'funny'?"

"Strange. Alone. Cast out. Nothing makes sense the way it did even a month or so ago."

"Your job isn't at risk, is it?"

Richard glanced at his wife. She was looking straight ahead. Whatever information she gleaned from him, Richard suspected, would be applied to whatever *she* was worried about, like their economic security.

"Richard?" she said. "Your job? Jason was worried."

"Nah. Nothing going on there. Except . . ."

"Except what?" Now she was looking at him. He could see the alarm on her face, the alarm that typically embroidered any discussion about the certainty of his job.

". . . Except that what I do for a living doesn't seem to make much sense." There, it was out. As lame and vague as it was, he'd said it. What he did from day to day at Cascade Enterprises, even hour to hour, seemed to have no point. He just did his job because he could, not because it mattered to the cosmos in any way. Most days he couldn't even remember what he'd accomplished, only that he had been busy.

"You're not going to get fired, are you?"

"Hell no," Richard said.

"Jason said layoffs at dinner."

"I've survived a half dozen of those, Alex."

"We'd lose everything if you got fired, Richard."

"We wouldn't lose *everything* if Cascade laid me off. Our *everything* would just change into something else, something *less*. Maybe being dead would be losing everything. But getting fired? Getting fired isn't death—even when you lose a good job."

Even Derek on the corner not far from Starbucks hadn't lost *everything*. Richard could feel the truth in that, a kind of peaceful verisimilitude that wanted to redefine for him the nature of what *everything* actually was.

Still here in the car with Alex, he decided to drop the subject of *everything*. "Maybe it's Derek Cavanaugh that has me preoccupied," he said at last.

"Derek made his own choices," Alex said. "He's not your responsibility. If he wants to be a bum on the corner, well, Richard, that's up to him."

"I can't help caring about his circumstances."

"It's your family you should be caring about. *Our* circumstances are your first priority. That's the way it *should* be."

All discussions between him and Alex came to a close this way. She repeated the mantra of what his responsibilities were and he found himself nodding, not in agreement necessarily, but to escape the routine in the conversation.

"I know all that," he said as he turned onto their street.

"You think too much, Richard."

"I know that too."

A moment later they were home.

"This too shall pass," Alex was fond of saying.

"Maybe I just need to get laid," Richard said more plaintively than he intended, as they walked the last few feet to their door.

"Oh Richard," Alex replied. "That awful rash, that allergy. It just completely turns me off."

IT WAS KIND OF AN ADDICTION, in Richard's mind, anyway. The walk down the street from Cascade towards Derek, on his way to Starbucks to buy Derek his coffee, placing money in Derek's cap first and saying good morning.

"I think I'm going crazy," Richard told his friend today, standing under his umbrella because it was drizzling with an unusual enthusiasm here on the street.

As was his habit, Derek waited to hear the rest of what Richard had to say before he contemplated any response. Derek wore a clear sheet of plastic in which he'd cut a hole for his head. It didn't seem to keep him very dry and it looked like hell, emphasizing his homelessness the way it did.

"You know how you can sometimes get a song running through your head?" continued Richard. "A line or two gets stuck in your brain, repeating itself over and over."

"An ear-worm," Derek said. "I've heard it called an ear-worm."

"Yeah. But in my case it's a phrase. There's no song, no tune. Just this one line. Four words. They repeat themselves in my mind most days, all day long. Four words."

"Which are?" asked Derek.

"*Everything just lives here.*"

Derek merely nodded, shrugged a bit.

"*Everything just lives here,*" Richard repeated with a kind of tired finality, trying to cast the four devilish words out of the church of his normalcy.

They remained silent for a time inside the hiss of the rain on the street. Richard had no questions for Derek today; he didn't want to hear Derek's evasive answers.

"I have a rash," he told his friend. "It's spreading. We haven't figured out what it is yet, what's causing it."

"A rash," said Derek.

"Yes. An allergy."

"You being tested?"

"I see a specialist next week."

Derek only nodded.

"You should put that twenty in your pocket," Richard said later, gesturing with a cock of his head towards the money he'd donated to Derek today. "It's getting soggy in the rain."

But Derek just left it in his ball cap, anchored by some rain-glistened coins. The cap was soggy too. Richard considered where he might go to get Derek a new ball cap, should he decide a new ball cap was a good idea. He had no idea where to find them. He didn't buy ball caps. Wal-Mart? Should he go to a ball game? Richard considered asking Derek his hat size.

"I think I'm allergic to you being homeless," he said instead.

"Rash and all?" said Derek.

Richard didn't reply. Derek's words just pissed him off.

LATER THAT MORNING, when Richard glanced up from a report he was writing on a laptop at his desk, he discovered Amanda Drew loitering in his doorway.

"Amanda," he said, "how long have you been standing there?"

She didn't answer him but stepped inside his office and closed the door behind her. Richard's was a relatively small office—she needed to take only a couple of steps forward to be standing directly in front of his desk.

Richard lowered the top of his laptop so that they did not have to peer around it to look at one another, and so that Richard could cover up his initial bolt of apprehension that she was here. He couldn't remember the last time she had visited him here; in just about every case, all meetings with Amanda took place upstairs in *her* office, after he had been summoned.

"What's up?" Richard asked.

Amanda took her time replying. It was clear she'd been thinking about what she wanted to say, yet didn't know quite where to begin. She gazed at him a moment longer. Then, "you never were a handsome man," she said. "But pleasant looking. You were always pleasant looking."

"Thanks—I think," Richard replied with a smile.

"Pleasant looking is attractive," Amanda mused. "Handsome is arresting. A man should never be handsome. It just causes trouble. It's better for a man to be attractive in that pleasant-looking way. Unless he's a celebrity, of course."

Richard shrugged, a trifle embarrassed by the apparent vacuity in her babble. "We get what we get, though, don't we? It's not like we order our looks from a catalogue."

"Of course not," she snapped. "But these days, Richard, you're not even pleasant looking. You're not in the slightest attractive."

Richard was helpless to answer, to defend himself. No one had ever spoken to him this way. He wasn't hurt; he just didn't know how to respond to such a matter-of-fact, yet insulting observation.

"You're pale and puffy," Amanda continued. "You've got a rash, this allergy thing."

"I'm seeing a specialist next week."

"Thank God for that," she said. "Thank God we live in a world where we can change how we look, if we're not satisfied with ourselves."

"Yes, we do," Richard said. "We live in a world like that. It's a comfort."

Amanda sighed deeply. "When you get this allergy cleared up, what are you going to do to fix yourself? What are you going to do to make yourself pleasant looking again? That's what I need to know. When you meet with people, you're the face of the company. People need to see that you're pleasant looking so that they know the company is pleasant."

Richard shrugged again, dumbfounded that a woman as intelligent as Amanda thought a giant conglomerate like Cascade Enterprises had any hope in hell of being *pleasant*. "I guess I'm focused on what the specialist says next week. First things first. The allergy, I mean."

Amanda made a show of taking in this information. "I want you to think about what I said, Richard."

"I will," he said, feeling uncomfortable and now a little annoyed.

"I want my vice-president of Communications Marketing to be pleasant looking again. I need him to be attractive."

"I hear you."

"Good." She stood there a moment longer, then glanced at her watch. "Look, I'm kind of busy. I have to get going."

"Okay," Richard said.

Abruptly she was gone. He didn't watch her perfect legs depart this morning. He couldn't. He was disliking her too much to pretend to admire her legs.

As the next few minutes passed, Richard found himself wondering again, sitting at his desk, if he was going crazy. There was something persistently wrong with his world these days and, accordingly, it made his life seem wrong as well, like he was at fault somehow. Being at fault meant he *had* to be going crazy, didn't it? What else could all this wrongness mean?

NO SOLACE AT HOME EITHER. Katie, his daughter, thought his allergy was "gross." When she told him so, Richard began to explain about the virtues of empathy, about consideration for the suffering, for people who weren't feeling themselves, for what could be construed to be an illness, but she put her hands over her ears and fled the room, histrionic as always. For some time now, empathy and consideration had been something Katie preferred to receive rather than give. He felt sad that this was the case. While he still held out hope that Katie would learn to feel a legitimate empathy for others, he was aware that the human majority was working against him because it too seemed to see little merit in compassion these days. Empathy? Couldn't hold a candle to the drive of the market to sustain what in his youth had been called conspicuous consumption. Of late, Richard felt a quiet, secret shame about this. No wonder he was pale and puffy. It had occurred to him, by exercising his profession in marketing, he had changed the world's idea of truth into something that wasn't true at all.

Just Saturday affecting his mood, he supposed. Saturday was a day—especially with May hardly arrived—when everyone in his household drifted from room to room, bored and dazed and uninspired. School and work, it seemed, provided a little structure. Saturday, though—unless something major was planned—evolved into a day without idea, a freeway of normally inspirational traffic now suddenly grinding to a halt, bumper to bumper.

When Richard sat down to have coffee in the kitchen, everyone was still in his or her room, including Alex. It wasn't early. Richard was not an early riser. It was just that everyone in his family was busy. Alex was probably reading. His children? He wasn't sure. Usually Richard would briefly corral each one as gradually, around noon, they emerged and found him reading the newspaper in a corner of the living room. He greeted each one as they passed.

"Hey, Kev. What's happening? Whaddyuh got planned for the day?"

"Not sure yet, Dad," Kevin would usually say. "I'm open to some good ideas."

Drake, on the other hand, was going to hang with friends.

"Whereabouts, Son?"

"The mall. Tony's basement."

Richard nodded.

Alex showed up at last, already dressed and made up. "Katie wants to go to the mall. South Shore. Can you get your own lunch? I promised her the food court. Lunch here sounded boring."

"Okay," said Richard.

In the end, it was just him and Kevin at home alone. "What about a western sandwich, Kev?" Richard said from over his shoulder at the refrigerator door. He'd seen eggs on the shelf. He'd felt strangely nostalgic noticing eggs this morning.

"What's a western sandwich? Does it ride a horse, shoot a gun, join a posse?"

"A *western* sandwich, not a *cowboy* sandwich."

"My mistake."

"A sandwich from my youth, smartass."

Kevin grinned. "Well, it looks like you survived it."

"Survived it? I thrived on it. Watch and learn," said Richard. "You're in charge of the fridge, okay?"

Kevin saluted.

"Eggs," said Richard, putting a frying plan on the stove, locating a mixing bowl and a whisk. "Milk, onion, leftover ham, green relish. And the item that makes it mine: cheese, the old cheddar in the drawer. You'll probably want ketchup too. Butter, can't forget butter. Bread. In formal terms, it's a *toasted* western."

"Toasted," said Kevin. "Of course."

Shortly Richard regarded his son with love in his heart, after Kevin had taken a couple of bites of one of his father's youthful pleasures. "So whaddyuh think?" he asked.

"It's good. Whaddyuh have with it?"

"Dip it in ketchup."

"Fries?"

"Sure," said Richard. "Fries on the side, dipped in ketchup too."

The sandwiches vanished quickly. They pushed their stools back a little, now meditative.

"School?" said Richard.

"It's okay."

"Marks?"

"Fine."

"But you don't like it."

"No."

Richard nodded. "Good practice for the world of work. You won't like *it* either."

Kevin thought about this a moment. "Seems like a strange thing to do then."

"What?"

"Work. Find a job. That kind of work."

"We need the money," Richard said, although his tone held little conviction.

"Yeah, but why would you work at a job you didn't like?"

Richard had no real answer. "It just works out that way. You start to make money and then you buy things. To buy bigger things, *more* things, you make more money. It's kind of a treadmill that most people get on."

"The rat race. Right?"

Richard nodded. "That's what it's called, yes. And society's entire system operates on it."

Kevin was thoughtful for a long moment. "Whaddyuh do if you don't want to be part of that system?"

"Good question, Kev. Something else, I guess. You do something else."

"Like what?"

"I don't know. That's the problem; I just don't know. I don't think we're programmed to know. Or, if we did know at one time, we get caught up in the tide of something else and simply forget."

They sat there in silence, privately mulling over Richard's answer.

"You know what I like about you, Dad?" Kevin said at last.

"What?"

"You never bullshit me."

Richard nodded ambivalently. He supposed this was true. While he felt acknowledged by Kevin's words, he found himself wondering if too much truth-telling was a failing on his part. Didn't children need to be taught parental myths to grow up safely? Parental myths are society's myths. Would children who didn't have faith in them find a way to fit into conventional society, to be accepted? Would they be prepared for what Richard called "society's mean streak?"

"What about friends, Kev?" Richard asked shortly. "Do you hang with anyone."

Kevin shrugged. "At school, I guess."

Richard waited.

Kevin shrugged again. "I'm different," he said at last.

"Of course. Different is good, isn't it?"

"Different is *okay*. People don't like it. Too scary, I guess."

"Scary?"

"It's not familiar," Kevin said. "Everyone I know feels safer when everyone's not very different from one another, when everybody's doing and saying the same thing. In my world anyway."

Richard supposed this was true but said nothing for the moment. The same personal ambivalence: should he be encouraging Kevin to be authentic or to blend safely with the crowd?

"How'd you end up doing what you do at Cascade?" Kevin asked suddenly.

Richard didn't know what to say at first. Then, his thoughts collected, he answered the question. "I needed a good job after university. I'd been trained for journalism but newspaper jobs were scarce and the pay wasn't good. Cascade advertised for a low level marketing job and, following an interview, they hired me. The money was good and kept getting better. Time passes. You settle in. The fork in the road where you chose right or left is way back *there*; you stop looking over your shoulder at it. You just accept the choice you made, put on your blinders and keep going."

"You buy things," Kevin said with a grin.

"For your kids too," added Richard, grinning along with him.

Kevin got up to go.

"Keep me posted, Kev."

"About what?"

"Everything. Anything you want."

"I will," Kevin said as he left the kitchen. "Thanks for the toasted western."

"My pleasure," Richard said.

HER NAME WAS VIOLET, she said after they had been talking for a few moments. She had green eyes, a freckle or two on the bridge of her nose. Strawberry blonde hair. She'd been leaning against a tough old cedar at the water's edge, gazing out over the quiet ocean. Thinking, Richard supposed. He hadn't startled her. Or if he had, she was so capable of calm—and this quality struck him right away—her surprise had barely registered.

"Sorry," Richard had said, about to turn away from the rocky shore he'd been exploring, now feeling himself briefly an intruder.

"It's okay," the woman had said. "Join me. Pull up a tree and rest." She smiled an attractive smile. Delicate lift at the corners of her mouth. It made him want to smile in exactly the same way, out of admiration. Shared sense of irony of some kind, he supposed. Teach me how to smile your smile, he thought, feeling strangely released by his secret reflection, by this gentle transgression.

He sat down and leaned against another cedar about a yard away from hers.

"You're new here," the woman said.

Richard hadn't thought about whether he was new or not until now— he didn't feel new at all exactly—but, yes, sitting here with this woman against a tree, he supposed it was true. "Sort of new," he said because "sort of new" was how it felt to him.

That was when she had said her name was Violet.

Then he said he was Richard.

They didn't comment further for a long time, gazing instead out over the water where birds flew and dove, feeding themselves, kingfishers, gulls, even a bald eagle that snatched up a fish in its talons, a sight Richard had never seen before but that seemed familiar to him somehow, a recollection gnarled within the fabric of his roots.

Richard stole glances at the quiet woman a couple of feet away. Sometimes he was aware she was stealing glances at him.

He remembered vaguely that he probably had a rash he should be worried about. He even nearly remembered the little bandages he wore to cover it up. He brought his fingers to his throat, but the rash and the bandages weren't there. Perhaps he had been imagining them all this time, perhaps he'd only dreamed them. And as he thought about it, as he tried to retrieve the accurate recollection of it, his memory of his bandaged rash dissolved even more, fading away to nothing.

"Sorry for staring," the woman, Violet, said, although she hadn't been staring at all. "It's just that you're new. Not new, but *new*. I couldn't help myself."

"That's okay," he said. And it was—her green eyes were wonderful. Pretty. Alert. He would have said: dancing, waltzing with calm. *Maybe* he would have said something like that just now. Yes, now perhaps, but not back *then*, whatever, wherever, whenever the faded "then" he could barely discern at this moment actually was.

"It's confusing being new," Violet offered shortly. "You're feeling the confusion of newness. It's a little like being a baby, an infant. I can see it on your face. You're wrestling with it. It's normal."

"But it feels old too, I guess. No wonder it's confusing."

"I don't know," said Violet. "I never thought of it as being old."

"Of course not," Richard said, thinking he'd insulted her. "You're young."

She seemed prepared to reply but, in the end, didn't respond to his words. "Am I the first person you've met?" she asked instead.

"Yes," said Richard, somewhat confused, only now realizing it was true. "I've seen others. But I haven't had time to meet them. Someone gave me a sandwich once." His voice trailed off. He was only making it worse. The confusion. And he sensed there was some other place where he had met people too but the memory danced away from him every time he tried to capture it.

Violet blushed for no apparent reason. "Oh my," she said, her fingers coming up to her mouth like a child's, as if to hold back anything else she might inadvertently say.

"What?" asked Richard.

"You're *very* new. You're *that* kind of new."

"I guess so," he said, not fully understanding her meaning. "If you say so, I guess I am. That's what it feels like, at least. I don't have much of a past and I'm wondering where the rest of it went. Amnesia?" He said this last word without alarm.

She gazed out over the water.

"You're very pleasant-looking," she told him then.

Strangely, Richard's hands went searching again for the rash he remembered vaguely from some other moment in time. Nothing. He was blemish free. "Thank you," he said at last. Had this woman been waiting for him here? It was an absurd and vaguely arrogant notion, and Richard felt embarrassed by it.

She continued to gaze at the ocean. He could see the smile at the corner of her mouth. He felt something calm and wonderful at this moment, not from her this time, but from within himself. He thought of it as resting in a womb. He was aware he would never be able to explain the sensation to anyone. Because the womb he was in wasn't holding him prisoner, it was too large and open for that. Here, he wasn't trapped. Just comforted, and gently pleased and excited. Yes, womb was the place it felt like, but a womb as large as a sunrise.

THE ALLERGY SPECIALIST was one of those doctors who have no time for anyone. He introduced himself as Dr. Newell. He called Richard Mr. Braddock. It made Richard feel older than he really was.

"We're going to need a lot of blood tests, Mr. Braddock," the specialist said without looking up from the information he'd received about his new patient, open before him on his desk.

Richard examined the doctor's profile, concluding the man was as handsome as a fairy tale prince. Echelons above pleasant-looking. Amanda Drew would think the doctor dangerous, if her view of such things was to be believed. Richard's instincts recognized that the doctor was cold. Business was business, was how it seemed with Dr. Newell.

"You'll have to fast for the blood tests," the specialist was saying.

"Fast?"

"No food or drink for more than twelve hours before the test. My receptionist will fill you in."

And so the tests began—another appointment was scheduled.

RICHARD TOLD DEREK all about it the next day they met on the corner to drink their Starbucks beverages. Now that it was May, the weather was getting better. Mostly, in the people who passed, one sensed a certain optimism, even the budding of joy. Yet, at the same time, car horns honked and invectives drifted by, sirens continued to cry out in the distance and people kept on hurrying. No wonder joy budded with difficulty—it had to hit a constantly moving target. People were on the go: they raced, they ran, they charged, they fled, they scurried. Richard hadn't noticed this until recently, how people lived their lives in a curious state of frenzy, hour after frenzied hour.

"Is the rash dangerous?" Derek wanted to know.

"I don't think so," Richard replied. "But I'm under a great deal of pressure to stop looking like hell."

"That's tough," Derek admitted.

"Yeah. Alex. And Amanda Drew, my boss. I'm no longer pleasant-looking, you see?"

Derek grinned and shook his head. "Pleasant-looking," he murmured somewhat incredulously. "Anyone interested in how you're feeling?"

"Not really," Richard admitted, thinking *everything just lives here* again, the way he always did when he was asked that kind of question.

"I dream a lot," he said. "At least, I remember having dreams. I think they're dreams. The sleeping part—I don't remember that. I'm not even remembering the waking up part very well either. The dreaming, the dreams, they kinda seem more like ideas, in a way, except I barely remember them. Because the waking up is so weird. It's not sleeping. You don't wake up— you emerge from it. It's more like just sensing things, sensing the memories, the dreams that have nothing to do with my normal life."

"Good or bad memories?"

"Incredibly pleasant and peaceful. The sense of it afterwards, I mean."

"That's something, anyways," Derek said, nodding his thanks to a woman from Cascade enterprises who put some coins into his hat. "Choice did that for me, Richie," he added after the woman was gone. "The pleasant, peaceful feeling."

"What choice?"

"*My* choice."

"What does *that* mean?" Richard asked, annoyed to be going suddenly down the same old road towards Derek's unwillingness to be clear, his need to talk about choice without being specific.

"It means we all choose differently, that's all."

"I couldn't be like you, Derek, the way things are right now. You here on the street? I couldn't do that."

"My point exactly," the homeless man said. "That's what I'm trying to say."

"Jesus," Richard muttered, frustrated by his friend's persistent obtuseness.

BAD FAMILY NIGHT. Not new. Not old. Same old same old, as far as bad family nights went. Squabbling among the children. Like most hostilities between the kids, it was difficult after it was over to remember what specifically had started it. This time, though, it went this way: Kevin and Drake. Everyone at the dinner table for the evening meal. Sunday night dinner, a tradition to Richard, though not so much to everyone else. He had given vats of blood on Friday for his allergy tests, and had felt fatigued all day Saturday. He hoped Sunday would renew him. He made barbecued ribs, one of his favourites, a reward to himself for giving so much blood. He'd stood outside on the deck at the gas barbecue, turning the meat, brushing on barbecue sauce, standing under an umbrella because it was drizzling.

"I keep saying we should screen in the deck," Alex said, poking her head out the patio doors not long before he was finished cooking. "This weather just proves my point. At least you'd have a roof over your head."

At her words, Richard felt something unhappy burrow into his chest. He didn't know why exactly. Not the money, per se. Something vapid and trivial about the perceived need? Maybe. Did they really need another project right now, another opportunity to spend thousands at the building supplies store? Richard didn't think so. He was tired of the routine: no sooner was one project completed than another one was conceived. It was like being constantly pregnant, in a state of endless reproduction.

At dinner, Drake asked Kevin to pass the pepper.

Kevin was in fantasyland and didn't seem to hear him.

"Hey asshole, pass the pepper."

"C'mon, Drake, not at *our* dinner table," Richard said.

"I just want some goddamn pepper."

Richard passed it himself, fixing his son with a stern glare.

Drake snatched it from his father's fingers.

"God, I'd rather be somewhere else," Katie suddenly cried. She sighed loudly and rolled her eyes. Richard had said Dougal couldn't come to Sunday dinner this time. Not enough ribs to go around. Besides, Dougal didn't need to be here for *every* evening meal. Privately Richard wondered why Katie couldn't find a boyfriend who was going to amount to something. In fact, why couldn't she find someone he liked to have over for dinner?

"Kevin!" Alex called.

"Sorry," Kevin said, snapping out of his reverie.

"You all right, Kev?" Richard asked.

"Asshole," muttered Drake.

"Okay, Drake. That's it. That's enough. Leave the table."

"Oh Richard," said Alex. "Don't over-react."

Drake pushed his plate away with violence, tipping over what was left of a tumbler of water. It spread enthusiastically across the table, soaking his mother's placemat. This he ignored as he stomped out of the room. "Fuck you," he said over his departing shoulder.

"Shit!" Richard muttered, rising out of his chair, tossing his napkin beside his plate, preparing to go after his son to straighten him out.

"I'll go," Alex said.

"No . . ."

"I'll go!" And Alex left the room as well.

"I'm outta here too," Katie said, standing.

"Katie? Sit down."

"I can't," she wailed. "I can't sit here with you looking so gross. You're killing my appetite. All those zits and bandages!"

Richard was dumbfounded. He could find nothing to say as his daughter left the room.

A couple of minutes passed and none of the others returned to the table.

"Eat up, Son," Richard said.

"Sorry," Kevin said. "I didn't mean to start this." He picked at his food half-heartedly.

"Eat up," Richard said again.

They chewed on their ribs in silence, conspicuously aware that they sat at the table alone.

"I was daydreaming," Kevin confessed shortly, by way of apology. "I wasn't ignoring everyone. I didn't mean anything. Sometimes I discover I'm not here when I think I am. Like I've zoned out."

"I know," his father said. "Happens to the best of us sometimes."

Kevin nodded.

None of the rest of the family returned to the dinner table. Richard and Kevin cleaned up the spilled water. They cleared the table of the wasted dinner, put things away, loaded the dishwasher, and filled the refrigerator with leftovers.

No one came back to apologize, to make peace. This bothered Richard the most. When had it become okay to just let things go? What was wrong with his family? Were they frying their lives in Teflon? Didn't anything stick? Richard resolved that night to find out what was ailing his children and the workings of his family.

The next day, alone on his computer at work, he paid a visit to Facebook.

RICHARD HAD HAD HIS USUAL DIFFICULTIES signing in on Facebook, creating an account, calling IT with some cock and bull story to permit him to scale the company firewall, connecting to the other members of his family. At least some of the difficulty had been his resentment that he was even compelled to take this step—he didn't *want* to be on Facebook. Yet here he was, giving in again. He also found the site complicated and demanding, this too no doubt partially a result of his resentful attitude. Not only did he not want to be on Facebook, he didn't even want to be on his computer. But here he was anyway, looking for a picture of himself to post, trying to sound interested about creating his personal biography. His resentment grew. He felt manipulated, controlled by circumstance. In a vague way, he felt pushed around.

He explored Alex's Facebook page first, in much more detail than when he had done so at home over her shoulder. Most of the exchanges, most of the posts were to or about their three children. Links, information, ideas Alex thought they would be interested in. At first, Richard found the tone of these postings comforting. Alex's focus on their children seemed normal to him, healthy. But soon he began to wonder when his family actually talked to one another without using a device as a medium. Did these electronic posts replace actual conversation, actual *private* conversations? Was it all concocted to be eavesdropped on by others?

Richard remembered, several months ago now, a Saturday afternoon when he'd encountered Katie and Dougal texting, sitting side by side on the sofa. He'd asked them if they were texting one another, basically to confirm his suspicions that they were.

"Yeah," Katie had said without looking up from her cell. "Jeez, Dad."

Later Richard had voiced his incredulity to Alex.

Alex was unperturbed. "All the kids do that."

"Why don't they just talk to one another? They were sitting beside one another."

"Young people today are different than we were," Alex said.

"And this is good?"

"Oh Richard, it just *is*."

"So it's okay with you."

"Richard," his wife said, "stop being such a dinosaur."

Now, with Facebook on his computer screen, Richard supposed he *was* a dinosaur. But this admission was followed immediately by another: he *liked* being a dinosaur.

Katie's Facebook pages were mostly about male celebrities with whom she would like to have sex. Richard sighed. And this was everybody's business? Couldn't she keep these fantasies to herself? He fled Katie's page with relief.

His sons were more circumspect in their posts. Drake posted music news, musicians he liked, others he despised. There were posts about computer games too. Kevin? Not much recently. There was a post, Richard found, about the toasted western sandwich he had served a few weeks ago. "Sounds awful," some girl at school had replied. Kevin had posted back that it was delicious. She'd replied that she hated eggs. Kevin had retorted that "eggs speak well of *you*."

Then, before he could close everything up, he found something Kevin had written to "update your status."

"Just wondering," he had typed. "'Everything just lives here.' Anybody know what it means?"

There'd been one response and Richard seized on it quickly. "Could mean a lot of things," someone Richard didn't know had posted. "Depends on how you say it."

Richard made a mental note to raise the subject with his son. It now seemed to him that the statement must be a popular song lyric; only this could explain why he and Kevin both knew of and were intrigued by the four mysterious words.

THEY TOOK A GREAT DEAL OF BLOOD from Richard over the next few weeks. Worse, they took it to no avail.

"You're a medical mystery, my friend," was how Fred Sexsmith put it to him, without showing any noticeable concern.

"I don't want to be a medical mystery," Richard replied irritably.

"Of course not," said Fred. "No one does."

"So we don't know anything?"

Fred considered his response before he spoke. "We haven't found the specific cause. Your blood work shows some elevations . . . ."

". . . Elevations?"

"It's complicated," said Fred. "In a more general way, in cases like this, we usually conclude it's pollution."

"Pollution? You mean the environment?"

"Yes. Air pollution. Climate change."

"Are you kidding? Are you saying climate change is giving me this rash?" Surely there would be thousands, millions of other people affected in this way, Richard mused. If so, that many victims wouldn't be content to sit around and endure an environmental degradation that was giving them a rash, would they?

"Not exactly climate change," said Fred. "Not literally. I mean in the more general sense. Damage to the environment might be giving you the rash. Allergens increase when everything in the environment is in decline."

Gobsmacked, Richard was silent.

"Then there's your psychological distress," Fred continued. "Your concern about your homeless friend, Derek. Work. Family. The times. You know, life."

Richard nodded. Life. He knew, in this context, what that was.

"Dr. Newell, of course, doesn't place as much credence on *those* circumstances as I do."

"Jesus, Fred, I'm under a lot of pressure to get this cleared up. Alex. Amanda Drew. Telling them it's just pollution isn't going to reconcile things for them."

"Which, of course, would tend to make it worse," said Fred.

"Yeah. I'll tell Amanda Drew I'm allergic to *her*. See where *that* gets me."

Fred grinned. He'd heard about Amanda Drew from Richard for some time now, enough to know what Richard meant.

"Well shit, Fred, I don't want to conclude that I'm allergic to life—it simply isn't true."

"Of course it isn't," said Fred. "That isn't what I meant. But life as you and I live it inspires a broad array of irritants, mostly environmental and sometimes psychological, which can give us an allergic reaction, a rash. There's no way that means you're allergic to *life*. It's just that life has its ups and downs, its issues. Sometimes we react to this and it's like an allergy."

Richard felt comforted after Fred's explanation. Knowing he had still more to confess, his doctor's words encouraged him to do so.

"I zone out, Fred."

"As do we all."

"I go to a different place."

"Of course," said Fred.

"I don't actually remember it when I come back, but I sense I remember it. The place, I mean. It's not clear in my memory."

"Sure," said Fred.

Seeing his doctor didn't truly understand, Richard hesitated before continuing. Then, "I sense that I like it there. I sense that, sometimes, I don't want to leave."

"The zone?"

"Yeah. I don't want to come back *here*."

"You need a vacation, my friend," Richard's doctor said.

"I'm worried, Fred."

"Worry is fear. Remember what Buddha said: the key to existence is no fear."

"Huh! Easier said than done."

"Puts worry into a different perspective, though, when you really think about it."

"What now, Fred."

"Newell isn't done with you. He wants to schedule a few more blood tests."

"Okay."

"And you have to stop worrying."

Richard nodded.

"Get control of your life. Stop letting it control you."

"Tall order, Fred."

"Sure is," said Fred Sexsmith. "If I could bottle advice like that and sell it, I would."

Richard stood up to go. "I'd order a couple of crates, Fred."

"I know you would," his doctor said.

THE SUN BOMBARDING THE BOARDROOM again. Everyone wearing dark glasses. Another report on new product development. A vice-president from the west coast droning on about a conference he had attended where the assembly had heard from a futurist. Gobbledygook, Richard thought not long after the man began to report his findings. Piffle.

He could feel Amanda Drew watching him and sensing his disapproval, but he couldn't be sure because she was wearing her dark glasses. Behind their shades, the entire room of people seemed to be playing a bizarre game of hide and go seek.

Richard pretended to make notes. "Three D printer will print out food," he'd written.

He glanced around the room again, still certain Amanda was watching him, maybe even glaring at him. This he might be imagining. The sun-filled room was too brilliant to confirm his suspicions.

Now the west coast VP began to talk about AI. Richard made another note.

Then . . .

. . . Violet introduced him to three new people on the beach. The three—Leon, Gary, and Isabel—had been approaching them along the shore for several minutes, strolling towards them from a great distance. Everyone walked slowly and it took a great deal of time for them to approach. Eventually, though, when they were close enough, they drifted to a halt.

"This is Richard," Violet said. "He's new here."

The others nodded and smiled happily.

"Richard may have questions," Violet said then.

Questions? Did he have questions? Yes, suddenly he did.

"What do you guys do?"

"I'm at the school," said Leon.

"Me too," Isabel said when Richard glanced at her. "I work with Leon at the school."

"I fish," said Gary.

"What about you?" Isabel asked Richard.

Unsure, he turned to Violet but she was looking at him in anticipation too.

"It appears," said Richard then, "that I'm here to tell the truth. Not sure what job that gives me."

Everyone expressed delight. Violet took his hand and held it in encouragement. "The truth is a virtue here," she explained. "We need and admire it here."

Here? He wondered about "here." Because, obviously, there was somewhere else—the *there* that was the antithesis of *here*—but although Richard sensed the other place, he couldn't remember it.

Violet still held his hand but soon gave it a squeeze before letting go. Richard enjoyed her touch. He'd begun to think Violet was wonderful, and exciting too. There was a faint notion in him that he shouldn't think so—a memory or instinct that it was somehow improper to think she was wonderful—but he couldn't remember why. As long as he kept his caring to himself, he supposed, everything would be all right, much of his confusion would simply melt away. Sometimes a man achieved wonders when he did nothing. . .

. . . Richard glanced at his notes. The meeting was being adjourned. The future the vice-president from the coast had been talking about was entirely technological, and this troubled him. Cars were going to drive themselves from destination to destination. Drones would fly overhead, photographing your garden, catching you leaning on your rake. The speaker hadn't discussed how people would feel, what they would think, how they would be governed. No, the future he discussed had concerned itself with trinkets. Product. Stuff. Ways to capture a life in pictures you'd be too busy photographing to actually live. The future wasn't going to be about people. No, it was going to be about people buying and using their *stuff*. Behind his dark glasses, Richard frowned. He felt strangely sad, realizing his career would require more elaborate dishonesty in future. He would have preferred to know he was going to be able to tell—and help people to find—the truth.

A RARE CIRCUMSTANCE—all the children were out. Just he and Alex at home. They'd flipped on the television and were watching a reality show. Some numb-nuts woman was crying over being ejected from the show. Richard was annoyed with her. Thankfully, the show went to commercial and, using the remote, Richard muted the sound. Television was now a freak show. He felt embarrassed to watch it. What was the word his children used? Skanky. He found reality TV skanky. He changed the channel to a show called

"Naked and Afraid." A trio appeared to be crossing the African Veldt entirely nude, in relative proximity to a Black Mamba, a dangerous and speedy venomous snake. The equally dangerous breasts and private parts of the program's participants were blurred for family viewing. Richard and Alex watched for two or three minutes, then changed the channel back to the other reality show. "This kind of reality isn't reality at all," Richard said.

Now, watching the first show—he thought it might be "Big Brother"— he was troubled by where he was and why he was here at this moment. "Are you happy, Alex?" he asked.

She looked at him over the top of her glasses. "With what?"

"Life? The world? Us?"

She sighed heavily. "You know I hate questions like that."

"Yes," said Richard. "The abstraction in them. I know. Too vague." He raised his arms and fingers to put "the abstraction" into quotation marks for her.

"Then why do you ask them?"

This time, *he* sighed. "It's the way I think sometimes. I don't do it to annoy *you*."

"I always think, when you ask me if *I'm* happy, that you're telling me *you're* not happy."

Richard nodded—he supposed he could see why she felt that way. And he was pleasantly surprised to discover that she might be concerned, on occasion, with whether or not he was happy.

"This is a bad time for you, Richard."

"Yes."

"That awful rash, the allergy."

"Yup."

"The rest of it, though," and she was peering at him over her glasses again as she spoke, "is just things about life you won't accept."

"I . . ."

". . . The show's on."

Richard hit the mute button again and the sound resumed. The cameras revisited the weeping woman, in case viewers had missed it or hadn't cared enough the first time around, or hadn't had a chance to feel superior yet.

"Can we watch something with a plot?" Richard muttered.

"Of course, Dear," Alex said.

"Are you having an affair?" Richard hid the question inside the act of flicking through the channels, looking for a crime show.

"You're kidding, aren't you?"

Richard hesitated. "Only partially," he confessed.

"Boy," said Alex. "When, where, how would I ever have an affair?"

"Yeah," said Richard. "Sorry."

"I'd be flattered, if I wasn't so insulted."

"I don't blame you," Richard admitted. "I guess I'm just wondering why we're in a rut."

"*You're* in a rut, Richard. *I'm* not."

"We don't have sex, Alex."

"I know we don't. Your rash, the allergy. It's almost hideous."

"Hideous? That's hyperbole and you know it."

She *did* know it but gave no sign.

"What about *before* the rash?"

"It hasn't been *that* long, Richard."

"Months, Alex. It's been months."

Alex just rolled her eyes, ending this exchange.

Richard knew what Alex had said was true. *He* was the one in the rut. Trouble was, Alex liked the rut that he didn't like. It wasn't called a rut if you liked it, right? Clearly she believed he'd created this impasse all by himself. Was that it? Was it *his* fault? Or was it really a rut that only he could see?

Damn, his life had gone missing, mislaid under the couch like one half of a pair of socks.

On the giant television screen cops chased robbers and bullets slammed noisily into walls and bodies, a world of shattered glass and squealing tires. Husband and wife watched this mayhem together, drifting down different tributaries. Richard thought about how wonderful it would be to have sex with Alex, right here, right now. "Wild monkey sex," he would have called it a couple of years ago. They would have laughed at his words. But they would have done it, laughing or not. Right here in the living room. With the kids out, away from home and not expected back? You bet. God, he missed that. Or at least he was convinced he did.

KEVIN WENT RUNNING with him over the holiday weekend in May. And Richard asked his son about the four words that continued to dance in a monotone in his mind, the four words that Kevin apparently knew about too: *Everything just lives here.*

A year or so ago Kevin and Richard had run together on a regular basis. Over time though, the regular running date had drifted away. Richard blamed himself for this—he'd been the one to let it slip. Kevin was the only other runner in the family. Richard regretted not making the most of it, renewing the event again as a celebration of their father and son friendship. And, on this occasion, he'd specifically made the running date only to be able to ask his son about *everything just lives here.* Suddenly he felt disingenuous.

"Saw it," Richard was saying. "On your Facebook page."

They were jogging along the trail that bordered the stream cutting through the green space at the rear of the street where their house was located. The fine gravel on the trail crunched loudly under their sneakers. With the dryness of summer still more than a month away, the brook nearby offered up a pleasant burble as it headed for the storm sewer a couple of blocks away.

"Thought you stayed away from Facebook, Dad."

"Yeah. Me too. But the rest of you guys are there. I thought I should show up and maybe join the conversation."

"I don't use Facebook much," Kevin said. "Not like Drake and Katie."

"I noticed that," Richard admitted. "But I saw the line—*everything just lives here*—and I wondered if it was a song or something. To be honest, Kevin I hear it all the time myself, several times a day in fact."

They rounded a bend, ran up a slight incline and emerged from the trail by the brook. Now they were back in the cloister of suburbia, running along streets that would lead them to the high school the three Braddock siblings attended. There, unless someone altered the ritual, Richard and Kevin would run two turns around the track before heading home the way they had come.

Kevin wasn't looking at him. "You mean there's a tune?" he said uncomfortably.

"Like a melody?"

"Yeah."

"No," said Richard. "No melody. That's what's so odd about it. It's not even a chant. It's kind of flat. A monotone."

Kevin said nothing.

"If you could hum a few bars, Kev, that'd be okay with me." Richard grinned to show that he was mostly kidding.

"I can't," said Kevin, still looking straight ahead.

They were both panting from the run now, although Richard was more breathless than his son.

"You mean you don't know the tune?"

Kevin was clearly a bit uncomfortable. "It's like you said," he told his father at last. "There is no tune. Not that *I've* heard anyway."

They ran on.

"How often in a day do you think of it or hear it?" Richard asked.

"A lot, I guess."

"Me too."

"I get to wondering if it's one of those things you think because you tell yourself not to think something. Know what I mean? The more you tell yourself not to think it, not to hear it, the more you think about it. That ever happen to you?"

"Yeah, it has," Richard said.

"Whatever," admitted Kevin, "I've stopped telling myself not to think it and I think it anyway."

"Me too, I guess."

"Besides, melody or not, it isn't that I think it. It's more that I *hear* it."

They ran on a few more yards.

"Want to take a break?" Richard asked as the high school came into view in the distance.

"Yeah. Sure."

They held up at the entrance to a cul de sac. The high school was visible in a large ravine at the end of the next block. Richard put his hands on his waist and bent over for a moment or two. "Phew," he said as he straightened up. "I'm getting old."

Kevin smiled, but through pursed lips. "What about you, Dad? You know what I mean when I say, *hearing* it?"

Richard nodded. "I *hear* it that way too."

"Like a song with no tune, right?"

"Yeah. A song with no tune."

"So you don't know where it comes from either."

"Nope."

"Weird," said Kevin. "And you don't know what it means."

"No. I hear it without inflection."

"There are four different ways to say it," said Kevin.

"Yeah. I've tried that. Changing the emphasis."

"Which one do you think is right?"

"I don't know, Son."

"Maybe *all* of them," Kevin said.

"Maybe."

They stood there together, looking down the street. Except for brief glances, they felt awkward catching each other's eye.

Kevin looked down at his feet. "It's not like it's a voice. You still *hear* it, but there's no voice. It's not female. It's not male."

"A whisper," Richard said. "As if it shows up from . . . inside itself somehow."

Kevin took a long, deep breath, shrugged. "How weird is all of this?"

"Weird enough," Richard replied, putting his hand on his son's shoulder. "But I don't think we have to hide the sharp objects in the house or anything."

Kevin grinned. "That's a comfort," he said.

"I'd race you to the school if I wasn't sure I'd lose," Richard said then.

"Yeah, Dad, you should probably take it easy."

"Watch the lip, buddy."

And with that, they were running again. Richard felt better. *Everything just lives here.* Fair enough, Richard thought. Fair enough. Like everything else, his rash, his discomfort with himself, the zoning out business, he supposed the repetitious chant would eventually go away.

JUNE NOW. HOT DAYS SOMETIMES. Sunshine. Humidity. On the street near Cascade Enterprises, there was an increase in the frequency of ill humour. Traffic was heavier on the street, on the sidewalk too. Exhaust fumes, horns, sirens, cries, the sound of shuffling, scurrying feet.

"It's the same today as yesterday," Richard complained to his homeless friend after a long glance around the street.

"What's the same?"

"Everything."

"You oughtta be me, Richie."

Richard glanced at Derek, somewhat ashamed. "It's all relative," he muttered.

They fell silent in the eye of the hurricane of street noise.

"What about your rash?" Derek asked.

It was Monday morning. The two men tended to catch up on things on Monday mornings. This was now the pattern in their meetings. By Friday they would be wishing each other a good weekend and Richard would feel miserable at the deep contrast their weekends represented. To wish Derek a fine weekend felt deeply hollow to him because, so far, he'd failed to do anything significant to help his friend.

"They've given up," Richard said shortly.

"Given up?"

"My doctors. Newell, the specialist, has concluded the allergy isn't life-threatening. He says it will go away in time. In an uncharacteristic moment of warmth and good humour, Newell told me that ninety percent of human ailments go away on their own. What it boils down to, he says, in blunt terms, is he can't help me."

"Wow."

"And Fred Sexsmith, my GP, tells me it's psychological."

"Psychological?"

"He says I need to change my lifestyle."

"Lifestyle," repeated Derek. "Now there's a word with some rash on it."

"Yeah."

A bike sped by, carrying a twentysomething female pedalling furiously. Two motorists honked their horns at her, apparently jealous of the bike's ability to smoothly glide through the traffic gridlock.

"How does Sexsmith think you should change your lifestyle?"

Richard shrugged. "He says take a break. Take a sabbatical. Cross the country. Take a long trip to Tahiti. Whatever I think might work. It's all vague and impossible."

"Is it really impossible?"

"Yeah. I have bills to pay. Children in school. Katie's going to university in the fall. Alex. Cascade. Amanda Drew. They all have their fingers at my throat in some way or other. No wonder I've got a rash on my neck."

"It's *your* life, Richie."

"No it's not, it's theirs. I live it for *them*."

Derek said nothing.

Richard said nothing.

Then, "I feel selfish when I talk like this."

"I know," said Derek. "It's the price we pay for wanting to be authentic. You get to drown in the guilt."

They pondered the conundrum further in silence.

But the street that surrounded them talked endlessly, babbling noisily, volleying relentless minutiae back and forth as it passed them by here on the sidewalk. Richard and Derek could hear how much of it seemed like nothing, so that Richard felt further trapped by his circumstances.

IN THE END, RICHARD INSISTED that his family take a vacation with him. This, he believed, might curtail his allergy. It had been five years since the last real holiday, his children much younger then, still capable of a physical kind of fun that didn't find its focus in technology. They'd spent three days at a water park, screaming on waterslides, delighting in the speed and freedom of their wet, resilient bodies. Whenever he recalled the vacation's various activities with affection, it was the water park that Richard remembered most.

"I need your support on this, Alex," he said, lying in bed with his wife one muggy June night, as they were readying themselves to go to sleep. "Put your book away for once and hear me out."

Alex sighed ever so gently in protest but placed her book on her night-table.

"Last time I saw Fred Sexsmith he suggested I need a vacation."

"To help with the rash?"

Richard hadn't thought about it quite that way until recently, but he was newly convinced it was true—the time away from work and home would help alleviate the various stresses Fred thought might be behind his allergy. "Yes," Richard said. "He thought it would help."

"You mean a full-blown family vacation? You, me, the kids?"

"Yes," said Richard. "Katie goes to university this fall. The boys a year from now. This summer is our last opportunity. After this summer, everyone will be too grown up, everyone meaning Katie."

"They won't go, Richard."

"I'm going to insist. With your support, of course."

"Where do you want to go?"

"I was thinking the East Coast. The Cabot Trail, Peggy's Cove. Newfoundland. The bay of Fundy. PEI. The whole East Coast nine yards. I'd rent a big RV, something that gave us lots of room."

"How many weeks?" asked Alex.

"Four or five. I have that much vacation time coming to me."

"I don't, Richard. I'd have to ask for extra time at the library. Don't forget I'm a part-timer."

"Tell them you need a leave of absence. Any money you lose, we'll make up out of the vacation budget. You know, your losses become part of the cost of the trip."

"Maybe," Alex said.

They fell silent a moment. Richard was aware they both were lying rigidly on their backs and that both of them stared at the ceiling as they talked. So far, they had not looked at one another. Was it the heat and humidity that kept them from touching, that forced them so far apart? Or were they nearly strangers these days? The air conditioning was on. Maybe it wasn't the heat— maybe it was *them*. Maybe the glue that held their marriage together was cracked and drying out.

"I don't know, Richard," Alex was saying now.

"Fred Sexsmith says I need a vacation. I think he's right."

"Sounds expensive," Alex mused.

"I don't care. We have the money."

"Katie won't go, not without Dougal."

"No Dougal," Richard said with a sigh. "Our last family vacation. Just the five of us."

"I know you don't like Dougal, Richard, but . . ."

". . . No Dougal. My final word."

"Katie won't go."

"She's going. She's not staying behind. You want to come back to a house that's been left to Katie for five weeks, that's been party central for that long?"

"No," said Alex after a moment's hesitation.

"Katie goes with us, Alex. This is important."

"I see that," Alex said.

"I need your support on this."

"And Fred Sexsmith says it will help with your allergy?"

"Yes. I agree with him."

"When are we talking, Richard?"

"Mid-July to mid-August."

"Katie's university?"

"All the paperwork and preparations done before we leave."

Alex sighed. "You have it all figured out."

"I do."

"Okay." Alex reached for her book. "Can I read now?"

"I need a family meeting, Alex. I need to tell everyone when we're all present. Can you keep it quiet until then? I don't want anything said until we've all gathered together."

"When?" Alex glanced at him for the first time as she opened her book.

" How about Sunday at dinner?"

"Fine. Anything else?"

Richard glanced at his wife, anticipating an ironic smile to accompany the mock obsequiousness in her question, but it wasn't there. Alex was already reading.

"DOCTOR'S ORDERS," was how Richard presented his vacation request to Amanda Drew the next day.

"Okay, okay," she said, raising her hands as if his request was an assault that she needed to ward off. "As long as I get back my healthy vice-president of communications marketing."

"You will," Richard promised, although he knew there was no guarantee.

"It's been months, Richard."

"Months?"

"Since you were pleasant looking."

"Oh."

"Anything else, Richard?"

He rose to his feet. "No. Thanks, Amanda."

She was making a note in her appointment book. She did not look up at him as he left. She was wearing a low-cut blouse and a push-up bra. He glanced at her fashionable cleavage, then away again, surprised that he was unimpressed. Everybody had cleavage these days. It was all part of the spectacle. Underneath it all, Amanda was being a bitch about his allergy. Attractive cleavage didn't alter the fact. Pleasant-looking my ass, he reflected. It wasn't like he was giving this rash to himself.

TO NO ONE'S SURPRISE, Richard's vacation proposal evolved in reverse. It *de*volved. He'd expected fierce resistance during the family meeting after dinner. Dougal had been there for the meal but Richard had asked him politely to leave, there was family business to discuss. There'd been the expected objections to the vacation—from Katie and Drake, with Alex acknowledging the fairness in their arguments—but the resistance hadn't been fierce. In the end, Richard concluded everyone was at least grudgingly on board.

But two nights later, Alex reported that it was doubtful Katie would go. "Not without Dougal," she said.

"Dougal's not going."

"Then Katie won't."

"Yes, she will."

Alex barrelled forward. "And there's too much to do to get her ready for university."

"She can 't stay here alone. I don't trust her."

Alex nodded but didn't say anything to that.

Two more days passed. Alex invited Richard for a walk in the neighbourhood. Wow, Richard thought. How long had it been, a walk together around the crescents and streets in the area where they lived? He tried to feel pleased but his pleasure was smothered by a growing apprehension.

"I have a solution to the Katie problem," Alex said at last, after they'd politely chatted about other subjects, more or less for show.

"What's that?" Richard asked.

"You won't like it."

"Go on." Richard already knew he wouldn't like it. At this moment it was clear this walk was happening specifically to convey news he wouldn't like. He already felt defeated.

"I'm staying here with Katie."

"Jesus Christ!" Richard muttered, although he felt no real surprise.

"I don't want to come back to a wrecked house."

"Surely we can tell her not to wreck the house and she wouldn't . . . you know . . . wreck the fucking house!" Richard glanced at his wife, catching her expression of incredulity at his words. Hearing them himself, he abruptly felt naive and embarrassed. Clearly, to Alex, his expectations of his children weren't realistic. Teenagers wrecked their parents' houses when the parents were away, everyone said so, it was the way of the world, everyone just accepted it.

"And I have to help her get ready for school," Alex said.

Richard said nothing. He realized, at this moment with a heavy heart, that he had lost the battle. He'd been kidding himself from the beginning.

"I suppose, if Dougal was going . . ."

"Dougal told her he wouldn't go. He likes the idea of four weeks in an RV with you about as much as you like four weeks in an RV with him. He told Katie he'd break up with her if she went."

"And she's going to let the little prick push her around, call the shots like that?"

"Oh Richard, she's just a child. She only turned eighteen in the spring."

"She can arrange for birth control but can't stand up for her rights to take a vacation? The incongruity is amazing," Richard said in a fury.

"I'm sorry," Alex said.

"Me too," Richard said. "I'm sorry too."

Drake—and nothing could surprise Richard now—opted out of the vacation too. Upon hearing that his mother and sister were staying home, he announced he didn't have to go either. "Do you want a miserable kid going with you on vacation?" Alex said, bringing him Drake's decision. By now, entirely defeated, Richard admitted that he did not and gave in.

"Take Kevin somewhere," Alex said. "You two are closer anyway. You have much more in common."

Richard said he'd think about it.

In the end, he asked Kevin what he would like to do.

"I wouldn't mind going camping for a week or two, like when I was young," Kevin said.

"Wilderness or car camping?" Richard asked.

"You'd really do wilderness?"

"Sure. I like wilderness camping. It's your mother who wants the car parked nearby. And we're both experienced. If we're going to go away, we should *really* go away, someplace where the cell phone can't reach us."

"We'll have to get outfitted, won't we?"

"Yup. Most of the old gear is gone. But that'll be part of the fun too, finding the stuff we'll need."

Kevin's broad grin went suddenly sombre. "Sorry your East Coast thing didn't work out, Dad."

"It's okay, Kev. Just between you and me, I can't say that I'm surprised."

THE PLACE WHERE RICHARD TOLD THE TRUTH, and where the truth was considered a virtue, inspired him to create a tiny newspaper. It was an old-fashioned and rather rough publication, barely a dozen pages of announcements and stories that this strange world considered news. Richard didn't question his new vocation. The notion to publish the truth in this way just came to him one day and he knew it was what he must do. He felt himself to be newly born, not like an infant, but as a brand new adult with a brand new responsibility. In a sense, running his little newspaper seemed to be something he'd always done. When he found himself in this place, time behaved strangely, simultaneously vast and shrunken. Vast because it went backwards into infinity, with memories he could barely detect and historic knowledge he only nearly remembered. Shrunken, because what lay ahead was small and unknown and didn't need to be considered beyond the vague notion that it was going to last some kind of near forever, and the forever it would last was going to be permanently serene. Violet had told him about the forever part, how long life was. He couldn't remember enough about the other world he inhabited to challenge what she said.

"This place is mostly set in the present," Violet said one day when Richard felt nearly clear enough about the question of time to ask her about it. "Past and future here, they're pretty small, because we can't do anything about them."

"Yes, I see," said Richard. "That's the way I feel it sometimes."

"But they're large and long too," Violet added. "Because much has and will happen."

"I feel that too."

"I mean, beyond learning from it, the past isn't something to worry about," she was saying.

"No," admitted Richard. "I suppose not."

"And the future? Too much concern about the future is the very definition of senseless worry. Right?"

"I suppose it is," said Richard.

"Worry is something we can do without. Right?"

When Violet said things like that, Richard was convinced she was telling the truth. Yet he sensed truth of this nature was difficult to hang onto. After all, there was that vague *other* place too that he could only occasionally nearly begin to remember, where he lived a different life in a more fragile truth. And he sensed it existed, catching glimpses of it out of the corner of his eye.

"I'm not dead, am I?" Richard asked, glancing at his companion a moment because he expected her to laugh.

"No," said Violet, shaking her head. "You're standing right here with me."

"I mean, this isn't heaven, is it?"

Violet thought for a moment while she shook her head. "Not in the way *you* mean it. It's not . . ." and she grinned . . . "life after death."

"It's just that it's wonderful here."

She glanced at him, a delicate smile on her lips. "You haven't seen anything yet."

He said nothing in reply, feeling cautious because he was aware that now he loved her, and that perhaps he always had, but . . .

"It gets easier to understand," Violet promised, her one concession to a larger future. "At some point, if you choose this place, you'll remember the other one much more clearly."

"Right now I'm kind of in between. Right?"

"That's one way of putting it," Violet said.

Even Richard's newspaper announced only small aspects of what lay ahead tomorrow. Something was happening at the school . . . everyone was invited to . . . people he didn't know were pleased to announce . . .

"What do you call your newspaper?" Violet asked him then.

"The Bulletin," he replied.

She smiled in approval.

And Richard smiled back at her.

"I'm here to tell the truth," he said nearly like a child, although Violet knew this about him already. Still, he liked to say so right out loud. And he often did. And Violet shared his pride immensely. The truth was no small thing to show up for, to live a life around.

RICHARD AND KEVIN left for their camping trip as if they were sneaking out of town. A Saturday morning. Tip-toeing through the house with their packs and other gear, closing the door each time they went outside so that the latch wouldn't click and disturb the slumber of the rest of the family, known to be crabby if their sleep was interrupted. Their rented SUV (Alex had insisted on keeping hers at home and the Audi didn't have space for what they were taking with them) glistened in the sunshine. Richard and Alex had said their so-longs the previous night, lying side by side in their bed, not yet reading, just gazing up at their ceiling the way they often did. Alex had asked him to be careful.

"Careful?"

"Bears and stuff."

He had purchased bear spray, the kind you wear in a holster on your belt, one for him and one for Kevin. He reminded Alex of this, even though, during all of the times he had camped, he had never seen a bear, not even in the distance.

"Come back healthy," she said.

Alex was referring to his allergy, he knew, but, "We will," he said.

It would have been nice to make love but he knew better than to suggest it—he was still spotted and speckled with bandages and ointment. In the end he fell asleep while she was still reading, feeling leprous and discarded in the way he usually did in recent times.

As for Drake and Katie, he didn't get to say goodbye to them. Both were out with friends when he got home from work and they weren't back before he went to bed. He knew better than to awaken them early in the morning when he and Kevin were departing—a goodbye interrupting sleep would not be welcome.

"Going to be hot," Kevin said as he climbed into the vehicle and reached for his seatbelt.

"Yup. Hot already."

And with the rest of the family undisturbed, they pulled out of the driveway, Richard behind the wheel, making for the nearest Tim Hortons. He felt a pleasant excitement about their going away. It paled by comparison with what he knew he would have felt had his original East Coast trip survived intact, but he was now looking forward to being away in the wilderness, a decent consolation prize. Kevin was good company. A break was a break. And family was family, no matter how splintered and separate from one another its members were. You took the moments you could get, however reductive they might be.

They wound their way through the drive-thru at Hortons—coffee and three breakfast sandwiches, one for Richard and two for Kevin (teenagers could eat)—then headed north towards Algonquin Park. Traffic was reasonably light; everyone else leaving the city for the weekend had left the night before. Richard could picture the slithering gridlock of vehicles that probably serpentined the freeways until nearly midnight.

Richard had said goodbye to Derek the previous day too. He and his friend were now a fixture on the corner, Richard's daily donation tucked into Derek's ball cap, their Starbucks coffees in hand.

"You'll be here when I get back, right?"

"Yes," said Derek.

"Unless something good happens."

Derek laughed. "You mean, if I win the lottery or something?"

"Something like that," Richard had said. "Of course you'd have to have a ticket."

They'd both grinned at this fairy tale.

Now, driving north, Richard felt a deep ambivalence about whether or not Derek would occupy the same spot on the sidewalk when he returned. If Derek was gone when he got back, he would never know if it was because something good or something bad had happened to him. Fearing this a few days ago, he'd invited Derek to go camping with him and Kevin.

"My place is here," Derek had said. "But thank you for thinking of me."

No surprises there, Richard thought now, as he sped along the highway. Derek, he knew, was afraid of losing his particular spot on the unforgiving sidewalk. As far as Richard knew, for much of the day it was the only home Derek had.

THEY PADDLED UP CANOE LAKE, stopping to visit Tom Thomson's Cairn. Here, they planned to have lunch. And they needed the break; there was a chop on the lake and too many motor boats. Both Richard and Kevin were rusty navigating a canoe on rough water. Laughing and embarrassed, they had to take two passes at the dock before they were able to safely grab hold to disembark. It was a large canoe. It had to carry quite a bit of gear. It was going to be a hefty craft to portage.

They climbed the steep incline up to the cairn. Kevin carried his father's pack, which contained their lunch. They'd been here before. They glanced at the bronze plaque honouring Thomson, then gazed out over the lake in silence, the heat of the day bearing down on them through a gap in the tree cover.

"I thought we could camp somewhere on Little Joe Lake," Richard said when they were done eating. "One short portage. Perfect for our first day."

Kevin nodded.

"You remember Little Joe, Kev?"

"Little Joe Lake? I sure do. We spent a long weekend there."

"Yes."

"You, me, Drake, and Kyle Bennett."

Richard nodded. Kyle Bennett. He remembered him. Chubby kid. Freckles. Runny nose. Great laugh. One of those voices, when he grew up, that would be perfect for heckling at a ball game. But Kyle had been glad when the weekend was over; he wasn't fond of the wilderness. He suffered fears of bears, of snakes, of the dark, and was bothered by the lack of conveniences.

"There's no roof on the outhouse, no walls," he'd complained. "It's just a . . ."

". . . Box," Richard had said.

"Yeah."

"Where's Kyle these days anyway?" Richard wanted to know now.

Kevin shrugged. "He went to a different high school. Haven't seen him since that summer."

Richard understood. High schools represented galaxies in their separateness, he remembered. In *his* day too. Growing up was like trying to function in a universe of empty space. He remembered faces from his own youth, loves, friends. All of them had disappeared. So important at the time of their being needed. Then gone, replaced by the new and briefly important. It was similar to what had nearly happened to him and Derek, the years they had been out of touch before their encounter on the street had inspired an unexpected reunion.

"Remember the loon swimming under our canoes?" Kevin asked.

"I do. Up close and personal."

"I didn't know loons were so big until then."

"No. Me neither."

"And those people who were sunbathing in the nude on Little Joe?"

Richard grinned. He'd forgotten the incident until this moment. They'd had to politely paddle around out in the lake, at a safe distance, while the nude sunbathers, six in all, hurriedly fled the shore to put on their clothing. Soon, dressed and mostly blonde, the sunbathers were paddling away—they weren't camping at the site and apparently had only stopped briefly to lie in the sun on the rocks. Richard and his charges had begun to pitch camp there as soon as the sunbathers were paddling away from the area. In the end, they hadn't seen much in the distance as the young people fled the shore. Pale buttocks. Bare legs. But his charges had found it titillating.

"You thought then they were Europeans," Kevin was remembering.

"The nudists?"

"Yeah."

"Because Canadians don't sunbathe together in the nude in Algonquin Park. Trust me on that—we're Canadians, after all. But Europeans? Different culture. Not so shy. Not so hung up about their nakedness."

Father and son walked to the cairn, took time to read the plaque. "In memory of Tom Thomson . . ."

"Well," said Richard at last. "I guess we should get going."

Carefully they made their way down the steep incline to their canoe and the rest of their gear. They put on their life jackets and pushed out into Canoe Lake's chop. They began paddling north towards their first portage.

RICHARD ENJOYED THE REWARDS of labour that wilderness camping provided. Work in the wilderness resulted directly in benefit. What a man did at his campsite corresponded entirely to his needs and nothing else. It wasn't complicated. Nothing was accomplished for some cause he was expected to blindly accept. No, a man found and chopped wood so that he could build a fire. He pumped water out of the lake so that he could purify it for drinking and cooking. He pitched his tent in such a way that it would keep out the rain. He tied his food supplies in tree branches overhead so that it didn't attract bears or skunks, so that it wasn't stolen by raccoons. There was a deep satisfaction in doing all of this work well. The rewards were obvious. Richard wished his professional life could be as direct as his wilderness obligations were, not the convoluted mess of complex vagaries at Cascade Enterprises.

Yet he felt childish for wishing this, selfish and irresponsible. And he thought about these things often when he and Kevin stared in silence into their campfire every night. He gazed into the gently dancing flames and, recognizing his inner conflict, succumbed to a vague but powerful guilt that he didn't seem able to be happier about what his life had accomplished.

The weather was good. They swam, they canoed, they shared domestic duties. They played cribbage and they talked. Alex was right. He and Kevin got along well. Kevin was the only one of his children he believed was also one of his friends. Richard felt mysteriously at fault about this but ultimately rationalized the various antagonisms between him and Drake and Katie, concluding they were probably only temporary. There was so much inner conflict in life, Richard decided. What a man *was* versus what a man *should be*. That was the crux of the human war, wasn't it? I'm this and I should be *that*. This makes *me* happy; *that* makes *you* happy. Existential crisis, Richard supposed. Everyone was mired in it. But no way of knowing how many *knew* they were.

He and Kevin canoed deeper into the park and found another site where they could camp.

"A change of scene, Kev," Richard said.

They broke camp early on the morning they left Little Joe Lake. A perfect day to move. Sunshine everywhere, the lake sounds barely a whisper.

"I think I'll just live out here from now on, Dad, if it's okay with you," Kevin said as they paddled towards a portage they'd identified on their map.

"Yeah," admitted Richard. "I know what you mean."

"Then again, there's winter."

"Yup. There's winter."

And they paddled quietly on, privately musing, Richard knew, about how wonderful life could be, each thinking his own thoughts, that were both different yet the same. It was so peaceful here. Even temporary peace was a state they coveted, yet felt strangely guilty about. Why, on a bad day, did peace seem to be a state of failure? What was it they had learned over time—even Kevin at such a young age—that convinced them tranquility wasn't worthwhile, that it reflected a lack of will or ambition? Good question, Richard thought. And no one around to ask.

VIOLET SHOWED HIM WHERE SHE LIVED. She was an artist. Her home, a wooden cabin like all the other cabins Richard had seen, included a corner room that served as her studio. Richard didn't know anything sophisticated about art, but he liked her paintings very much. They compelled him to reach out and touch them. He didn't do so but he wanted to. In fact, his arm reached out a couple of times, then froze in mid air, indicating his resistance. Violet smiled with pleasure when she saw him gesture in the direction of her work, clearly needing to get closer to it.

"They're me," she said. "My voice."

"Of course," Richard said. "I hear it too. And I see it. Your voice."

He and Violet made love for the first time that day, on a cot a few feet from a pair of easels, near some of her most recent paintings. Their lovemaking was gentle, exciting, almost virginal: yes, almost like the first time, Richard thought, though less clumsy. Although he couldn't remember his actual first time—it was off to the side somewhere, out of his field of vision— he knew this wasn't it. Something in his past about sex, in another world that he couldn't quite remember. At this moment, though, there was only this joy, this pleasure with Violet, and nothing else seemed worth trying to clarify. They made love several times, that day, because it was wonderful each time, even ecstatic, neither of them wanting to stop, neither of them wanting it to be over.

Richard loved her now. Like he never had before. Like he always had. Naked, Violet looked like everything he had never seen before and more wondrous than he could have imagined. To his fingers, she was a thousand images he hadn't touched before. "This place," he whispered to her. "It feels like love itself." Her flesh, her cot, this room, her cabin, this world. One or all of these together, it didn't seem to matter which. Love in this time and place was everywhere he looked. And in everything his fingers found to stroke.

"IT'S A SIGNPOST," Kevin said one night as they stared into yet another campfire. The flames were burning down to coals. Night had gone deeply black around them. Soon, as they had done on many nights this trip, father and son would crawl into their tents for another peaceful night of wilderness sleep.

"What's a signpost?" Richard asked.

"*Everything just lives here.* I think it's a signpost."

"To what, Kev? To where?"

"Something much better than we're used to."

Richard studied his son's face while Kevin gazed into the fire. Kevin looked happy, satisfied. It was a shame they must go home in a few days.

Kevin glanced at him. "You still hearing it, the phrase—*everything just lives here?*"

"Yeah," said Richard. "I hear it."

"I think it's talking about some other place."

"Maybe," Richard said, although he was troubled by his son's words. He didn't know why. Maybe it was the woods. For nearly two weeks, nothing had seemed crazy out here among the rocks and trees and water. But "some

101

other place," the implication in a phrase like that, troubled him deeply. Was he talking about an afterlife? Was Kevin going religious on him? Was he becoming delusional?

Time passed. The flames burned down further. Mostly coals now. Richard had nothing against spirituality. But organized religion, in these times of intolerance, seemed like a malevolent force to him. Narrow. Constricting. Prison-like. A reason to make war on the innocent. A reason to blame everything on *someone else*.

"Dad?"

"Yes?"

"Do you still zone out?"

"I don't understand," Richard said, although only some of his reply was true.

"Around the time we went jogging," Kevin explained. "You know, around the time we first discovered we both knew about *everything just lives here* . . ."

"Yup."

". . . I told you I zoned out sometimes. You said it happens to the best of us. I don't remember when exactly, but I remember you saying, 'it happens to the best of us'."

Vaguely Richard recalled the exchange. "Yes?"

"So I'm wondering. Do you still zone out? Like I do?"

"I don't know, Kev. I don't remember it much."

"I think *everything just lives here* is connected to zoning out."

Richard poked at the embers of their fire with a stick. No flame now, just the pulsating coals, an occasional blue flicker. "Sounds kind of weird, Kev."

"Yeah," Kevin admitted. "Dad?"

"Yes?"

"I think there's this other place I don't remember."

Richard considered what he could say in response, believing he should be cautious. "You mean, where you zone out?"

"Sort of. Where I zone out *to*. *That's* what I mean."

Richard said nothing.

"You know what I mean?"

"I guess so," Richard said. "I think they're just daydreams."

"I don't know, Dad. I've had *daydreams* and they're usually pretty lame. This is different. And I *remember* my daydreams, the good ones, anyway, so I can daydream them again if I want to. But these other times—the zone-outs—I can't remember them except for a feeling afterwards."

A couple of minutes passed.

"Anyway," Kevin said, getting up from his camping stool, "everything's cool about this?"

"Yeah," said Richard. "It's incredibly cool."

"You don't think I'm crazy, do you?"

"Of course not," Richard said.

And he stood up too. They said goodnight to one another, then parted, heading into the darkness to have a piss in privacy.

For a long time, though, Richard was troubled. Inside his tent, sleep evaded him for the first time during their trip. Mostly he felt he'd let Kevin down somehow. He felt Kevin had reached out to him and he'd failed to accept his words, which, while bizarre, were also frank. Had he lied to Kevin with his silence? And, if so, what had he lied about? And why was this all so difficult to understand? Why was there something out there he couldn't remember? What was it? And why could he only *nearly* remember it?

Tomorrow, he decided, he'd talk to Kevin again. To Richard, morning was a better time of day than night for trying to get to the bottom of something.

KEVIN HAD THE COFFEE PERKING on the camp stove burner when Richard crawled out of his tent. It was cloudy and sombre, chilly. There was a mist over the lake, soft as fine yarn.

Kevin waved. He'd also started a fire and was feeding it.

"Going up to the box," Richard called, turning away.

When he returned, he bent at the water bucket, washed his hands, and dried them with the towel they left hanging on a shrub.

Kevin handed him his coffee when he approached the fire. Out here, they drank it black.

"Might rain," Kevin said.

"Looks like it."

They both stood, sipping their coffee and watching the slow dance of the mist.

"Last night," Richard said. "I'm not quite sure how, but I feel I let you down. I feel like I wasn't completely honest with you."

"About the zoning out thing?" Kevin said.

"Yes."

Kevin stood there, looking out at the lake, waiting.

"I *do* zone out, Kev. I told Fred Sexsmith about it. He said I needed a vacation."

"Makes sense," Kevin murmured.

"What you said about the signpost. That makes sense too, Kev. *Everything just lives here* as a signpost to some other place. I haven't seen it in my mind, but it's possible." Awkward with his son, Richard glanced at the ground, distractedly considering the dirt on his sneakers. He moved them in the dust, pushing pebbles around with his toe. "I don't know. I feel stupid talking about it. I feel a little crazy. There's nothing substantial to explain. It's too fuzzy to find the words. I *feel* what I'm talking about but I don't *know* what I'm talking about."

"Me too," Kevin said.

Richard thought for a moment. "We can't both be crazy. At least not in exactly the same way."

Kevin found the notion funny and laughed. His laughter was infectious and his father laughed too.

"Anyway," said Richard shortly, "I'm just telling you that I don't think you're crazy."

"Dad, I don't think you're crazy either."

Richard looked at his son. "Zoning out is embarrassing for a man my age."

"No problem," said Kevin.

"You could be right about the signpost thing, though. I just wanted you to know that." Richard put his hand on his son's shoulder. "I guess we just have to wait and see. Lots of things go away when we're done with them, when we don't need them anymore. Then, over time, we completely forget about them."

"Well," said Kevin, grinning broadly. "One thing, if we're both crazy, maybe they'll lock us up in the same place and we won't have to figure out how to visit one another."

"That's true," Richard said.

"It's all so weird," Kevin said then.

"Weird is right."

They drank more coffee and dealt separately with the strangeness they'd confessed jointly, finding a kind of solace in the normalcy that replaced it. Soon they broke camp. It was time to go home, Richard thought, as they paddled away from shore—what could be more normal than that?

This place, this generous park, his thoughts answered. Not much could be more normal than paddling this peaceful lake.

"I feel sad to be going home," Richard confessed then.

"Me too, Dad," Kevin said.

AMANDA DREW ASKED RICHARD to see her Friday morning at ten the following week. "In my office," she said.

That day, Richard put everything he was working on into his briefcase; she hadn't told him what their meeting was about and he thought he should be prepared. One didn't know with Amanda; sometimes there were snares.

She had a leather couch in her office, oxblood in colour, expensive, she'd told him, and often this was where they sat down to meet, him at one end, her at the other. But today she remained behind her giant desk, which held a large desk blotter and a pair of gold pens in a black marble holder. Her lap top was situated to her side and it was closed. She gestured in the direction of the chair in front of her desk. No couch today, no leg show. Richard felt mildly and aesthetically disappointed.

"What did you do on your vacation?"

Richard stationed his briefcase on the right side of his chair. "Took one of my sons wilderness camping in Algonquin Park," he replied.

"How was that?" She glanced at him as she spoke but Amanda wasn't a camper and didn't hold his gaze. She'd asked the question out of politeness. She did not notice that his entire family had not vacationed with him.

"It was great," Richard told her, feeling more mild disappointment.

They sat there a moment in silence. She seemed distracted, distant.

"You look good, Amanda." And she did. She'd added a perfect tan to her arsenal of weapons while he was away.

"Thank you," she replied.

More silence.

"What's up?" Richard asked at last.

Amanda leaned forward a little as if she was about to whisper a secret.

"We're making some changes around here," she said.

"Change is always good," Richard remarked without really thinking about it.

"Yes," said Amanda with a trace of a smile. "We're letting you go, Richard."

"Ah," he said. "I see." He felt no surprise, no outrage. Maybe he was in shock, but as soon as he considered this possibility he knew that he was not. Perhaps death would be like this too, not so bad after all, the anticipation harsher, more fearsome, than the event.

"We've got a package for you. Two years salary and a bit of a bonus."

Richard nodded. On days he had speculated about this particular moment in his career at Cascade Enterprises, he had imagined he would feel Amanda's words like a blow to his stomach. But, to his great dismay, he felt a relief so provocative he was forced to resist an urge to squeal with glee. He had no idea where the sensation of glee came from. Was he hysterical? Was this moment a state of epiphanic inevitability? Was everything one dreaded in life like this? Just a relief after it arrived?

"That's very close to a million dollars," Amanda was saying. "You'll have to sign the usual agreement not to sue for wrongful dismissal."

"Yes, I see," he said again.

"This is effective immediately," Amanda said. "The agreement not to sue is down at the main desk. You sign it on your way out."

He was tempted to utter another "I see" but managed to merely nod instead.

Amanda handed him an envelope. "Your letter of dismissal and the cheque," she said.

Richard took the envelope and lifted his briefcase to his lap, intending to place the envelope inside.

"Come on in," Amanda said to no one in particular, startling Richard thoroughly.

The door opened and a security man came in. He had a bud in his ear and it was clear he had been waiting, that he had listened to their entire conversation, that Amanda's office had been bugged for his firing. Understanding then what was supposed to happen next, Richard handed the man his briefcase. The security man, much like a bouncer at a nightclub, blonde, large, heavily muscled, intent on being expressionless, took the contents from his briefcase and placed them on Amanda's desk.

"Anything personal here?" Amanda asked.

"No."

"Your personal stuff from your office. It's down at the main desk."

"Okay. They're quick. I've only been up here a few minutes."

Amanda didn't comment.

Richard got to his feet. The man from security was much taller than him.

"I'm sorry to see you've still got your rash, Richard," Amanda said then.

He nodded. "Yes, it's a stubborn allergy."

"You're not excited about working here anymore," she added. "We need someone to be excited."

"Yes," said Richard. "Of course."

"Just a minute." Amanda suddenly rose, came around the desk and hugged him. It wasn't much of a hug—most of her body avoided touching his. It was, at best, symbolic, nothing more than a gesture. And he knew she was still deeply repulsed by the bandages on his neck.

He gave her A-plus for closure anyway. He smiled politely.

"Good luck, Richard," Amanda said, backing away.

"Thank you. You too."

"Thank you," she replied.

The security guard escorted him down to the main concourse in a ceremony of silence, watched while he signed the letter awaiting him there, then gestured at the two boxes on the counter. "I'm required to help you to your car."

Richard nodded. "Of course." Cascade owned everything, even the subterraneous parking lot to which they were headed.

Carrying a carton each and resuming their silence, both men headed down into the earth. The guard took Richard's plastic parking pass, snapping it in his powerful fingers, putting the pieces into a breast shirt pocket. Absurdly Richard thanked the huge man with the muscles.

Richard kept thinking how extraordinary it was to have reached his car all the way from Amanda's office without seeing anyone he knew. Even Cecily, Amanda's secretary, had been away from her desk when he left Amanda's office. The world was easily embarrassed, Richard knew. At Cascade Enterprises, when the going got tough, everyone disappeared down the same burrow, washing their hands at every intersection to stave off any chance of infection.

RICHARD HAD TO PARK FOUR BLOCKS AWAY before he could walk back to Cascade to tell Derek he'd been canned. In the interim, it had clouded over and was threatening rain. Richard kept going anyway, hurrying as best he could along the sidewalk where other people hurried as well, talking on cells, barging by one another, focused on whatever matter currently preoccupied them. He wanted to tell Derek he was unemployed; it felt important to him. In a purely superficial way it seemed to equalize their relationship somehow and Richard suspected feeling equal to Derek would enhance their friendship in some mysterious way. As he approached Derek's corner, Richard glanced at his watch. Just after eleven. So much had happened in less than sixty minutes.

"I've been downsized," Richard said as soon as he was within earshot.

"Downsized?" Derek echoed.

Richard hesitated a moment. "Fired," he amended. "Let go. Canned."

Derek nodded. He was waiting for the rest of it—the story, the version, the truth, whatever Richard had in mind.

"Two years severance and a bonus. Effective immediately."

"Well, *that* gives you time to find something else," Derek said at last.

"Yeah. And we can trim our expenses until I do."

Derek said nothing else for the moment. Then, "Did you see this coming? You haven't said . . ."

". . . No, I didn't see it coming." Richard fell silent a moment, thinking. "Then again, I didn't *not* see it coming. Know what I mean?"

"Yeah," said Derek, "I think so."

"You know what's really incredible? I think it was mostly my rash that got me fired."

Derek merely nodded.

Richard glanced at his friend's grimy ball cap, saw that his twenty dollars from earlier this morning was still there, pinned against the fabric by a collection of coins. There was no breeze in the heavy air, not even from the passing traffic. The bill just laid their limply, waiting for the rain to fall on it.

"Going to be difficult to meet you for coffee every morning," Richard said then.

Derek grinned at his friend's euphemism for their arrangement. "It's okay, Richie. Not your fault."

Richard swallowed. "It's just a matter of logistics. I'll still be able to make it most days. I'm gonna try. Every day if I can manage it."

"Cascade people might see you," Derek said, looking up at him to gauge his reaction. "They'll be going by."

"Not an issue," Richard said. "They'll be strangers because I have no job. There'll be no reason to speak to one another. In a way, they've probably already begun to forget me."

"Friends at the office?"

"Cascade doesn't like current employees to fraternize with employees who've been canned. It's not a policy but it's understood. We just know."

Derek nodded.

There were a few drops of rain falling now. Richard felt them on his face and saw them begin to form dark splotches on the pale sidewalk. Looking down at Derek, he felt a powerful urge to sit down beside his friend as some kind of gesture of friendship and loyalty, of solidarity. In the rain, it would mean something. They would share equally the misery caused by a heavy rain. He nearly did it, but he was wearing one of his best summer suits and he would need to keep it sharp for the job interviews he believed would lie ahead. Derek wore his piece of plastic, the one with the head cut out of it. At this moment, to his dismay, Richard envied his friend's chances of staying dry because he had to admit they exceeded his own.

The rain came down a little heavier now.

"I have to get inside," Richard told his friend. "I'm going to need this suit for interviews." His words sounded disingenuous and Richard was saddened by them. He wasn't good when he stood outside the confines of conventional success. He had spent years working in a different world that didn't much value honesty. Stuff—he thought of it as stuff on purpose—just rolled off people's tongues like pranks, like the dialogue bubble in a magazine cartoon. Like you wrote and then lived in your own fairy tale. Like he was doing now. If you don't know what to say or the right answer, make it up; if that doesn't work, make something *else* up. Coming to these conclusions again in the rain, maybe he deserved to be fired. "Gotta go," he said now.

"No problem. Sorry you were let go, Richie."

"Yeah. I know." Then, "Alex will be upset."

"I know. Get going. It's going to pour."

Richard made it into Starbucks just ahead of the heavy shower. Inside, he found a crush of people much like him, seeking shelter from the storm.

HE HAD TO FACE HIS CHILDREN FIRST. All of them were home. Summer vacation. Boredom. Rain. They were inside where it was dry. At least Dougal wasn't there yet. Richard decided to talk to them before Dougal showed up. It was important that he get to explain to his kids privately how he had apparently let them down.

It helped that he was in shock, that he was dazed. He'd never been fired before. It happened to all kinds of people these days but this, his first time, entirely befuddled him. He felt like a rock, hard but permanently asleep. He took his children to the dining room table. Katie was texting someone.

"Send that," Richard told her, "then put the phone away."

"It's important," Katie said.

"Not as important as what I have to tell you."

Katie sighed deeply. But she finished her message and put her phone on the table.

Richard felt strange, split into two beings. One, his truer self somewhere overhead, close by, but above him, coldly observing what his other self was doing. This powerful duality tended to compromise the significance of his announcement somehow. Just for a second, Richard wondered if he had imagined the whole thing—his being fired, the crush in Starbucks during the rain, even these first few moments before he told his children their father was out of work.

"Dad?" said Katie. "This is boring. Sitting here. It's boring."

Richard glanced at her but wasn't aware of seeing much. He glanced at his sons too. He continued to feel his twin overhead, watching this other self trying to talk to his children.

"Cascade Enterprises has let me go," he said at last.

No one replied.

"I've been fired."

Strangely, his children just seemed puzzled.

"I've lost my job."

Nothing. What was it going to take?

"I've been downsized," Richard said, seizing on the popular euphemism.

"Gee, Dad," Kevin said.

"Yeah," added Drake.

Katie hesitated, then asked, "Are we screwed?"

"I shouldn't think so," Richard replied.

"Mum's gonna be upset." Katie reached for her phone, compelled by it.

"Not yet, Katie," said Richard. "No phone. Okay?"

"But this is *huge*," said Katie. "You've had this job *forever*."

"No phone, Katie. I mean it. This is private family business until I talk to your mother."

"Mum will be pissed," Drake said.

"Well, being pissed won't help," Richard countered, feeling peevish and truculent, knowing his son was right.

"So what's going to happen?" Kevin asked at last.

"For the foreseeable future, not much," Richard replied. "I was given two years severance. I would think I can find another job in two years. Until then, it's business as usual. Everything stays the same."

The relief around the table was palpable. Two years, for his children, was an interminable time. Through the window Richard could see that it had stopped raining. He realized he was no longer in shock. It struck him that a million dollars was probably an opportunity, although he doubted Alex would see it that way. She would feel vulnerable, citing the mortgage, the things they would not be able to do or purchase, the high cost of university for their children. Yes, Drake was right. Alex was going to be pissed.

"You're all right for school," Richard reassured his children. "All of you. You've covered. This Cascade thing won't change that."

"You're going to pay for our university, right?" Katie asked.

Richard nodded with solemn enthusiasm. "Absolutely," he said.

"What about the house?" This from Drake.

"The house should be cool." Richard took a deep breath, collected his thoughts. "Look, the severance means I'm still getting paid for the next two years and then some. Full salary. It's like, for two years, everything is the same. By then, I'll have found something else. You see? Until then, my job is finding another job."

One by one his children nodded.

Richard grinned. "But wish me luck with your mother."

"Drake is right," Katie said, getting up from the table. "Mum is going to be pissed."

"Good luck, Dad," said Kevin.

"Yeah. Me too," said Drake.

INDEED ALEX WAS PISSED. Because the future was uncertain, even if two years away. Uncertainty made her feel vulnerable. When she felt vulnerable she grew frightened. Fear reduced her to ashes. Richard couldn't remember when she had become this way, but it seemed like a long time ago now.

"I mean, Alex, it's nearly a million bucks."

She was crying. "A million dollars isn't much when you have so much future, so much responsibility ahead of you. For all we know, we won't be able to do *anything*. Then, before you know it, you'll be retired and you won't have any money."

Richard gazed at her, realizing he truly did not understand her at times like these. He sat at the same table where he had told the kids about his job being gone. It had felt strange enough then, but here, with Alex, he realized how different she was from him, how much of a stranger she had become during the two decades of their marriage. A million dollars was still a lot of money. In some destitute regions of the world, it could buy a minor state. He told her as much.

"How can you be flippant at a time like this?" she cried.

"Alex, I'm not being flippant. I sit here before you a modestly wealthy man." He reached out to touch her hand in reassurance but she snatched it away. He thought her reaction childish. Now *he* was getting angry too.

"You have to go to Cascade and beg for your job back. Tell them you'll work harder, be a better employee."

Richard gazed at her, dumbfounded, insulted.

"This is all a mistake," she added. She dabbed at her eyes with a tissue. She blew her nose.

"No," muttered Richard in annoyance.

"No, what?"

"No going to beg for my job back. Think it through, Alex. I already have more than my next two years salary. It's nearly a million bucks. If I get my job back, they take back the million bucks. It's not smart to beg for my job back. Okay? They don't want me. I don't want *them*. Let's leave it that way while I find a new job."

Gradually, as they had talked, they had moved into the living room, drifting there along a current of angry exchanges. Now Alex sat at one corner of the sofa, a box of tissues on the coffee table nearby. He was leaning forward at one end of a loveseat. He waited for her to understand the most recent point he had made.

She sighed, that was all.

"I'll find a new job."

"A good one?"

"No," he said. "I want a terrible . . ." He stopped. "I hope so," he said after a moment.

"Who's going to hire a man with zits all over his neck?" she asked then.

He could say nothing to this and didn't. "Rather than a setback, Alex, we have to consider this an opportunity."

"I don't suppose we have any choice."

"Not today, no."

"This is awful, Richard," she said.

"It'll be all right." Abruptly he stood up, wanting to conclude the discussion.

"And you seem almost happy about it. Are you happy about it, Richard?"

"Of course not," he snapped. But privately he knew this wasn't true. At some point, something buried deep inside him had decided it was better to be fired than to keep working at Cascade Enterprises. In a way he couldn't define, it just made more *sense*. "This is the first time I've ever lost a job, Alex. I'm not happy about it and I'm not headed down some rocky road to irresponsibility."

"I'm not sure I can trust you on that," Alex murmured, her voice sounding sad and strangled.

Richard gazed at her, offended further. "Suit yourself," he said before storming out of the room. "Until then, you'll just have to take my word for it."

RICHARD'S LIFE SETTLED INTO A DIFFERENT ROUTINE. He began to look for another job. He prepared a job search strategy, typing it out on his laptop. He researched how to write a successful modern CV and then wrote one. He checked the want ads in the major newspapers and search engines. He telephoned some agencies and asked people there to call him back. Dutifully, at the end of each day, he reported his progress to Alex.

Alex responded most days with a tearful purge that infuriated him.

"You're worrying the kids for nothing," he told her.

"It's not for nothing, Richard."

"Yes, it is." But he couldn't win this argument. No one could.

He got on with it, dry-cleaning all of his suits to be ready for interviews.

He resumed having coffee with Derek, driving downtown and parking in a lot a few blocks away. He resumed putting twenty dollars into Derek's cap.

"Are you sure, Man?" Derek asked the first time his friend put the money in his hat.

"I'm sure. Just don't tell Alex." Richard smiled wanly to soften the blow of his remark.

Derek grinned. "Except for the news you bring me about her each day, Richie, Alex and I are out of touch."

Of all of his activities in the first week or so of his unemployment, going downtown to talk with Derek was the most pleasant, that and the fact he had resumed a regular running schedule with Kevin. "I need to be in shape to get another job," he told Alex. This, at least, was something with which she could agree. "You need to get rid of that rash," she added, though.

Derek thought the rash was improving, what he could see of it, that is, at the edges of all the bandages and ointments.

"Me too," said Richard. "I think it's slowly getting better."

Summer was still in full bloom and Richard wore jeans and a t-shirt. His battle with his allergy was more visible here on the warm street where he didn't wear a business suit. Even though he was out of business uniform, people from Cascade Enterprises tended to recognize him at times; leggy administrative assistants with fashionable cleavage, whose names he didn't remember or maybe never knew, and some of the other VPs with whom he had met in the solar furnace boardroom on the nineteenth floor of the Cascade building. Some of these various people nodded at him as they passed. Others spoke his name like a chant, a toneless two-syllable acknowledgment clearly intended to stop short of conversation. These incomplete exchanges tended to make Richard feel like a spectre and he detected an air of embarrassment as everyone passed, like two cultures were clashing—one the world of work, the other some slum on the street where people didn't do much. Richard didn't feel embarrassment about himself, though. He felt it emanating from the co-workers he used to know. It was *their* embarrassment that caused him to feel he was imagining himself.

At home, his progeny were in getting-ready-for-school mode and the normalcy of this ritual made his own state of unemployment feel routine as well. Katie was all wound up—university was "hugely" different from high school, she mentioned several times a day—but the melodrama of it all was normal too. And it kept Alex busy; else she might have found the couch and wept all day instead of every other day. Was she behaving this way at work? Not likely, he thought. There, he wouldn't be able to witness her concern. There he would miss her anxious reminder that currently he was a failure.

"Why the endless weeping?" Richard asked. "Embarrassment?"

"I can't help it," Alex replied.

"Everything's all right," Richard protested. "It's going to be all right for another couple of fucking years!"

"I can't help it, Richard."

His voice softened. "Well try. Please?"

She nodded nearly imperceptibly, although the crying persisted.

Kevin was quieter these days. He would go missing by times, then seem to reappear. He had things to do, he said. Still, he ran regularly with his father, unusually subdued, apparently caught up in his own affairs.

"You're not saying much these days, Kev," Richard said as they jogged the streets of their suburban neighbourhood.

"No."

"Everything all right?"

"Absolutely," said Kevin.

"You'd tell me if there were problems, wouldn't you?"

"I would," said Kevin with a smile. And he placed his hand on his Dad's shoulder like *he* was the father and *Richard* was the son.

Each day, Richard went downtown to tell Derek about these things. In every way, he said, he felt himself to be existing in a state of waiting.

"Waiting for what?" asked Derek.

"Something better, I guess," said Richard.

THINGS MIGHT HAVE GONE ON THIS WAY forever—stalled, in a state of anticipation, in a holding pattern—had Kevin not made the choice he did sometime before mid-September.

Everyone had gone back to school. Katie was in university, in residence in another city a few hundred kilometres down the highway. She telephoned her mother most nights, in need of constant advice. She only spoke with Alex. Dougal, at college here in the city, wasn't taking their separation from one another very well. When the young people did connect, they fought. Alex gave advice most nights on the blow-by-blows. On the one occasion Richard asked about his lack of role in this, Alex said he wasn't the kind of man people came to for advice. He supposed this was true, that he lacked the patience for teenaged romantic melodrama. His own had been worthwhile, he admitted with some levity, but Katie's was another matter. As for Drake and Kevin, they were back in high school, their last year. Nothing different there. They left each day for classes like tired old soldiers, clearly bored, vaguely slouchy, yet committed to the cause.

Richard wasn't getting anywhere looking for work. He did everything he was supposed to do but there were no interviews. Richard travelled downtown to talk to Derek most days, the way he had since their reunion in the spring. There, people passed them by. There, the street teemed with apparent purpose, although both Richard and Derek couldn't figure out what that purpose was and why most of it took place on a cell phone or tablet. For one thing, the people who passed in clusters were separate from one another in their pods, only their physical proximity to one another an indication they were relating in some way. While he was still working, Richard hadn't noticed this strange separation between people, the silence, the lack of conversation. Now he was aware of it constantly.

Alex still cried most days. And Richard wondered why her misery continued despite what he maintained was his moderately wealthy state of unemployment. It was too early for her to feel the kind of fear she currently exhibited. How could she not relax until the actual point in time when she might feel more legitimately concerned, two years from now?

And so on, Richard thought, into the third week of September.

Then Kevin disappeared, and became a forgotten young man.

GONE. TOTALLY GONE. Literally as if he had never existed. These days Richard jogged alone. The room that Richard and Alex would have remembered as Kevin's room, had they been able to remember Kevin, was a guest room in their spacious house. Kevin didn't leave any possessions. There was nothing to leave. Richard hadn't gone camping in Algonquin Park the past summer; he had not wanted to go alone. He'd stayed at home and worked around the house, the way Alex needed him to. Of course, all this took place before he lost his job.

There was the sense that something—even a person—might be missing to Richard, but it was really only a sense. Hardly even that. Whatever was missing was not there enough to be considered a true sense of loss. So far away from a memory, it simply could *not* be remembered. Kevin, and everything about him, wasn't even a figment of his and Alex's imagination. He was not only absent in the present, he'd been removed from the past. And there was nothing of him remaining to *live* itself into the future.

A YOUNG MAN RAN UP to Richard and Violet as they walked along the beach one afternoon. He seemed to evolve out of the sunset, as the sun was dipping close to the horizon. He was wearing running gear, headband, shorts, t-shirt, but he was barefoot to accommodate the sand of the beach.

Barely breathless, he seemed so perfectly young.

"Dad?" he said as he clumsily took Richard into his arms.

Richard partially accepted the young man's embrace but stepped back apprehensively.

Violet peered from one to the other, an enigmatic smile forming on her lips.

The young man seemed to realize what he had done, what had actually happened here. "Sorry," he said to Violet, although he clearly felt no regret. "I'm Kevin. And this man is my father. He's just not remembering me yet."

Richard stepped back another pace, a little alarmed by the young man's words.

But Violet was now grinning broadly. "How wonderful," she said. "I'm Violet. I'm the woman who loves your father." And she took the young man named Kevin into a warm embrace.

Richard stood there taking all of it in. In this place where everything was calm, where nothing else was required beyond a series of basic needs, in this place where there was only truth and nothing was a lie, Richard was mystified by what had just taken place.

"You're my son?" he murmured, still sounding very surprised.

"Yes, I am," the young man replied. "I'm Kevin. I'm your son."

Richard nodded agreeably enough. "This will take some getting used to."

"Yes, it will," Kevin said, glancing at Violet, in search of her reaction.

"I think it's wonderful," Violet said, taking his hand, then one of Richard's, and holding both hands, father's and son's, tightly in hers. Connected in this way, they absorbed what was now happening to and between them as best each of them could.

If there's police where there is no crime, then the police are *the crime* – Kevin Braddock, just sayin', while talking on the beach to his father, one sunny evening in Oblivion

NOW

"WHAT IS THIS PLACE?" Richard asks Violet hours after Kevin departed their company to resume his barefoot jog down the seemingly endless beach.

It is later now, dusk, and they walk under glowing streetlamps along a village street, holding hands, making their way to Violet's cabin where both of them anticipate making love for a while. Solar streetlights gently guide the way while ample light from upstairs living quarters purrs out of windows overhead, providing the illusion that the street is dissolving more gently into darkness than it actually is.

"You mean here, the town?" Violet wants to know.

"No," says Richard. "I mean this whole place. This whole world. What is it? That kid, Kevin, apparently my son. What's he doing here and where is *here*? *What* is here? I don't have a lot of memories here and I'm a grown man. I'm disoriented." He smiles, uncertain why what he is going to say next may be slightly comical. "I feel like I was born yesterday."

Violet grins but hesitates over his onslaught of questions for a moment. "Everything just lives here," she says eventually. "It's the best place for me to start."

For Richard, Violet's words seem vaguely familiar but he can't quite get a grip on the where or how. "Okay. But doesn't this place have a name?"

"Oblivion," Violet replies. "It's known to us as Oblivion."

"Oblivion?" Richard is horrified by the word and comes to a halt at Violet's side. At this moment, he glimpses clearly that he is a man who exists in two distinct locations, in transition, caught somewhere in a deep, baffling middle country that he does not understand. Then, worse, "You mean I'm dead? You mean I don't exist, I'm gone?"

Violet smiles and touches his arm. "Oh Richard, you're as alive as you can be."

"But oblivion, oblivion is nowhere, isn't it?"

"Not exactly," Violet replies gently. "Officially, by definition, Oblivion is the place where you're no longer remembered." Now that this important conversation has begun, Violet guides him to a bench along the sidewalk where they can sit down. There, she takes his hand and holds it in both of hers, tucking their entwined fingers between her knees.

"Jesus," Richard says.

"I know," replies Violet. "I had this very same conversation some time ago with an elder I know here. I remember how difficult it was to understand at first."

"Okay, let me try to figure it out. You're saying this is a place where I'm no longer remembered, right? Is that what you just said?"

"Yes."

"By whom? No longer remembered by whom?"

"Them," replies Violet.

"Them?"

"The people we knew before we came here," she adds, no longer hesitating over his questions. "And the world where they live and function. It's the world where *you and I* used to live and function."

Richard nods, although he is still unable to fathom what she is truly saying. He is only slightly aware—barely at all—of people back in some other *there* who might know who he is when he walks among them.

Still nodding, Richard says, "I feel like I go back there. But I don't remember it. I feel like I *might* remember it at some point, but it doesn't happen."

"Yes," says Violet. "I was forgetting that you haven't decided yet."

"Oh," replies Richard, perplexed.

"It's okay." Violet leans to kiss him briefly on the mouth.

"It feels okay," he admits after a time. "You. Kevin. Both of you so patient."

And it does feel okay. Here, even while he is unable to clearly grasp that other world back there, he cannot help but feel pleasantly mollified by Violet's explanation. He sits beside her, enjoying the *feeling* of her answers to his questions, more than any dull pondering he might consider over the implications in her words. He has learned there is a prevailing calm in this place she calls Oblivion, an atmosphere of tranquility. And even terrifying possibilities or potential *im*possibilities are viewed in a serene way; their logic, their potential to inspire apprehension or fear is defused entirely by the atmospheric serenity of this place. Richard has noticed that it is a compulsion here, not merely a choice, to view everything in a calm, transcendent way. Clearly, in Oblivion, as Buddha predicted in that *other* place, the key to existence is no fear. He remembers Buddha from the other world, that one thing that Buddha said, quoted to him once by someone he can't quite remember. That's all. Buddha's words drifting in the dense mist that is his memory. But not much more.

"Richard?"

"Sorry," he says. "One more question, okay?"

"Yes?"

"Everything just lives here. It sounds familiar to me. But how do you say it?"

Violet nods. "All four ways."

"Tell me."

"Okay," she says. "*Everything* just lives here. Everything *just* lives here. Everything just *lives* here. Everything just lives *here*."

He nods and smiles.

"You've heard this phrase before, haven't you?"

"I feel like I have. Again," he says.

Violet repeats herself. "Now you," she instructs.

Richard repeats the sentence as she has taught it to him, in the same four ways, shifting the emphasis to each word as she did.

"Everything just lives here," she repeats once more, without emphasis. "All four ways are true. You see?"

"I see," says Richard, smiling broadly.

Violet squeezes his hand. "There's so very much more to understand. We can't be in a hurry."

Richard nods.

"I want to go home," says Violet. "I want to make love." She gets up from the bench.

Richard follows suit. "Oblivion," he murmurs gently. A question arrives from that other place he knows is out there but cannot remember. It stumbles out of his mouth before he can really think about it, an unexpected revelation. "Is this place like Shangri-la?"

"Yes," says Violet calmly. "This place is exactly like Shangri-la."

KEVIN BEGINS TO SEEK HIM OUT in Oblivion. They are two extremes in an as yet unresolved juxtaposition where Richard remembers nothing about their past together and Kevin apparently remembers everything. Although Kevin is patient with his father's *amnesia*, Richard occasionally feels like a failure. Kevin sits on the beach with him sometimes, his knees drawn up, his arms locked around them. Patient, so patient, waiting for his father to remember: him or the other place where they both were aware equally that they were father and son.

But Richard doesn't remember him. Not really. He believes that Kevin is his son because Kevin has said he is, and everyone in Oblivion appears to have no inclination for anything but the truth—Richard has seen this for himself. Still, he doesn't remember when he was a father. And he doesn't remember *his son*. Except *here*. Except here in Oblivion where he remembers the Kevin he sees each time he is here. Kevin says he lives in Oblivion permanently. Richard, though, continues to deal with the fact that he comes and goes between this world and the other one, remembering events and knowledge only about the world that he happens to be visiting during the time he is there.

Yes, Richard is away sometimes and he never quite resolves the dilemma of having no control over his coming and going. Still, he knows he goes back there, where Kevin is no longer anybody and, now, never was. Kevin has told him this and Richard believes it to be true, although it seems impossible to understand.

RICHARD'S ALLERGY IS DEFINITELY IMPROVING, even Alex has noticed it. Fewer bandages, the blemishes now revealed are drying up. On good days she admits this will help him to get hired, if he ever gets an interview. It's still September, barely more than a month since Richard was dumped by Cascade Enterprises. But when Richard reminds Alex that he still has two years before they need to fret about their finances over his lack of a job, before his generous severance is used up, she simply finds something else to worry about.

"Katie and Dougal. They're fighting. Her heart is broken. She's too far away at school. It's all over Facebook."

Richard cannot fathom Dougal as any kind of a heartbreaker. "Never mind Dougal," he says. "Never mind Facebook. Is she keeping up her studies?"

"She says she is," replies Alex.

"She'd better be."

"Where's your empathy, Richard? Your only daughter is in pain."

"I'm saving it up," he says, "my empathy. For a situation that actually requires it." He feels guilty after a remark like that. He shakes his head. "Sorry," he mutters. Then again, how much responsibility is he supposed to shoulder for his daughter's immaturity? "When they expose themselves on Facebook, their 'broken hearts' it's one more public performance, not a legitimate expression of love or loss."

"You can't know that," Alex says.

"Not for sure, but that's how it feels to me."

As usual, when Richard and Alex have these conversations, they are on their backs in bed, a foot or more of separation between them, their remarks, their retorts shot from anxious lips at targets in the general direction of the ceiling. They are not getting along. Both of them feel cold and angry, both of them feel wronged.

"I hardly know you these days, Richard."

"How so?"

"I look at you and I don't see all the wonderful things we used to share. I can't even remember what those wonderful things used to be."

"Do you think it's me?" Richard asks, feeling hurt. "You think I'm the cause of this? I mean, exclusively? You think it's just me?"

"Something about you—some of who you are—is missing."

"Maybe we should make love. Maybe some mutually pleasurable intimacy would bring things back to the way they used to be."

Alex makes no move to endorse his proposal. She just lies there like a board, in silence.

"Strange," muses Richard then. "To me, *you're* the one who's changed."

"And how have I changed, Richard?"

"Well," he replies, gathering his thoughts. "For one thing you won't have sex with me. For another, you're worried all the time. Needlessly afraid, in my opinion. Irrationally fearful."

"'Needlessly? Irrationally?' For Christ's sake, Richard, you're out of work!"

"You were worried constantly long before Cascade fired me. You've been worried constantly for years."

"Oh, Richard, I have not."

"Yes you have. No matter how well we were doing, it wasn't going to be good enough. Alex, even though we had plenty of money, there was never enough money."

Alex stiffens. "You think it's greed, don't you? It's not greed, Richard. Don't make it sound like greed. The world is more complicated than it used to be. The future doesn't take care of itself. There are things we need to have, to do, to stay in control of our economic situation. If we fall behind we'll have no one to blame but ourselves. No one is going to do it for us. No one is going to help us. We have to plan ahead. Planning ahead isn't greed, Richard. It's being prepared in an insecure world. It's dog eat dog out there. You, more than anyone, should know what a nasty world it is out there."

For the moment Richard says nothing; he hardly knows where to begin. His position is indefensible. As a marketer until recently employed by a giant transnational conglomerate, Richard is keenly aware that he and others like him—marketing admen, communicators—have planted a fear of inadequacy in modern society. A preoccupation with retirement plans, status symbols and distractions. Alex's fear has been abetted by people like *him*. He feels ashamed. He swallows. People like *him* do this, people in marketing and advertising. No better than pushers, he decides. What they sell is now addictive, including the notion that people are mean and naturally self-serving, and the only way to survive in society is to be meaner and more self-serving than your competition. At this moment, Richard regrets every television and radio commercial he has ever ordered, every billboard, the magazine ads, the nagging on the Internet he has put in place. Richard has no strength to explain such things to his wife. It's too big and relentless and omnipresent. To explain is to speak in ancient Greek. It will take them along a tangent she will not understand. He feels the tension of his inadequacy burn in the pit of his stomach. As a professional purveyor of fear, he cannot find a way to reverse the damage he has helped to cause. "I'm sorry, Alex," he says, frustrated by his conclusion.

"I know we've done well, Richard," Alex replies. "But we can't *stop*. We can't say this is *good enough*."

Richard glances at her profile on the pillow. It is a handsome face. He can remember when he loved her handsome face, looking at it, touching it delicately with his fingers. But handsome faces, he reflects, do not survive a long parade of disagreements, shame or guilt. "Why not?" he asks, still wanting to explain in philosophical terms what has gone wrong for them.

"Whaddyuh mean: 'Why not?'"

"Why *isn't* it good enough?"

She hesitates a moment. He wonders if he has scored an important point. But then, "We have a lifestyle, Richard. *Everyone* has a lifestyle. Our job is to maintain it, enhance it."

"Why?"

"If we don't, we'll slide into . . . oblivion."

"Oblivion?"

"Yes, Richard. We'll be left behind. Our children will be left behind. All we've worked for won't be enough for us in retirement."

"Alex, we have more than we need to have a good life. We should look at our current situation as an opportunity."

"For disaster," Alex mutters.

"No. For change. Our current lifestyle isn't the only lifestyle we have to have. We could live, say, in Costa Rica or something. Walk the beach. Learn how to do new things, learn how to be different from ourselves, learn how to be more authentic people."

"For God's sake, Richard, now you're just being ridiculous. Costa Rica? Do you want to discuss this seriously or not? Whatever could be going on in our lives that isn't authentic? To say we're not authentic, well that's just philosophical balderdash."

"You're taking me literally. Costa Rica was just an example."

"The place doesn't matter, Richard. What's wrong with right here, with where we live right now?"

Richard remains silent for a full two minutes. He would argue but feels fatigued by the prospect. Then, at last, he asks, "When did I lose you, Alex?"

"I don't know," she replies. "I guess it was when you gave up."

"Gave up? I gave *up*? How did I give up?"

"You stopped caring. About what we were doing, where we were going."

"Maybe we need to go somewhere else, head in a different direction. Maybe I just need the going—the *place* where we're going—to be different from what it's been up until now. That doesn't mean I don't care. I just want to care about some different things for a change."

"I guess that's our basic problem," Alex says after a moment's consideration. "You want to care about vague abstractions, ideas we don't share. I want both of us to care about what we have, what we've worked so hard for. You want to change things and I don't. And *our children* don't either."

Having reached this particular impasse, Richard feels an even deeper loss. He clutches at the first straw he encounters. "Maybe there's a happy medium we can find," he says.

"I'm tired," Alex replies. "There is no happy medium. That's what *you* don't understand. By now, where happy mediums are concerned, you should be all grown up." And she turns away from him, lying on her side. She is angry now and there is nothing he can say.

"Alex, this will all work out. It *will*. You'll see." But his words sound lame, even to *him*.

No wonder she doesn't answer him.

IN OBLIVION, KEVIN BRINGS UP THE SUBJECT OF JOGGING. "You run in the other place," he informs his father.

They are waiting in a cafe for Violet to join them after she finishes framing a new painting she has completed. It is mid-afternoon and a gentle drizzle falls outside. No one minds the rain here in Oblivion: it is understood and accepted that it is good for a variety of crops and that it has its own richness to the touch, on everyone's skin, caught in everyone's clothing and hair, a rain to be stroked by the fingertips. Kevin clearly loves the rain in Oblivion, its translucence, its frequency, the way it is not polluted by the antics of mankind.

"Back there, Dad, it was full of smog and chemicals," he says.

Richard nods. Kevin teaches him much.

"Strangely, the lack of control over Mother Nature here is what makes everyone in Oblivion feel that they are *in control*," Kevin says. "The idea is not to be in control of Mother Nature, but to be in control of your own fate, each person controlling his or her own days."

Increasingly Richard has seen indications of this for himself, but now he *feels* their veracity too, through his own perception, because it seems he comes to Oblivion more and more often.

So much to learn and understand, Richard reflects. Kevin—who is getting used to this world and clearly remembers the other one—comments unabashedly that their coffees here in the cafe have arrived with no expectation of payment. "No need for money," Kevin says.

"Money?"

"You know, cash, VISA, Mastercard, debit, the way we paid for things back there."

But Richard, when he is in Oblivion, only remembers Oblivion. Here he has never heard of cash or credit cards. He doesn't know what Kevin is remembering, what he is talking about. But Violet too teaches him to notice how things function in this world.

"Oblivion is a world of plenty," Violet says. "There's more than enough for everyone."

Kevin nods in agreement. "When you eat, say, an apple, you're not taking anyone else's apple—there are more than enough apples to go around. There is no greed here. In Oblivion greed makes no sense: for one thing, it's unnecessary; for another, it's dishonest. There's nothing dishonest in Oblivion so greed can't exist. There's no greed in Oblivion so *dishonesty* can't exist. Greed and dishonesty have no perceived value here, Dad. What could be more unnecessary than something with no value?"

"I see indications of this," he says because he has seen so much himself. But Oblivion's contrast to the other world? This eludes him still. When Kevin or Violet decry the other world where greed is considered a virtue, the measure of someone's ambition, Richard hears only the words and doesn't *live* their meaning. Then he feels separate from the young man who appears to be his son, and from the woman he loves so much.

"There are no banks here," Kevin is saying now with a kind of glee.

"Banks?"

"Places that hold and lend money, the conduit of an economic system."

"Oh," says Richard, not really remembering banks or what they did.

"A few people had just about everything, many more had some or a bit, and far too many others didn't have anything at all." Kevin sounds faintly bitter.

"I don't remember," Richard says.

"Here," continues Kevin, "in Oblivion, instead of money or plastic, it's kind of an indirect barter system. We exchange needs. The exchange satisfies the need and everyone goes on. You write The Bulletin and people need it for information. You need food, drink, a new shirt, shoes, because they can't be repaired, you get them. At some point, without anyone keeping score, an exchange is made. Or you grow your own food and make your own shirt. If you have more than you need, you share it. For one thing, it's no good to you if you don't need it. For another, someone else will appreciate it. No banks, no loans, no interest, no factories, no mass production. You see? We don't amass things here. Why would we when we have everything we need? With more than the basic necessities available to everyone, and no one going without, who would need an economic system to distort or corrupt that balance?"

But Richard hasn't understood any of this. In Oblivion, he can't remember a state of affairs that is any different. Richard knows Kevin means well—he wants to explain the differences in what Richard usually sees for himself. It must be difficult for him to notice his father doesn't truly understand.

While they sip coffee and wait for Violet to arrive, while the rain comes down in a drizzle and whispers as it falls, Kevin returns to the subject of jogging.

"Back there," Kevin is saying, "you and I used to run together."

"We did?"

"Yes. Around the neighbourhood."

Richard wishes he could remember this.

"We could run here too, you know. Along the beach. Or up on the trails that run through the woods."

"You mean together?"

"Yes," says Kevin.

"I'd like that," Richard says.

"Me too," replies the young man who not only says he's his son, but is gradually beginning to *feel* like one.

ONE DAY IN OCTOBER, on the Wednesday before Thanksgiving, Amanda Drew walks by with an entourage of her Cascade underlings. It has become somewhat chilly at this point in the autumn season and Richard wears a flannel shirt over his t-shirt and blue jeans. But the sun is shining and he sports his shades, the same glasses he was forced to wear on the nineteenth floor of Cascade Enterprises when he and the other vice-presidents gathered for Amanda's meetings. It is still early autumn, but the sun's arc is already flattening out here on the street and people walking along the sidewalk are like spectres backlit by the sun's rays. Derek sits in his usual spot, his weathered ball cap in front of him on the concrete. Inside the cap, Richard's daily twenty fidgets among some coins in the day's light breeze. It is nearly lunch-time and they have finished their Starbucks coffees some time ago. The empty containers are visible near the top of a wire mesh waste receptacle that threatens to spill onto the street. It is approaching lunch time and Richard has been considering going home.

Everything just lives here, he thinks at this moment, in the way he still frequently does.

He nearly misses noticing Amanda, then recognizes her as she appears on the sidewalk. He doesn't have much time to decide whether to acknowledge her or pretend he hasn't seen her. They inhabit different worlds now, two solitudes after all. Amanda is dressed in a long, knitted jacket, longer than her short skirt. She looks rich and spoiled and beautiful. But hardly has his appreciation of her begun when it vanishes; it is a feeling unexpectedly superficial to him. While Amanda is beautiful, the street remains ugly. Apparently beauty needs more than Amanda's efforts to make itself exist in a more permanent state.

Amanda's entourage consists of four well-dressed men, three of whom are busily tapping out messages with their thumbs on cell phones they hold out in front of them in that gesture of pagan offering with which Richard is so familiar, texting people far away or maybe even one another. Now that he hasn't been working for a number of weeks, Richard doesn't text much beyond an occasional encouraging message of some kind to his two children—the only way they seem to want to communicate—or a message to Alex even less frequently, usually to make some kind of routine arrangement. He now realizes a man without a job tends to drift towards digital silence. Unemployed, he's more attracted to people who want to talk face to face.

Strangely, though, it is Amanda's cell phone, it's musical ring-tone, her twisting to the right to reach for the device in her bag, that causes her to notice Richard not far away, where he is leaning against the building wall. Her glance falls on him, then slips away, then returns in recognition, all of this obvious to him even though her eyes are concealed behind her dark glasses. She speaks briefly into the ether of her telephone, then shuts it off, turning to the men in her party to say something to them or give them instruction, words Richard is too far away to hear. Richard interprets this to mean

Amanda might snub him. A moment later, though, the men move on without her, walking and texting, and Amanda comes over to him where he stands beside Derek. Not surprisingly she puts on an air of exasperation that he is interrupting the many important things she has yet to do today.

"Richard," is all she says.

"Amanda. How are you?"

She glances down at Derek seated on the sidewalk, a split-second of disdain taking shape in her smile, but quickly vanishing again in case someone, least of all Derek, should happen to see it and hold it against her.

"This is pretty freaky," she says, not answering his question about her welfare. "You standing out here by the building where you used to work. Some would say you haven't moved on," She waits a moment for her words to sink in, then asks, "What are you doing here?"

"Visiting my friend, Derek."

She glances down again at the homeless man panhandling here on the sidewalk and manages a weak smile. "Oh yes," she says, remembering Richard's revelation about Derek from a couple of months ago when they still worked together.

Just for the fun of it, just to see what happens, Richard formally introduces them, but neither one of them apparently wants to shake hands. Amanda busies herself with the cell phone in her bag, turning it back on, Richard supposes. Derek does not get up, although Richard can see he was tempted to do so at first, some remembered notion of gallantry perhaps, when he was a lawyer and not a homeless panhandler. Instead, Amanda and Derek say "how do you do?" in perfect unison.

"Your rash is all gone," Amanda says.

"Just about," Richard replies.

It's true. Only a couple of grimy bandages remain. He should remember to remove them tonight. The last remnants of his allergy should be left to dry up.

"We gave up on modern medicine too soon, I guess," says Amanda.

We? Richard ponders in silence.

"No job yet?"

Richard shakes his head.

They stand there in silence, looking at one another, not quite sure what they're doing here. Richard can see Derek is watching them, a hint of a smile forming along his mouth.

"Derek, Amanda is the woman who had to fire me," Richard explains.

"I figured," Derek says pleasantly, completing the smile that, to this point, had been merely a work in progress.

Amanda considers them together a moment, glancing first at one, then the other. "Do you two meet here every day?" she wants to know.

"Pretty much," replies Richard.

"Can't be very productive," Amanda remarks.

"Actually we're planning a takeover bid, you know, we're gonna buy Cascade Enterprises."

Derek just smiles.

"Once we figure out exactly what Cascade Enterprises does," adds Richard.

"You've grown sarcastic," Amanda says, seeming legitimately hurt by his remark.

"I hadn't realized," says Richard. "Sarcasm could be a side effect of being without a job."

"Well, this is awkward," the Cascade president says. "In view of your settlement, I didn't expect you to be so bitter."

"You look great, Amanda," Richard tells her, more or less to tug them off the rugged ground on which his snideness has placed them, but believing he means every word of his compliment.

At his statement, all the tension that has passed between them in the past few minutes is instantly forgiven. "You too, Richard. I like the jeans. They're you. Blue jeans and a flannel shirt, they're a good look for you. And that awful rash is gone. That rash was terrible. I'd look at it and just think: god, it's going to ooze."

Richard nods, tempted to mumble some kind of misplaced thanks.

"I wish we could talk, Richard. I mean, *really* talk." She glances down at Derek who is making a point of looking elsewhere, preoccupied in some way. "At dinner or something. You know, just you and me. Catching up. Working on those bygones."

"Yes," says Richard. "The bygones."

"Do you still have your cell?"

Richard reaches into his pocket and flashes his phone at her.

"Same number?"

He nods.

"I'll call. Or text."

"Okay," says Richard.

"I mean it."

"Okay, Amanda."

She turns to the homeless man at her feet. "Nice to meet you, Derek."

"Me too," Derek replies.

Richard glances at his friend as Amanda turns away. Maybe Derek meant it, then again maybe he didn't.

TO RICHARD'S ASTONISHMENT, Amanda actually calls a couple of days afterwards and invites him to dinner, something he was convinced she wouldn't do. "You ever been to that place, The Victorious Vegetable?" she asks.

Richard holds back a snort of mirth. These days, restaurants are like modern rock bands. It's as if the only names left in the lexicon are terms he would classify as dregs.

"Can I eat meat there?"

"Chicken or fish," Amanda replies, "if you insist on having something with flesh."

"Sounds fine."

"Dress casual," instructs Amanda, still sounding like his boss.

When he reports the news to Alex, she is excited by the prospect of him having dinner with Amanda. "Maybe you can get your old job back," she says, putting a hand on his arm.

"Or a promotion," Richard remarks drily, surprised when his response apparently placates his wife.

The Victorious Vegetable is dark and moody. It is decorated for Thanksgiving—pumpkins and various gourds are arranged on every windowsill and in locations along the bar. In the darkness, these vegetables appear to puff up in size, displaying a kind of phallic menace in the shadows. Privately Richard muses about the various squash as monsters and, in his mind, he renames the restaurant The *Vicious* Vegetable.

"What?" asks Amanda as they are seating themselves, apparently noticing the first split second of his grin.

"All the gourds in the windows," he replies. "Private joke." He declines to mention the new moniker he's given the restaurant, knowing Amanda will not appreciate it. Amanda is strangely loyal to what is new to her, but disdainful of what she used to care about. She leaps from trend to trend like a lumberjack crossing a log boom.

"I like the fact it's dim," Amanda says now, with just a hint of mischief. "It makes it intimate here."

Richard looks around the restaurant again and, not feeling it as Amanda does, doesn't know what to say. He falls back on Amanda's addictive need for compliments instead. "You look terrific, Amanda," he says. And she does. Lowcut teal blouse. Dark jacket with a crisp pin-stripe. Matching short skirt.

"Thank you," his former boss replies.

But their server has arrived—his name is Matthew—and Amanda is ordering what she calls her usual, which Richard knows will be an expensive red wine.

"And you, Sir?"

"Glen Livet, please. A double. With ice."

"Perfect," says Matthew, hurrying away with their order.

"*Perfect* is bearing down on the word *awesome* as the buzz word of the decade," Richard remarks with a smile. He remains an English graduate and likes words to mean what they really mean. He likes them to resist hyperbole. Amanda, he knows, suffers from no such ailment. On the single occasion he can remember remarking about the rusting out of the English language a year or so ago, she bluntly cut him off with a topic change.

This time she ignores him.

Richard opens his menu. "I guess we should decide on something to eat," he says.

Amanda works the enigmatic version of her smile. "Sounds like a plan," she replies.

They discuss menu options for a while, until Matthew shows up with their drinks. They order fish. Both of them.

"Perfect," says Matthew just before he takes the menus away.

"So," says Amanda then. "How's Alex?"

"She's fine."

"How's she taking this business of you looking for a job?"

Richard wants to answer with platitudes, but he wants to be truthful too. "Not well," he says at last. "Over the years, Alex has learned to worry with skill."

"I'm sorry to hear that, Richard."

"Thank you," Richard says.

"But you're not worried, are you?"

"No," he replies. "Not yet."

"The severance?"

"Yes, I suppose. It makes for some breathing room, to me, at least."

Amanda lifts her wineglass. "Here's to a short and successful job search." Her wine and his scotch dance as their glasses clink. They drink.

"Wonderful," says Amanda then, "to see you looking pleasant looking again."

"Wonderful to *be* pleasant looking again."

"You're pissed at me, aren't you, Richard?" Amanda says after a moment.

"Not really," he replies. And he *isn't* pissed with her. At this moment, it is clear to him that he mostly disapproves of her in some vague way. She is beautiful and ambitious, but these characteristics don't impress him the way they might have once upon a time. These days he finds himself seeking a deeper quality in the humanity he encounters. Sometimes he and Derek actively look for that kind of trait in people who pass on the busy sidewalk, when they meet each morning on the street to watch everyone go by. He and Derek talk about it a lot. What they don't see—simplicity, openness, clarity. What they *do* see mostly—a morning parade of envy and contempt—people limping or scurrying by at great speed. It's as if everyone is being chased by a childhood boogeyman that has pursued them into adulthood, injuring them along the way. And something about looking up to someone and down at someone else feels like it will wrestle the monster to the ground, although it never does.

Amanda has been studying him. "I've missed you, Richard," she says. "We used to have fun. I think our relationship at work was special."

"You've given me the opportunity to reconsider my priorities," Richard tells her.

"You mean what you're going to do when you grow up? You're thinking about *that* again?"

"That's one way of describing it."

Matthew is back. "Another Glen Livet?" he asks.

"Why not?" says Richard.

"Double?"

"Why not?"

"Are you uncomfortable having dinner with me?" Amanda asks after Matthew has gone.

"Wondering why a little," he replies.

"Me too," she admits. "It seemed like a good idea at the time, the other day on the street. I don't know. You're pleasant looking again. I guess we'll have to find out together what my intentions were."

"Fair enough. Alex was happy we're doing this."

"She was?"

"Yes. Probably thinks you're going to offer me my old job back."

"Would you take it?"

"No."

"Good," says Amanda, visibly relieved. "And I'm not offering. Giving you your old job back would be the *last* thing on my agenda."

AMANDA'S AGENDA. At some point Richard begins to suspect Amanda has decided to sleep with him. He's not quite certain when this possibility occurs to him—sometime near the end of the main course and the beginning of dessert—and he is equally uncertain what he would do if the opportunity to do so ever arose. The most he will admit to himself, he concludes during an interlude when Amanda is in the bathroom, is that he is ambivalent about the prospect. Amanda, with her perfect legs and short skirts, is a beautiful woman but his appreciation of her, if not pragmatic, feels at most only aesthetic. Is the *idea* of sex with Amanda his only enticement? Richard thinks so and, in this case, an *idea* of desire feels a lot less inspiring than desire itself.

He watches Amanda return to her seat. He sips coffee. She has freshened her make-up in the bathroom. She looks stunning. He wishes he cared. He wishes Alex would resume having sex with him. He feels a sharp pang of sadness. At this moment, sitting here in The Victorious Vegetable, he feels entirely devoid of love or desire, like both have moved away a few feet to taunt him from the edges of his peripheral vision.

"You're finding all of this tough, aren't you, Richard?" Amanda says at last. "This period in your life, I mean."

"I suppose I am."

"Two kids. One in university, one heading there next year."

"Yup."

"And Alex."

Richard waits for her to continue. What about Alex?

"About now, Alex is probably fed up. Right?"

Richard feels a familiar need to protect his wife from potential attack, but he remains silent.

"You get laid much, Richard?"

"Alex?"

"Yes."

"No. But I have fond memories."

"Your rash is all but cleared up."

"For some time now my entreaties have fallen on deaf ears," Richard admits.

"How awful."

At this point, Richard endures another one of those long moments in which he seems to be viewing himself from overhead. He can look down and see himself at a table with Amanda Drew in a dim restaurant. And he wonders what the Richard he is watching can do, is supposed to do, would do, will do. And all this wondering, this distant observation, is curiously flat.

"I used to think it was too bad you and I worked together," Amanda is saying. "That I was your boss."

"Oh?"

"It made things complicated. You were shy. I didn't want to be accused of sexual harassment."

To his utter dismay, Richard feels he might blush. He sips more coffee. When in hell did *he* take up blushing?

"You were always pleasant looking, Richard. I *like* pleasant looking. A *lot*."

"Thank you."

She hesitates, then plunges on. "We don't work together now, Richard."

Richard realizes clearly at this moment, now that it's out in the open, that he doesn't want to have sex with Amanda Drew, although something inside him feels he should—those perfect legs perhaps, or Alex's unwillingness to be intimate with him these days—but he thinks he should tell his former boss a sudden, unexpected, confusing truth.

"But there's someone else," he says, his words surprising him, his reason to decline sounding strange in his own hearing. What did he just say? But there *is* someone else, he can feel it. But where is she? Is it the memory of Alex when she was someone needing more intimacy than she does now? Is this who he wants to be faithful to? Or is it just some principle that holds his loyalty? The puzzle defeats him. Still, he is glad what he has said is definitely the truth.

"I thought Alex was . . ." Suddenly Amanda chuckles, only now believing she is seeing the light. "You rascal," she says.

Briefly Richard is confused by her words but manages not to let on. Then, after a moment, he understands the conclusion to which Amanda has jumped.

"I see. I get it," she is saying, entirely unperturbed that she has been rejected. "Nothing ventured, nothing gained."

"Sorry," Richard murmurs, amused by Amanda's conclusion that there is another woman in his life besides Alex, but feeling safer now in its wake. He finds himself wishing he'd thought of it himself. Or did he? If so, why? Something in the scotch?

Amanda digs in her purse, comes up with a company credit card. She sticks it in the wallet containing the check. "Don't be sorry," she says. "It makes too much of it. It's just sex, Richard, in *my* experience, anyway."

"I enjoyed seeing you again, Amanda."

She gazes at him a moment until she decides to believe him. Then, "ships passing in the night," she says, pushing back her chair and standing.

Richard rises too, placing his napkin on the table. "Thanks for dinner, Amanda. I really appreciate it."

"My pleasure." She smiles at him somewhat mischievously. "You know you're going to hate yourself for this in the morning, don't you? For saying no, I mean."

"I hate myself already," Richard says to please her.

"Too late," Amanda remarks, then turns with the check and her credit card and heads for the bar where she will pay.

Richard watches her legs vanish into the gloom of the restaurant. Standing there a moment to give her time to leave, he is distinctly aware that he doesn't hate himself at all. He is distinctly aware that he likes himself just fine, although why, precisely, at this moment, he doesn't know for sure.

"HOW WAS YOUR DINNER WITH AMANDA?" Derek asks when they

meet the next morning on the street.

"Fine."

Derek's gaze is intense, but laced with good humour.

Richard says nothing.

"She offer you your old job back?"

"No. But then I didn't think she would."

"Alex must have been disappointed."

"Alex has no reason to be disappointed. Believe me, Derek."

Derek nods, then thanks a passerby for the fifty cents she dropped into his ball cap. "So is that it?" asks Derek. "Amanda rides off into the sunset?"

Richard nods. "She said I'd hate myself this morning."

"And do you?"

"Not in the slightest."

FEELING GRATEFUL ONE DAY FOR VIOLET and the depth of their love for one another, Richard asks Kevin if he has a girlfriend.

"No," says Kevin. "I'm afraid I have to wait for one to show up."

"Why?"

"I haven't met her yet or she isn't here."

"Here?"

"In Oblivion."

Richard considers his son's words a moment. "What will make her show up in Oblivion?"

"Choice," replies Kevin. "That's what an elder told me."

"You mean she'll choose Oblivion over the other place?"

"Yes."

"Like you did?"

"Yes."

Father and son sit on the beach together. They have jogged through the wooded trails on the hills behind them for an hour and have emerged from the trees here on a trail leading to the shore, their run complete. They sit at the water's edge.

"You know I go back to the other place, intending to actually remember how different it is from here," Richard admits after a moment. "And vice versa. But I can't do it. Here I remember you, Violet, other people I've met, my work on The Bulletin, all this," and he waves vaguely at the beach, the ocean, the woods that rise behind them, "but it's gone when I get back *there*. I know there is a *there*, Kevin, like you do. But I can't remember it the way you do. I'm sure, sitting here now, I don't remember here when I go back *there*."

Kevin has been nodding at his father's words. "I know," he says at last. "And, of course you can't truly make comparisons, sort out the contrasts."

Richard nods. "Maybe I should talk to an elder."

"In time."

Richard glances at his son. "Are you telling me I'm not ready?"

"It's not for me to say, Dad. It's all inside you. It's what you decide."

"You're saying I have to make a choice?"

"That's how it worked for me. Choice is the only ticket into Oblivion."

People continually stroll by between where they sit on the beach and the water's edge. Richard and Kevin watch them in pleasant silence. Many are lovers, like Richard and Violet. Richard misses her at this moment but it is a calm, even wonderful feeling. It contains no fear of loss. Missing her feels more like an act of giving: not empty, but full. Love without trepidation; love with trust.

"So someone will choose to come here," Richard says after a time, "and you two will meet and become lovers or friends. Permanent companions."

"I guess so," Kevin says.

"What if you have to wait until you're older?"

Kevin grins. "I'm told I won't be appreciably older."

"You mean you'll be much the way you are now?"

"Yes."

Richard gapes at him. "You mean being here in Oblivion goes on for good? Just like this?"

But Kevin only shrugs. "Time moves slowly here towards its conclusion, if there *is* a conclusion. *Very* slowly, I'm told. We don't pay much attention to it."

Richard contemplates what Kevin has implied. Immortality? Or something nearing it? It is impossible to imagine, even impossible to imagine truly wanting it. He gives up.

But Kevin has been watching him. "We don't know about what you'd consider The End. You see, we don't think ahead that far and time moves slowly. It's not immortality—people die here. But we don't dwell on death, on the end of things. Whether that means there is no end or not, doesn't really matter. There's basically just now and the rest of the day."

"But aren't you impatient for your, uh, companion?" Richard wants to know.

"A little," Kevin says. "But only a little. This is Oblivion. We only feel modest periods of anticipation here. We get to have everything we need. Ultimately I'll have everything I need, too. Too much long-term anticipation would be just a kind of greed. I won't be denied what I need, anyway. It's not like anything is going to be permanently missing. In the other world, most people waited and anticipated constantly, like there was a deadline approaching and they were going to miss it. And, even when something wonderful arrived, they waited for and anticipated something *else*. Life slipped by while they waited and anticipated. Sad," murmurs Kevin, "now that I look back on it.".

Richard considers Kevin's words and feels loss. Beyond words, he has no idea what is true or false; the *feeling* of knowing continues to elude him even though he reaches out for it.

"I feel like a double amnesiac," Richard remarks shortly, a trace of frustration in his voice.

Kevin nods.

"Like I have two lives but this business of only remembering one at a time makes me a little crazy. Here I am, supposed to make a choice about which world to live my life in when I don't have the tools to do it."

"Yes," says Kevin, "I suppose that's what it amounts to."

"But that makes no sense."

"Yes it does, Dad. It makes perfect sense. Without the contrasts, you get to choose what you want instead of what you *don't* want. If you're happy there, in the other life, you'll choose there. If you're happy here, you'll choose here. It's a matter of choosing, not a matter of *rejecting* something else. You choose what you want; you don't decide *against* what you *don't* want. I know it's a subtle difference, choosing *for* and choosing *against*, but it's still the choice, when you get right down to it. Dad, I tend to think of choosing *for* as a matter of free will. Choosing *against?* Well, to me, that's letting dread push my buttons. You see what I mean?"

"I do, Kevin. What you say always makes sense. . ."

"But?"

"But I can't *know it* the way you can."

"I know."

"You remember both worlds, right?"

"Right."

"Because you made your choice?"

"Right."

"And you're happy with your choice?"

"Yes," replies Kevin. "Now that I can see what I chose. But I chose this because this was what I wanted, not because the other *wasn't* what I wanted. Once you choose Oblivion, you can remember both worlds so that you know why you chose the one you did and why you continue to value it."

"You can't go back, can you?"

"No. But I don't want to. This place is how I want to live my life."

Richard ponders his son's words a long time in silence. Then, "I'm going to need to speak to an elder," he says.

"Talk to Violet about that," Kevin says. "Ask her if you should be seeing an elder."

"Okay," Richard says.

"But remember," cautions Kevin. "The answers, the choice, are within *you*. The elder can only answer the questions he or she can answer."

ALEX WANTS TO KNOW how it went with Amanda at dinner. It is two nights later that they talk. Alex has been busy on the telephone and the Internet with Katie. Katie wants to leave school because it keeps her away from Dougal. So far, Alex has prevented their daughter's defection. She's going to drive Dougal down the highway a couple of hundred miles to visit her daughter for the weekend. To Richard, this plan of bringing the young people together for a visit is the lesser of evils, less than having his daughter drop out of university because she thinks she's in love with a jerk, less too than driving over to Dougal's house and beating him to death for romantically harassing his daughter when she should be concentrating on her studies. The lesser of evils. He tells Alex so. An investment in their daughter's future.

"Dinner with Amanda?" Alex repeats, chagrined that Richard has drifted away again into a world of his own thoughts, forcing her to ask the question again. "How did it go?"

"Fine."

"I'm gathering she didn't offer you your old job back."

"No," says Richard, seeing disappointment blemish Alex's profile. "Then again, she didn't ask for the company's million dollars back either."

Alex frowns at his remark.

They are cleaning up the table after having pizza and salad together. He is glad tidying up keeps them busy—it is easier to say nothing about Amanda's sexual proposition and the fact he turned it down, or his confession to Amanda that he wouldn't take his old job back even if she were to offer it to him.

In the kitchen, they silently load the dishwasher, then take turns wiping down the counters and the stove. Drake has missed dinner again. Alex has admitted their son no longer calls to say he will not be there. How long has it been since Drake joined them for a meal? A long time, Richard realizes, feeling deeply the new normalcy of him and Alex being alone together at this time of day, on the precipice of evening.

"Any idea why our son still isn't eating with us?" Richard asks at last.

"It's what they do at his age. Everyone says so."

"Trends can be changed, you know."

"It's a small slice of independence."

"It's a major slice of inconsideration."

Alex is done wiping and is hanging up the dishcloth. She says nothing.

Richard leans on the kitchen island counter on his elbows. "I'm concerned about our children. Everything is fucked up." He gazes at his wife intently. "But we don't do anything about it. Everything is all fucked up and we don't do a damned thing about it; we just accept it and drift on to the next issue."

"Oh Richard," Alex says with a sigh. "Don't be so melodramatic. It's the way things are these days. This too shall pass." She pauses. "Now I know where Katie gets her flair for melodrama."

Finding this latter remark preposterous, Richard is compelled to silence.

"We can't keep the world the way it was when we were young," lectures Alex. "It's not the way things go. Things don't stay the same. Mores and values change. Don't be a dinosaur."

"Not everything that was done before today was done badly," he retorts.

"Or vice versa," says Alex. "It wasn't all *good* either."

Richard gazes at her without a word, unable to find the energy to speak. They look at one another for a full minute while no one moves.

"Your job is to get a job," Alex says eventually. "I'll handle the rest of it."

Richard straightens up from the counter. He stands there feeling vaguely overwhelmed and hugely insulted.

"Everything just lives here," he mutters under his breath.

"What was that?" his wife asks.

"Nothing," Richard replies, turning away from her. "Just thinking out loud."

IN OBLIVION THERE IS SOMEONE for everyone. Strangely it is Richard's conversation with Kevin that underlines this truth for him, bringing it into clearer focus. Until now, he has been too close to Violet, enraptured by what she is and his feelings for her, for him to truly grasp the love and companionship that exist between so many other people in Oblivion. But since talking with Kevin, Richard continually notices the varying kinds of intimacy and companionship a tranquil Oblivion generates. Age is not a factor. Nor is sexual orientation. There is no greed about love, no need for more affection than a person can provide, no abuse, no cruelty. There is no apparent sense of loss, of disappointment, no ideal against which a love relationship is found to be lacking. The love you need is the love you get; it has nothing at all to do with the love *anyone else* needs or receives, or the love others would *have you* need or receive. Violet is for him, he needs no one else. He does not have to accept Violet by rejecting the idea of someone else. The people he cares about in Oblivion are quick to mention Oblivion's ease of love as a great contrast to love in the other world, where, ironically, an ideal of love is what mostly *spoils* love.

"Yes, here, you find the love you need," Violet has told him. "It's never more than you need, and never less."

"Yeah," Richard muses. "It's never wrong. It's wonderful. I can see that for myself."

Richard and Violet discuss this topic often, as if playing inside it like otters.

"WHAT DO YOU NOTICE ABOUT THIS WORLD?" Derek asks Richard one morning as they meet once more on the street, gesturing with his arm to indicate the traffic, the tall buildings, the preoccupied passing pedestrians, the noise, the hubbub, the steadily unfolding treadmill.

"Whaddyuh mean?"

"You're an intelligent man. What's wrong with this planet? If you could change it, what would you change?"

"Jesus, Derek, Pretty big question for a chilly October morning."

"Not so big," argues Derek. "You must like it here. You must find it interesting or worthwhile. You come down here every morning to stand here with me and watch it all unfold, slurping your coffee and grunting in some vague, perpetual dissatisfaction."

"I don't want to drop out, Derek, if that's what you mean."

"Drop out?"

"Become homeless. Sit here like you every day, exposed to the elements and the whims of stingy passersby."

"Is that what you think I did? Drop out?"

Wary now, Richard glances down at his friend. "You often talk about choice, Derek. I thought being here every day in these circumstances was what you meant."

Derek nods thoughtfully but doesn't respond. Both men are silent for a time, working through what they might say next.

"There are many choices a person can make," Derek says at last.

"Of course."

"It isn't just this—where I am every morning with my cap on the sidewalk—or that out there . . ." and, as he did a few minutes ago, he gestures to take in the busy street. "There are many choices in between those options, and many choices that overlap."

"Yes, I imagine that's true."

Derek accepts his friend's acknowledgment without comment.

"Life used to make more sense to me when I was younger," muses Richard shortly. "Now it's going in a direction I don't appreciate. The times— these times—I want to get off the bus."

"Progress bothers you?"

"I just feel we've gotten stupid, all of us. Personally I feel too stupid to figure out why I'm stupid. I'm complacent. I'm too exhausted by my complacency to do anything about it. In the end, like everyone else, I just shrug and go shopping." He glances at his friend in search of some kind of response.

"What's caused that, Richie?"

"I've been thinking about that."

"And?"

"I'd say it's too much self-interest. Every man for himself—women too. Self-interest. I think that's at the root of human failure."

"I wondered," Derek says, after considering Richard's words. "I have these thoughts as well, even more than you do."

"I feel like a cranky old bear, Derek."

"You're a little on the young side for that, my friend."

"Huh," retorts Richard. "I'm not letting my relative youth hold me back. Who says you have to be old to be cranky?"

ANOTHER MORNING DEREK SPECULATES about Richard's allergy.

"The rash. The doctors concluded it was an allergy, didn't they?"

The rash is gone. Apparently Richard's memory of it wants to be gone as well. "They never found out what caused it," he says at last. "I'm already getting used to not having the rash. I'd almost forgotten it."

"By the cause, you mean what you were allergic *to*?"

"I guess so."

"Aren't you curious?" Derek asks.

"I'm just glad it's gone."

The two men consider this fact a moment in silence.

"I have a theory," Derek announces at last.

"Okay. Let's hear it."

"I think you were allergic to your job."

Richard grins, thinking Derek might be yanking his chain.

"I mean it, Man. I think you were allergic to what you did for a living."

"Really?"

"Yeah."

"Like what? Specifically what was I allergic to about my job?"

Derek considers the question a moment. Then, "I understood you to say you didn't know why your job existed, at least not in a significant way."

"True enough," Richard admits. "It's complicated."

"Complicated bad or complicated good?"

"Just complicated. Because the important things about working, about doing your job, are obscured by minutiae."

"Yes. Minutiae. Much ado about nothing."

"And there's so much of it, so much small stuff that you can't find your way through it to get to something important. My job was like that. I was always spinning my wheels, going through the motions. At the end of a week, I wouldn't know what I had accomplished. Reports about nothing. Meetings about nothing. It was endless. New products that didn't have any function or use to humankind but their salability. I was spending my career marketing trinkets to keep people at home amused or entertained. It wasn't important. It didn't help humanity. If anything, the products I promoted put everyone to sleep, dumbed things down further, put shutters over any important issues human beings might have been better addressing. I wanted to work at a newspaper, writing stories that helped people connect the dots. Instead, I ended up making all these additional, unconnected dots. I just added to the confusion. By the time I was released from, uh, dot making, there were hardly any newspapers left. Nowhere to go."

"Good reason to get a rash. As good a reason as any," Derek says with a grin.

Richard just nods. In fact, the two men fall comfortably silent. Derek sits waiting for coins to be dropped into his hat. Richard shivers—it's late October—and watches the various aspects of this busy city street go by.

"It's all minutiae," he says much later.

"True enough," agrees Derek from his place on the concrete. "I remember entire days of errands, fixing computer glitches, surfing the net, checking email, looking for the right-sized screw, just looking in store windows, wandering Wal-Mart, wishing, hoping, and just plain worrying. All that used up days, weeks, months, years. For some, it's lifetimes. I remember. My collection of minutiae is smaller than yours now. But I used to have a big batch, believe me."

Richard nods. "I do. I believe it."

"So what are you gonna do?" Derek asks.

"I don't know," Richard replies. "Something, I guess."

"I seem to recall your doctor . . ."

"Fred Sexsmith."

". . . Yes. Fred Sexsmith. I remember you telling me he thought you might be allergic to a number of aspects of your life."

Richard considers this a moment. "I remember."

"To be honest, I'm coming to the same conclusion about you."

"But my rash is gone. In effect, it disappeared with the job."

Derek shrugs. "Do you think it's as simple as that?"

"Sometimes," Richard admits.

"There's a lot more to life than our work," counters Derek.

"But there's a lot *less* to the *more* these days." Richard's gesture takes in the entire street. "You can see it for yourself."

"That's for sure," says Derek. "I see it."

"If Alex was okay with it, I'd take a year's vacation, or even six months."

"Alex wouldn't even agree to six months?"

"Not a chance. Not a fucking chance. Alex believes we should keep our noses to the grindstone. That way, an economically uncomfortable future won't catch up to us and bite us on the ass."

"Do you need her permission?"

Richard tenses. "Now that's a much bigger question with much bigger repercussions, my friend."

"This world obsesses," Derek says.

"It's terrified."

"You too?"

Richard shrugs.

"Lousy way to live your days."

"Totally lousy."

And, having said these things, the two men nod in unison at the passing evidence of their conclusion.

STILL ANOTHER MORNING DOWNTOWN. The last nice day of autumn—both Richard and Derek are convinced of this. Not the date, but the nature of the day. The cold is sharp, its touch metallic. It is as clean and solid as steel. But the mess of winter, it warns, is brooding on a horizon not far away.

"The worry on this street is palpable—you noticing that, Derek?"

"Yes," replies Derek. "Fear."

Richard nods. "Everyone is afraid, like Alex is afraid."

"Scared to death," Derek remarks. "Loss of job, fear of being broke, fear they won't be loved, fear that they'll be hurt, fear that someone is looking at them, fear that someone *isn't* looking at them, fear that they haven't made muster, fear that they don't have anything, fear that they don't have *everything*, fear that they're not good enough . . ." He falls silent.

"And many other things too," adds Richard.

Derek nods.

"There's one good thing about being unemployed," Richard says.

"What's that?"

"I have time to consider the larger questions about my life."

"Yup," says Derek. "That's a bonus, pure and simple."

"Imagine if we all had more time to think."

"Yes."

"I mean think about things that mattered."

"No minutiae, no duty on the treadmill stuff."

"Yes. Just a few hours a day to take everything in our lives and connect them in a way that makes sense. *Why* we do what we do."

Derek is nodding. "You mean living in a context."

"Yes. Not *outside* the context like little robots, but *inside* it, our lives the *reason* for the context."

"You make it sound easy, my friend."

"It *is* easy. This . . ." and Richard gestures at the busy street . . . "is complex and difficult, especially since it's outside the context we need to have rich, personal lives."

"Well said, Richie." Derek raises his hand as if in a toast.

Richard merely shrugs.

The two men watch the street go by in a blur. Standing here with Derek, Richard feels removed from the bustle and is gleeful in gratitude. Often, though, immediately after he leaves Derek, he becomes convinced that he is only kidding himself. How can he *not* be part of a mess that he used to promote to the masses? Richard feels more than unemployed. He feels betwixt and between. He orbits some ever more complex simplicity or some ever simpler complexity. He's not sure which. It feels right to wait. It feels *wrong* to wait. But he waits anyway.

NOVEMBER. WINTER PRICKS RICHARD'S NOSTRILS. His concern for Derek intensifies.

"I could find you a place for the winter," he tells his friend.

"I know."

"Will you consider it?"

"No."

"Why not?"

"I need to be here," Derek says.

"I don't understand."

But Derek cuts the conversation off with one of his observations. "The fear we see downtown all the time—you know what makes it contagious?"

"What?" says Richard.

"We look at our peers to see our reflection. But our authenticity isn't there. So we look again. Some piece of dread reveals itself and preoccupies us. We worry at it like a jackal at a piece of tendon. And, gradually, we begin to be afraid of more and more things, gnawing on each one of them endlessly—most of these things some version of *what will people think of us*— and we become part of the mirror everyone looks into to see if they are worthwhile, to see ultimately if they exist. We all do it. We're not self-possessed enough to live our own lives."

Richard considers Derek's words.

"Do you see what I'm saying?" Derek asks shortly.

"I do. But I want to find you a warm place to spend the winter. I think you're stonewalling me right now. Philosophical distraction tactics."

In the cold, Derek's ball cap nets a larger number of loonies and toonies than usual—never many but, today, certainly more than normal. Derek just grins and shakes his head. The two men drink their coffees in silence, considering the various matters that seem to present themselves each morning at this location on the street.

"Socrates and Plato," Richard murmurs at one point.

"That's us, I guess," Derek admits.

"PEOPLE HAVE CHILDREN HERE. Children are born here, right?"

Violet glances at him, amused. "Richard, you've seen the children here. You've seen the school!"

"Yes. If Kevin found a companion here—whatever it is that happens to bring people together the way you and I came together—and Kevin and his companion wanted children, she could get pregnant, right?"

Violet nods.

"Can you get pregnant?" Richard feels himself blush slightly at his question. It's not that her potential for pregnancy is a worry for him. To the contrary, sometimes he wishes that she could have a child with him, a tender, not very urgent wish he cannot explain to himself. He supposes it's just that he loves Violet in a way that would make him happily a father. There is nothing difficult to understand about this in his mind but putting it into words is another matter: he has determined the urge is too fundamental for explanation. And Violet, he believes, in partnership with him, would be a good parent.

"You and I can't have children in Oblivion," she explains, rising to clear their plates away from the porch table in her cabin where they have eaten.

"Oh," says Richard. He gets up to help her and they are quickly done.

"We've already had children . . ." and here she indicates with a vague flourish a world they cannot see together . . . "back there."

"Like Kevin, you mean. Kevin is my son from *there*."

"Yes. I have children from there too."

"You mean your children are still back there?"

Violet hesitates. "Their choices are or were their own," she says at last.

"Of course," says Richard.

"When you've had children back there, you can't have children here."

"And Kevin?"

"Kevin will be able to, if his partner *here* hasn't had children *there*. You see?"

Richard nods. "You're saying Oblivion doesn't cross breed with the other world. The only doorway into Oblivion is choice. You don't get here by cross pollination."

"Wow," says Violet with a broad grin. "I've never heard it put *that* way. It sounds . . . so *botanical*. You learn quickly, though. That *is* what I'm saying. Cross-pollination would usurp a child's ultimate ability to choose."

Richard shrugs.

"Don't forget," adds Violet. "When we're forgotten back there it's a forgetting that is complete. It's entire. It's like we never existed."

"Yes. I know."

"And we all take responsibility for the children here in Oblivion. All the adults here have a parental role. It isn't left only to the natural parents."

"I've noticed that," Richard says.

"Children born here are Oblivion's responsibility."

Richard nods. He raises Violets fingers to his lips a moment, then kisses them.

"You won't care that we can't have children here, Richard. And Kevin's in Oblivion of his own choice—you're a lucky man. Few people have progeny here from the other place, because people need to make their own separate and individual choice to live here. We don't arrive here with families. We can't *bring them* here. They have to choose it on their own."

"I get it," he replies. "I'm fortunate on both counts. I just love you Violet, down to every last freckle, and I feel something *fatherhoodish* about it sometimes."

"I know you do," she says. "That's just love being a great deal of itself, as close to everything complete as it can get."

"A great deal of itself?"

"Yes," says Violet.

Richard gazes at her with longing.

Violet gazes back at him.

Time passes easily. Hours go by. "Your children could still make Kevin's choice, couldn't they? They could still show up in Oblivion, couldn't they?" Richard asks that evening because he's been musing on the subject most of the afternoon. "I mean ultimately it could happen, couldn't it? I met someone elderly the other day at the village cafe, you know, a man in his mid-sixties, and he said he was a recent arrival. So one or both of your children, even in their mature years, could make the same choice you did, couldn't they?"

By now they are strolling the village streets, holding hands. At his question, Violet gently squeezes his hand in a way that conveys appreciation, acceptance, even encouragement. Several minutes pass before she answers.

"It's too late for my children now," she says at last.

Richard glances at her in dismay. "How so?"

"I've been here a long time, Richard."

It takes him a moment to grasp the implication in her words. "You mean they're gone now, they're . . . dead? You mean they can't choose Oblivion like you did because they died?"

"Yes," says Violet. "You see, I come from an earlier time than you. My children have no doubt passed on by now. Back there, I mean. And, when I came here, back there they ceased to be my children to anyone but me, here."

Richard feels deeply sorry. He says so.

"It's okay," Violet tells him. "There are children here at the school I get to love and cherish."

"I know that," Richard says.

"But I remember my children from before too. I still care about them, about their memory."

"I see," says Richard.

They walk on in silence. Then, "My life back there in the time before your times, all of that will be difficult to explain to a man like you, who hasn't yet made his choice. From the vantage point of *here*, of Oblivion, you won't know what I'm talking about."

"Because I can't remember the history of the other place?"

Violet nods. "Not while you're here. All that history is forgotten. At least for now."

They carry this conclusion with them in silence along the quiet street.

"I hope you'll try to explain anyway, Violet," Richard says finally. "At least a little bit. That world's long past isn't beyond *your* ability to recollect or describe it."

At first she doesn't respond beyond gently squeezing his hand again. She sighs, but not with impatience.

Richard waits in silence.

"What I remember most, dear Richard, about the time of my choice, is that the world had just gone through a great and stupid war, a terrible, terrible war."

And Richard wonders, here in a tranquil Oblivion, what she means by war.

ALEX TELLS HIM ABOUT KATIE after it's all too late. He gets the news nearly a week after she took Dougal to visit their daughter where she is in school. "Katie and Dougal are moving in together," she announces.

"What? In residence? They *allow* that kind of thing?"

"Of course not," Alex replies. "Do you really think the school would allow it?"

"These days nothing would surprise me."

Alex waits for him to calm himself, although clearly he continues to fume. They are in bed, staring again at the ceiling they know so well, the ceiling that has witnessed so many unhappy conversations in recent years. It's a ceiling he doesn't want to know as well as he does. Even with the distraction of Katie's latest misadventure, he has a moment to contemplate the personal wreckage gathered on his ceiling.

"Katie's left school."

Although the news is something he has been expecting with dread for weeks, Richard is still deeply angry. "Jesus Christ!" he says.

"You knew it was coming, Richard. You had to know it was coming."

Richard fumes. It is the waste of it all that angers him: the tuition, the books, the effort to get her accepted, even the stress and melodrama before classes began. Didn't she know before she applied that she didn't want to go, that she wasn't ready yet? And now the opportunity to do well for herself has been squandered too. And Dougal? Dougal has never been and never will be anything but the booby prize at the end of a race to the bottom.

"Why didn't they find a place in the student ghetto? They could have moved in together there. Katie wouldn't have had to leave school."

Alex has pulled the comforter up to her chin so that she can wear it like armour. No wonder they don't make love anymore, Richard concludes; the bedroom is used only for sleeping, or argument, or the announcing of bad news.

"Katie wasn't ready for university," she says eventually. "If you had been paying more attention you would have noticed that. Not mature enough scholastically."

"Not mature enough, period." And he wonders in silence what he was supposed to have noticed about Katie's immaturity in school when he was working all day or when his daughter spent her entire time in his presence dancing her thumbs over the face of her cell phone. Katie had made a vocation out of ignoring him, out of never relating to him. He would offer to take her shopping; she would decline. Go to Dairy Queen for a treat? She visibly turned up her nose.

"No. I suppose not," Alex is saying. "I admit she could be childish."

"But mature enough to move in with that asshole Dougal."

"Jesus, Richard," Alex mutters.

"C'mon, Alex. You want me to just accept everything without a fight. Dougal. Katie's fancies and whims. I'm just supposed to give over to whatever happens next in our kids' lives, no matter how much of a disaster it happens to be. What are we afraid of? As parents, I mean. Them? Our children? Not being cool? Are we afraid to take charge, to lead? It's kind of our job, isn't it? Leading. Isn't that what we're supposed to do?"

His wife considers his words a moment, though not very seriously. "I know it's hard," she says at last. "I know it's a disappointment."

Richard lies there in silence, thinking about how impossible everything is. It occurs to him then that he is a very unhappy man and no one cares about his unhappiness. Not a soul. He hardly cares himself. And he wonders how it came to this. He wonders how he came to be unhappy and where he misplaced the ability, the volition to correct the situation.

"Richard," Alex says shortly, "you miss working. You're depressed because you lost your job."

But Richard doesn't feel depressed, particularly about being unemployed. He doesn't miss his job. He didn't really like the people at work all that much in recent times and he didn't really know in the end what he was doing at Cascade exactly. A number of weeks ago at dinner with Amanda, when she brought him up to date on the news at Cascade Enterprises, what was happening to whom with whom, the information had bored him silly. How can Alex be so wrong?

"Once you get back to work, you'll be a changed man. Dougal and Katie won't matter in the same negative way they matter now."

Richard says nothing to this.

"Richard? You asleep?"

"Goodnight, Alex," he says, turning on his side, away from her. "I need to be alone with this. It's too much bad news to digest all at once. And this parental impotence, this laissez-faire attitude? I need some private time to figure out what in hell it gains us."

To this, Alex merely grunts.

THAT WEEKEND, RICHARD ENCOUNTERS DRAKE in the kitchen. Mid-morning. Early by Drake's standards, at least on a Saturday or Sunday.

"My god," Richard says, pouring himself a coffee. "It's my son. He is not a figment of my imagination. He actually exists."

Drake is gazing into the refrigerator, one hand on the door, the other on the wall of the device. "Very funny, Dad," he says over his shoulder. "You should do stand-up."

"And you should come home for dinner."

"I come home for dinner," argues Drake, his voice echoing in the fridge.

"When was the last time?" his father wants to know.

Drake doesn't answer. He emerges from the refrigerator with a carton of orange juice. He closes the door, opens the carton's cap and tips it back for a long guzzle.

"Can't you use a glass? People use that spout for pouring."

Drake sighs. "I'm thirsty. I'm going to drink all of it."

Richard stands there in silence, realizing there is little argument he can offer when his son's preoccupation with only himself is so apparent, so bald. A reasonable argument or instruction only works on someone reasonable. With Drake, these days, he might as well talk to someone from another universe. Pick your battles, Richard, he tells himself. Fight the big ones and let the brush fires burn themselves out.

"You have to come home from school for dinner or else call to ask why you shouldn't have to."

Drake won't look at him. During conversations such as this one, Drake shuns eye contact. "Is this, like, a rule or something?"

"Yes."

"It's stupid."

"I don't care if you think it's stupid. It's a rule. It's a matter of family consideration. People in families cooperate with one another. Your mother does, I do, you have to too."

Drake prepares to argue further—his body takes the shape of argument, hunching slightly, coiling like a spring—but he reconsiders his tactics and takes another long drink of orange juice. "Whatever," he says at last. "I have to go," he adds.

"So, do we understand one another?"

"Yeah, yeah, I get it."

And then Drake is gone.

GRADUALLY VIOLET BEGINS TO TELL HIM what her life was like in the other world before choosing to live in this one.

"So you had two children in the other place?" Richard asks. They are eating together at Violet's cabin. They are flushed. They have been laughing. They are happy with one another. They have already made love.

"Yes, two," Violet replies. "A son and a daughter."

"I'm sorry," says Richard, in case he has caused her pain. "When I bring it up, I don't want to make you sad."

"It's all right," says Violet, placing her hand on his. "I didn't leave them. They didn't leave me."

"But you remember them. And I gather, after you chose Oblivion, they wouldn't remember you from that point."

Violet considers his words. "Yes. But when people die it's the same— we remember them; they don't remember us. This is much better. Even when they were alive with their choice and I was alive with mine, there wasn't much room for pain. I remember them and I enjoy the memories. I believe, Richard, that at least some of our grieving isn't over what we had with people, but what we *wished* we had or regretted *not* having when we had an opportunity. It's a sad conundrum about being human. As for me, I don't need to be remembered. We've talked about this before. In Oblivion, the past is small, even considering what happened in the other world. The future too—small here in the sense that it isn't bloated by worry, the potential for disappointment or anticipation. Only the present is large and, as you can see for yourself, the present is wonderful. It just goes on and on in a state of peace and plenty."

"I'd like to hear more about your children," Richard says when Violet finishes speaking.

"Okay," she replies. "That would be nice."

They move to Violet's porch. Of an evening, Violet likes to drink a pot of tea here and Richard has taken to joining her sometimes. Here on a loveseat, with evening arriving gently shapeless, they talk in a way that reminds Richard of making love, peacefulness, slow caresses of conversation so delicate and tender they are like sex.

"My husband was a farmer like his father and his father's father. He courted me rather relentlessly. I thought he was a nice man. It wasn't a matter of love, not in the romantic sense. An idea like romantic love wasn't that popular at the time. Too fanciful. Not practical. It was a matter of making a good, reasonable choice. Was he a good man, virtuous, kind, caring? That's what women like me were brought up to look for in a husband. We weren't looking for magic. We were looking for someone solid."

"And your husband was like that?"

Violet nods. "His name was Nathan. And yes, he was like that. Until after the war."

"The war." The word feels strange on Richard's lips, without understanding the concept in Oblivion.

"War," Violet admits, "could be difficult to explain." She sips at her tea, which is hot. She slurps gently. "Imagine all the people you've met so far in Oblivion choosing up two sides, digging trenches to defend themselves, taking the rifles they use here for hunting game, and using them to kill one another. Hiding in the trenches and shooting at one another. Inventing machines to blow one another up more efficiently. Imagine that. Day after day, on and on, pain and death and damage. For years."

"Okay," Richard says, though hesitantly.

"Imagine that, only thousands of times worse."

"I'm not sure I can," admits Richard. "It's too crazy. But you're telling me people died?"

"Millions of them."

"What? Millions?"

"Millions."

For Richard only one word comes to mind and he asks it. "Why?"

"Countries trying to build empires. Jealous heads of states. Profits on making weapons and other goods. National pride. It's called nationalism. Hatred. You find someone to blame for all your ills and then you try to kill him in war. And if you're really cynical, you sell him the bullets to shoot back at you."

Richard says nothing. Violet's words are clear but their implications are beyond his imagination.

"My husband went to that war and wasn't killed. But he came back broken, with scars and a limp. He came back periodically mean and enraged. He taught my children to be periodically mean and enraged too, both of them, Emily and Tom. Not on purpose, just mostly by example. Ultimately, to varying degrees, they became like him and turned against me. I was different from them, they decided. Inferior in my gentleness. Husband, son, daughter. I existed to serve them. They existed to complain and not feel well enough served. I was a compassionate person, Richard, by nature, I guess. My husband and my children interpreted my compassion as weakness and their lack of respect for it as strength and power."

"Oh Violet." Richard lifts her hand, gently kissing her fingers.

"War," she says then. "It conscripted my family and they never were released from it."

"Your children didn't conceive of a different choice?"

"Apparently not. I nearly didn't find one myself. That other world is powerful and cruel, and it makes a virtue of self-interest, making it seem like a normal and forgivable motivation. I don't mean self-possession, which is a benign self-interest. But the "me-first" kind. The "what's-in-it-for me?" view as a fall-back position. Few of us see or imagined anything different back then. Few got to choose. Few *bothered* to choose."

"But you did, Violet."

She nods. "Ultimately there was nothing holding me back. I began that drift—I think of it as drifting—that is discovering Oblivion. Dreaming. Waking up. Dreaming again. Getting a handle on the idea that there can be choice. I'm talking about *real* choice. I began to hear Oblivion's four words of welcome; you know the words: *everything just lives here.*"

"It's powerful," Richard murmurs.

"And I began to teach children here. And sometimes, whenever they wanted, some of the children would visit me here, at my home, like sons and daughters in a way, like my *children*, although of course they weren't my children. They are *Oblivion's* children and, as Oblivion's children, they are my children too. Then, one day, I was here for good and not *back there* for good. I could remember the world back there where I was forgotten. I could see and remember the differences between here and there. I realized I had chosen. I realized I was now a permanent resident of Oblivion."

Having heard Violet's explanation, Richard is silent, considering, as he frequently does, how he inhabits Oblivion and the other world too, the one that knows well what war is. At this moment he feels even more stuck. It seems apparent he will make a choice at some point soon but he feels a delicate impatience that he has not yet done so. He feels imprisoned by his inertia, even though it is an inertia he isn't able to control.

At last he asks, "Did something trigger your choice? Did something significant happen to make you choose at the time you did? Was there a specific moment? Something that pushed you from one place to another, that other world to this one?"

Violet squeezes his hand, knowing as well as he does that the man she loves feels trapped in aspects of two disparate worlds. "It's not like that," she replies. "Nothing dramatic. We don't choose Oblivion to *not* choose the other place. At some point, though, we discover Oblivion is better and Oblivion is what we want. And we choose it. When we do, we arrive in this wonderful, wonderful place."

RICHARD AND DEREK SEE THE WHOLE THING. The accident. It enters their perception in slow motion, allowing them to comprehend every laborious second of it, as if both men are compelled to be witnesses even before there is something to witness.

A woman in a Mazda. Texting. Richard sees this from his vantage point where he stands leaning against the wall. The woman—soon to be revealed as in her mid-thirties and on her way to a meeting—is gazing at her cell phone, glances up, then down again at the phone. The car grinds towards the sidewalk at a relatively slow rate of speed.

"Shit," Richard remembers saying.

Derek gets up off the sidewalk with surprising nimbleness.

The woman realizes she is headed for a hydrant and a parking sign, and the waste receptacle where Richard usually disposes of his and Derek's empty coffee cups. The woman can see she is veering off the street but, to Richard's astonishment, she glances down again at her cell phone to consider one or two more words, reading them in the second or two before the crash, or punching "send" with her thumb, using that second or two of knowing that her car is out of control and she should take the steering wheel with a fist instead of her forearms, or hit the brake. Hitting "send" instead is the woman's mistake. The mistake is why she crashes.

Priorities, Richard has time to think before the crash, and later he will remember this thought frequently.

Pedestrians scurry out of the way before the car crunches to a halt against the hydrant. A couple of them are already texting or tweeting this important news to their friends or followers, even as they hurry away from potential injury. Some lift their phones to take a photograph to be sent along to friends or posted on Facebook.

It's the garbage receptacle that sustains the most injuries, that makes the most noise, that sprays its contents over the sidewalk and the edge of the street. No human is hurt. The damage is relatively slight. No air bag pops out of the steering wheel. The woman gets out of the car, remembering quickly to slip her phone into her purse, preparing the lie she will tell that excludes her phone from this event and gives the authorities a better version of what happened to her, now that it is against the law to be texting and driving at the same time. All of that done, she stands there a moment surveying the damage, acting like it happened to someone else.

A cop has shown up already, almost as if he knew about the accident in advance. "You okay?" he asks the woman, interrupting a conversation he is having with a device attached to the collar of his uniform.

She nods unhappily.

"Stay there," instructs the cop who, though not a big man, brings an imposing demeanour to the proceedings.

Again, the unhappy nod.

The cop glances at Derek who has sat down now on his piece of cardboard and has brought his ball cap protectively an inch or two closer to himself. The cop dismisses him, a homeless man, from his list of potential witnesses and shifts his gaze to Richard, capturing him with striking blue eyes.

"You see what happened?"

Richard glances at the driver who is looking back at him. There is no entreaty in her gaze, rather a confidence that they are peers who probably understand one another and, in this case, a shared notion that the cop is being a nuisance.

"Yes, I did," Richard replies at last.

"So what happened?"

"She was texting," Richard says. "The rest is fairly obvious."

"I'm going to need your name and address," the policeman says. "Wait here."

"Okay," Richard replies.

The woman is coming over, perhaps to argue her case with the cop, perhaps to tear a strip off Richard for incriminating her the way he did, but the cop doesn't want any conflict between witness and perpetrator, and quickly steers her away.

"Do you have a cell phone?" Richard hears the cop ask as he and the woman move away.

"Might see you in court, my friend," Derek murmurs carefully when the policeman and driver are out of earshot.

"She could have hurt someone," is Richard's response. "On a *bad* day, she might have killed someone. I had to tell the truth."

RICHARD FEELS DEREK WATCHING HIM. He glances at his friend and, from habit, shrugs. It is now a couple of days after the accident involving Richard as a witness. Derek has stated more than once in the interim since the incident how proud he is of his friend for not backing down in the face of his responsibilities. Richard has thanked him each time.

"You're deep in thought, my friend," Derek says today. "What's on your mind?"

"War," replies Richard. "And the military-industrial complex."

"Wow," says Derek. "Is there something going on I don't know about?

Have we declared war on somebody? Are the Americans involved?"

"Probably," Richard says. "But, no, there's nothing new for us to know about. Just the usual. There's always a lot going on with the military-industrial complex that we don't know about."

"So your funk this morning is nothing specific."

"No, I've just been thinking about it—I don't know why. Something I read in the paper this morning, I guess."

"Any conclusions you want to share?"

Richard nods. "Just that running your economy on war and death doesn't seem humane to me. It feels like murder."

Derek nods, says nothing.

Richard looks at his friend to share his speechlessness with him. There's nothing else to be said when you've brought up murder and identified society as the murderer.

"Interesting," Derek remarks a few moments later, "that you still read a newspaper." Clearly he has been thinking about this. "Most people go to the internet for their news these days."

"True," says Richard. "But I want the newspaper. I want my news from professionals. I want my news to be long enough to be complete. I want thoughtful analysis. Generally speaking, the Internet has too many amateurs. Even the professional sites, CBC, for instance, are racing to the bottom to keep up with the amateurs. Every time I read a report or story, I end up with more unanswered questions than I had when I started."

"That's not good," remarks Derek.

"No, it isn't. And the story selection sometimes—my god, what are they thinking? The other day there was a report about a woman who found a grasshopper in her salad. And every story has a number of tweets posted in it. Let's hear from the amateurs on Twitter. I don't want to hear from these twits, pejorative noun intended. I want to hear from news people who are trained and know what they're doing."

"Phew," says Derek with a grin.

"Yeah, I know," replies Richard. "It winds me up."

Derek considers this and shrugs. "I guess you'd know, Richie. You studied journalism in university. You always wanted to work at a newspaper."

Richard nods. "Yeah. I've given this a lot of thought. There are prevailing falsehoods about the Internet. One myth would be that what is there is true. But there's no vetting of what's there. No editor. Anyone can post anything and say it's true. Bloggers and amateurs. There's no moral compass, no professionalism. Most of the audience doesn't care that these standards are missing. Many are too young to have ever known the period when our standards were higher."

"Some argue," counters Derek, "that the Internet is the new commons, that it gives everyone a fair shake at being heard or seen."

"Sure. But the commons exists even without the net. Professional writers did the bulk of the public writing in the old days, but people also talked. That's a commons too. The technology we have now waters down what is seen or heard. And the quality—the truth and comprehensiveness—of what is seen or heard drifts consistently to the bottom. People still yapped before Twitter or Facebook existed—they just did it in person or in letters and manifestoes. There has always been a commons."

"Wow," says Derek. "And I'm being a devil's advocate here—but some would say you're being a snob. Only the accomplished get to have a truly public opinion?"

"That's not what I'm saying at all," counters Richard. "Opportunity should be egalitarian to be sure, but if everyone decided they were a doctor, the way they decide they're a journalist, we'd be dealing with an infestation of quacks. Everyone should have an equal chance to be a doctor, to stick with the metaphor, but they should have the aptitude, training, and skills to be a doctor. Simply wanting to practise medicine isn't enough on its own. Not everyone ends up being able to *be* a doctor. Likewise, not everyone is a qualified journalist. Not everyone is an . . . elder."

"An elder?" Derek laughs. "What an unexpected word. Elder. An interesting choice of term, Richie."

Richard's own look is puzzled. "It just popped into my mind, I guess," he says in a moment.

Derek nods, still amused.

"The Internet," says Richard then, "gives everyone a say. Fine As long as we all know that not everyone *has* something valuable to say, that's important too."

"That's harsh," says Derek.

"But true, in my opinion. Even if everyone can talk, not everyone has something earth-shattering or new, or thorough, or true to say. That's just the way it is."

"Harsh, man," says Derek. "Harsh."

"I know," splutters Richard. "I know. I'm a sonofabitch."

AS WINTER CONTINUES ITS RELENTLESS APPROACH, the two men on the street, both jobless, one homeless, find more to complain about. They have assumed their usual morning places downtown along the wall of Cascade Enterprises, not far from Starbucks. This morning they are bulky in new down-filled winter coats because it has been cold enough to snow a little a day or so ago, although the snow shortly melted away. Overhead, the sky has assumed a pale gray pout, filled up with November slop that only the optimistic would call another coming snowfall. Richard bought Derek his coat yesterday, relieved that it fit Derek's lanky frame, and told him they were finished as friends if Derek didn't wear it. "I'll wear it, I'll wear it," Derek said. "And thank you, Richie," he added. This war of words represents the latest volley in their ongoing argument about how Derek is to be protected from the onslaught of serious winter weather a month or so away. Derek complains the coat makes him look prosperous and will discourage his panhandling success. But Richard has no sympathy for his friend's argument. "You'll be fine," he replies. "It'll imply you buy clothing instead of booze with everyone's donation. Or some charity has come along to help you out."

On the street, the world goes by this morning in a more miserable way than normal. Fear of coming winter is now piled into the shopping cart already brimming with all the other ongoing human fears the two men believe they have witnessed on the street.

And it strikes Richard then, not at all good-naturedly, that if he isn't careful the allergy he suffered, now blamed on the vacuity of his job, could come back, should he let the street get to him much more. If his rash comes back he'll never find a job, Alex will leave him, and—this is the ironic part—he'll be stuck being modestly wealthy on his own, without purpose or provocation or need for anyone's approval. All of which, for some reason, strikes him as rather funny. Imagine having everything you need only to feel abandoned by the endless act of needing, he reflects. Doesn't the need have to be insatiable to represent true need?

"Jesus," Derek mutters from his place on his sheet of cardboard. "I sit here remarking on how people are too clumped together to ever truly know themselves, and you stand there with this wry grin on your face."

It's true. "Sorry," Richard says. "I went away there for a moment. Didn't hear what you said."

Derek just shakes his head, although clearly his displeasure is mostly feigned.

"I'm interested, though," adds Richard. "Please continue with your remarks."

"I was saying: How can you make a choice in life if you have to consider how you look to everyone else, how that *choice* will be perceived by everyone else? Can you be authentic if you have to seek everyone else's approval?"

"You argue a good case, Counsellor," Richard tells his friend, reminding himself and Derek too that Derek was once a lawyer.

"We appoint our peers to be our judges. You ever feel this way, Richie? You ever have these thoughts?"

"Sure do," says Richard without hesitation. "These days more than ever. When I was in marketing just up the street . . ." and he gestures in the direction of Cascade Enterprises . . . "I used to talk in meetings about something called 'slow motion smug.' Mostly in our television commercials."

"'Slow motion smug?'"

"Right. It's where the commercial's main actors—because *they* use the product or service being promoted—glance at themselves or the losers who aren't in the know all around them with this look of smug superiority. If you want to motivate consumers to enjoy a product or service, you have to show them they'll get to feel superior about it. Gaze into the human mirror of *loserdom*, if you will, to confirm you enjoyed said product or service. Worse yet, we emphasized this smugness as a good thing, by offering it in slow motion, like a winning goal in hockey or a successful slide into second base in baseball. How's that for narcissism?"

Derek nods. "I get it. And, in a way, they know you're doing it, too," he says, gesturing at the passing crowd, even as a well-dressed woman bends down to leave behind a few coins in Derek's ball cap. "That's the strange thing: I bet just about all of them know they're being played. But the need for approval is too powerful to resist. Few of us fight back."

Richard considers this a moment, the next question obvious to him. "What's to be done, my friend?" he asks. "It can't all be blamed on advertising."

"Well," replies Derek then. "If I weren't some homeless guy with a frozen butt on a piece of cheap cardboard on a November sidewalk, I'd tell *them* to stop it."

"Stop it?"

"Yeah. I'd say, *you're not having a good time. You're a mess of anxiety and fear. So stop it.* That's what I'd say."

"You'd say: stop it?"

"Yeah, stop it right now."

"Stop it right now. That's it?""

"Yup. Stop it right now. I think it's as simple as that: stop it right now."

"You're saying, choose a different way, a different motivation in life."

"Yeah. Stop *this*, choose *that*."

They fall silent for a moment or two.

"Sometimes I love you, Derek, you know," Richard remarks at last.

"Thank you," Derek says.

"You're welcome."

"One more thing," says Derek. "These people. Just think what a wonderful life they would be having if they didn't have to tweet everyone about the wonderful life they're pretending to have."

"Good point, my learned friend."

"Fucking right," says Derek before downing his last swallow of coffee. "That's what I'd do," he mutters shortly. "I'd tell them to fucking stop it. Then again, here I am on the sidewalk, homeless."

Richard gazes up and down the street, seeing dozens and dozens of people whom he believes will never stop. He glances at Derek. "Choice," you say. "Right?"

"Right," replies Derek.

RICHARD HAS THIS IDEA that he and Derek, being of relatively like mind and sound body, could set up some kind of small business together.

"Something brainy, honest, and true," he tells his friend.

"Right," says Derek.

"You know, with some of my severance from Cascade as seed money. Maybe in a smaller city somewhere. Somewhere quiet. I'll sell my house. We'll move. Get you off the street."

"Right," says Derek again. "And I can handle your side of the proceedings when Alex divorces you."

Richard ignores him, continues. "We're smart—I'm a journalist, you're a lawyer. We agree on many things."

But Derek just shakes his head. "You ever see Paul Newman and Robert Redford in *Butch Cassidy and The Sundance Kid*?"

"Yeah, of course."

"And Sundance says, more than once, as I recall, 'You just keep thinking, Butch. That's what you're good at. You just keep thinking.'"

"And?" says Richard, knowing what's coming.

Derek is looking up at him from the sidewalk, a broad grin on his face. "You just keep thinking, Butch," he says. "You just keep thinking."

THE DAY OF RICHARD'S CABIN-RAISING ARRIVES without notice or forewarning of any kind. The activity gets underway not long after Richard joins Violet on the porch of her cabin, drinking his first coffee of the day with her. Approaching is a parade of people, wagons, horses, bicycles and carriages. It emerges out of the morning sunlight like a long snake of conversation, clopping hooves, laughter, joking and gaiety.

"Ah," says Violet before Richard can ask, peering into the distance along the dusty road. "The time has arrived."

Richard too can make out the procession, men and women, a throng of conversing voices. "What's going on?" he wants to know. "What is it?"

"We're building your cabin today," replies Violet.

"What?"

"We're building your cabin today."

Richard looks at her, dismayed.

Indeed, Richard's cabin is the plan. They intend to build the structure in one day, two dozen or more of them, on a small, flat piece of land they stake out a few yards from where Violet lives now. Once he gets over his surprise, Richard discovers how he can help with the work, although he needs detailed instruction each time he places and hammers a board. In his time of visiting Oblivion, Richard has seen a cabin raising only once and only in the distance. Up close, he discovers, it is a marvel of expertise and cooperation. There is a foreman, John Naylor, who directs the willing members of the crew to their specific assignments. Measurements are taken, footings are dragged into place and made level. Beams are sawn, joists constructed, floors insulated and laid. Wall frames are put together and lifted into place. Plumbing is installed. An additional crew digs and builds a grey water pit. Meanwhile, when the structure is complete, the porch is erected at the front: the skeleton continues to take shape like a being alive. Richard has always loved the smell of wood; today he inhales the scent with an even more profound joy and love.

Food has arrived with the workers and a few of them stop work on the cabin around one to set up a lunch, repeating this process five hours later when the assembly breaks for dinner. It's not fancy. They eat from planks they place across sawhorses assembled for that purpose. Yet, but for these two necessary interruptions, they spend the rest of the time constructing Richard's small structure, putting in windows and doors, shingling the roof and installing wiring. A team erects his solar panels, then installs the solar generator and his compost toilet. Cement is mixed, a brick chimney is erected and a wood stove connected to it. The men and women here, builders all, are specialists, save for Richard himself and Violet and Kevin who are here to help out where they can.

There are only a handful of basic models for cabins in Oblivion. Kevin has already explained to his father that there are no large, ostentatious homes to convey status or class superiority. Instead, all cabins are merely functional and, save for what the resident does to the inside of a structure to meet his or her specific needs, do not have any other purpose than comfortable shelter.

During the process of construction, Richard has additional questions, as he often does, which either Kevin or Violet answer for him.

"These materials," he asks during the shared break for dinner. "The solar panels, the bricks, the wood and electrical equipment. Where's it all made?"

"Here in Oblivion," Kevin replies. He sits beside his father, enjoying a meal of chicken stew that has been simmering on Violet's stove for a number of hours.

"Here? By whom?"

Kevin gestures at the throng partaking of the meal with them. "These people working with you today. You write The Bulletin. They make building supplies and tools and solar panels and electrical boxes."

Richard nods.

"And some people build buildings," adds Kevin. "Because they love to do it."

"In exchange for what they read in my little newspaper, right?"

"Yes. Although they'd do it even if they didn't get anything back right away."

"Artisans."

"Yes." Kevin thinks for a moment before embellishing his explanation. "No factories and production lines like they have in the other world. And no large economy. Dad, we only make what's needed and we exchange it—in the larger, looser sense—for what *we* need."

"Like you've said before: no money."

Kevin nods. "We don't need money for a system like this. Life has purpose without it."

"I've seen rifles for hunting."

"Made by a gunsmith."

"And the steel?"

"A forge."

Richard nods now too.

"In Oblivion, everything you need is here. The raw materials. The skills and talents that turn them into the necessities we use. And the people with skills and talents get to work at what they enjoy and what they're good at. Simple."

Richard gazes at his nearly completed cabin. He grins in appreciation.

"Of course you have to paint the place yourself," Kevin says. "And before you ask me, the paint is made by the paint guy." He follows up this remark with a broad grin.

"The paint guy. Of course."

"Of course," says Kevin, still grinning.

"WHAT IF I DON'T PERMANENTLY USE THE CABIN?" Richard asks Violet later that evening, long after darkness has fallen.

They have been sitting on Violet's porch, gazing at the new structure, which looks closer in the darkness than it actually is, enhancing Richard's nearly worshipful astonishment that he has a cabin of his own.

"What do you mean?" asks Violet.

"I worry that I won't choose Oblivion even though I want to."

Violet nods. "You want to when you're here. You have to want to when you're there, that's all."

"But how?"

"I don't know," Violet admits. "I only remember how it happened to *me*. Which won't help *you* at all."

"No wonder I worry."

Violet touches his hand, then holds it. "As for the cabin, if you don't choose Oblivion, someone else will need it, that's all."

"You'll have a new neighbour," Richard says, trying to cover up his sorrow, his sadness at the prospect that the neighbour won't be *him*.

"I suppose I will," concedes Violet. "But Richard? Just don't worry. Worry doesn't accomplish *anything*. Oblivion is not a place where people worry."

Still, Richard remains morosely silent for a few moments. "You know, Violet, should something in me choose the other world, it won't be because of you. I want you to know I've chosen *you* completely."

"I know that, Richard," she replies.

"I want to be here with you."

"I know," she says. "I want you to choose Oblivion. But none of this is up to me. And your choice can't be about only me. It's too large a choice for that. It's too vast. I'm only part of what comes your way when you celebrate a life of free will. Besides me, there are so many things to see and do, to experience."

Richard nods, sighs. "I don't get it," he says at last. "Wanting to choose and not being able to—I don't get it."

"None of us ever did," admits Violet. "Not until afterwards. Not until we chose."

KEVIN EMPHASIZES OFTEN THAT THE PEOPLE in Oblivion don't sell their labour to the rich. "We exchange our labour for the goods we need but there are no rich or habitually idle people here, and we don't work for them."

Richard takes all of this in and nods thoughtfully. Father and son are playing chess—not very competitively—and long gaps of inactivity punctuate each turn. As always, they are enjoying their conversation more than the reason they have contrived to share each other's company. And it is raining in Oblivion, which it does with such a balanced frequency that everyone finds it refreshing instead of tiresome. The natural environment in Oblivion is pristine; sunny and rainy days take place with a resulting normalcy. Chess on Richard's new porch on a rainy day? Why not?

"And the other world, I gather," Richard replies, " sells its labour as a commodity."

"Yes."

Actually Richard can glimpse this fact in the murk of his memory. He senses a kind of "us" and "them" in people there. Everyone is put to use to maintain the system.

"Back there," his son is pointing out, "in that other world, there were once places that the world's population collectively used. Oceans, forests, mountains, jungles. The commons. It wasn't a matter of owning them. It was a matter of being free to use them. Like here in Oblivion. People met their needs in the commons. Thirsty, they drank. Hungry for meat, they hunted. Wanting fish, they fished. Needing shelter, they cut down trees or found stone to build cabins and other structures. And the commons replenished itself."

"So what happened?" Richard asks.

"The wealthy and the greedy took them over, to exploit what was in or on them."

"And everyone just let it happen?"

Kevin nods. "They were persuaded to allow it. The invention of the steam engine, the Industrial Revolution. Remember that?" Kevin hesitates when his father shakes his head. Then he goes on.

"First of all, people were persuaded that they needed a different kind of plenty. Instead of two shirts, they began to think they needed ten shirts. Twenty shirts. Everyone became convinced that you were a better, more successful person with twenty shirts. As well, everyone became convinced that this kind of amassing of material goods was human nature. As for the commons, the places everybody owned, the *nobles* took them. It became divine right that the nobility deserved to own what they surveyed so that it didn't fall into neglect or disrepair, left to the whims of the ordinary man or woman."

"Who came to that conclusion?" asks Richard.

"The nobles who wanted to own it. It was bullshit, of course."

"It sure is in Oblivion," Richard admits.

"Yes, it's the opposite here. In Oblivion we know the person who wants it all will destroy it. Here, everything is shared by everyone who has a need. And we're sure everyone will look after it. Besides, it's not our alone. It *belongs* to *everyone*. In the other world, amassing wealth and selling your labour to do it is natural to many. Some even consider it mankind's loftiest virtue. Amassing wealth as the only motivation for work, you see?"

"And everyone just goes along? It sounds so inhumane."

"Well," says Kevin with a shrug. "Historically, in the other world, there have been threats, punishments. Deception. Death and oppression whenever there was a revolt. Ideas can be fists—they beat you down and beat you back. Today, though, it's often more subtle. Bottom line? If you don't, as a member of society, embrace the system, you are, in one way or other, left to eke out subsistence. Indirectly you are shunned and condemned. You are left to be homeless, which is where you ultimately die."

"That's awful."

Kevin nods. "And unnecessary. Look around you, Dad. Do you see many people looking for someone to look down on or up to?"

Richard nods in understanding, though sadly. "Are you supposed to be telling me this, Son? Are you selling me a choice I'm supposed to make on my own?"

"No," replies Kevin. "I don't think any information I give you will make any difference. Choice comes from within. I've learned here in Oblivion that choice and its responsibility aren't really learned. It's inside us. I think you're hearing some of my anger about where I used to live. I guess I'm just letting it out."

Richard reaches out and touches his son on the arm. He nods.

"But it's all true. The other world can be a cruel and selfish place."

Richard nods again.

Kevin takes a moment to shrug off the sadness he and his father apparently share. At last he sighs. "As you can see, Dad, Oblivion is entirely an opportunity to share the state of plenty."

"I see that, Kevin."

"You don't need ten shirts. This world, even with no one owning swaths of it, doesn't fall into neglect. And in Oblivion, you don't need to sell your work. You just exchange it for what you need in your own good time. Everything else that makes life wonderful is here. And in our ability to enjoy simplicity and tranquility."

"Is there a difference in size?" Richard asks. "You know, scale?"

"Whaddyuh mean?"

"The other world—it's huge, right?"

Kevin nods.

"Maybe Oblivion couldn't exist on a scale that large."

"You need to see an elder," Kevin says. "I'm told Oblivion is gigantic."

STILL, SELF-INTEREST COULD BE A MATTER of human nature, Richard reflects one day on the street where he has again joined Derek to watch their world go by. More wet snow is falling, the kind that often defines

November. Rough winter ahead. Derek will want to stay here, ensconced on his piece of cardboard. Derek won't want to move. Richard believes he will have to insist that his friend let him find a place for him to stay protected from the elements. Derek maintains he has spent other winters on the street like this and he has learned to survive them. Richard counters that all bad things must come to an end. "Assuming it's bad," argues Derek.

Maybe Derek knows that it's human nature to be self-interested, to be a bully or be bullied. Maybe it is these characteristics that Derek has rejected by living on the street. Certainly there are people who believe self-interest is basic to human nature—Richard has recently worked for people who make vast profit from their faith in peoples' self-interest. It's human nature to want things, they say. But is it? Maybe not, Richard thinks. *Everything just lives here.* But not in the world of this busy city street, Richard concludes this morning. It isn't *everything*. And it certainly isn't *just* and it isn't very *alive*. In a way, with so much missing, it isn't really *here* either. No, it's a here that is actually *elsewhere* somehow, although, as he considers this, Richard feels suddenly forlorn and lost. What is *wrong* with him? he wonders. Before he lost his job, would he have thought this way?

"You know something, Derek?" He says at last. "Something rather wise—I think it's wise—has occurred to me just now."

"I'm all ears," his friend replies.

"If people were aware that their abilities—however great or small—gave them more opportunity to share, to give of themselves, instead of more privilege, this world would be a better place to live in."

Derek thinks for a moment, then nods. "Good luck with that one my friend," he says.

"But it's occurred to me it's true."

"I have to admit it would be nice," admits Derek. "But all this world's various pressures focus on convincing us to prefer privilege over sharing."

"I know," says Richard. "I know." His coffee is getting cold. He drains it, falling silent for a long time.

"You okay, Richie?" Derek asks from his spot on the sidewalk, aware of his friend's continued distraction.

"I've gotta get you inside this winter," Richard replies then.

"You've got bigger fish to fry, my friend."

"The hell I do."

"The hell you *don't*. You've just been talking about it."

And they fall silent at that point, at well-intentioned loggerheads.

Sometimes Derek pushes *him*, Richard realizes, the way that he pushes Derek to come in out of the cold. But Derek's pushing is subtle and Richard doesn't entirely understand where Derek's prodding is finally supposed to take him. Richard is one man—what's he supposed to do? And here he is standing on the street when he's supposed to be finding himself a job. At this moment, defying the system seems just an excuse for not finding his place in it.

KEVIN ADMITS THE NEED TO OWN the commons has a long history with humanity. "Even back to primitive man," Kevin tells his father, "it was a territorial thing. Even primitives were territorial. Other animals too, I gather. You don't have to be highly intelligent to be territorial."

"So humans have an excuse for wanting to own it all," Richard ventures.

"Yes and no," says Kevin. "Primitive man is one thing. He was ignorant in many ways, at least. Later, though, he could comprehend the bigger picture and had enough information to make a different choice. Later we had the intellect to know what was best for us as a species. We had the ability to think on behalf of our collective, aware we could live unselfishly with success. We could see how we'd corrupted nature with our territorial stewardship."

"You mean, when we got smart enough not to be territorial, we didn't get *kind* enough?" suggests Richard.

Kevin nods. "When we figured out we had a choice, we chose not to share the commons."

"But in Oblivion . . ."

". . . Precisely," Kevin says. "The choice to come here is a choice for the commons and the tranquility of the collective."

Richard nods slightly because he seems to understand.

Kevin is watching him. "I know both worlds," he says at last. "This one—Oblivion—and that one. I can't believe how many people were unwilling to choose to share. I look back into history and wonder, as we became more intelligent, why we also became more sophisticated about being selfish. It's like we took the wrong fork in the road and then assumed we couldn't go back." He shrugs, plainly dismayed.

"We chose badly?"

Kevin nods again. "It was the worst choice people could have made. Billions of us. No plan. Be on top or be victimized on the bottom."

Richard gazes at his son, perplexed, as always frustrated that his knowledge is caught in purgatory, trapped with him inside his own apparent failure to choose.

Kevin, as always, remains aware of his father's confusion. "I know, Dad. You want to take my word for it, but it's difficult. I'm just a kid, notwithstanding Oblivion's different pace of time passage, compared to the other world. Even here, I'm still young, I suppose. In fact, in your eyes, I'm still your teenage son, whether you remember me then or not."

"A smart kid," Richard says with a grin. "And my son. That makes you a chip off the old block, doesn't it?"

"Taking credit?" Kevin says with a broad grin.

"Maybe a little."

"But don't forget the child is father to the man."

Richard nods. "Especially in Oblivion," he says.

RICHARD AND ALEX MUST HELP KATIE AND DOUGAL MOVE. Richard does so in a state of fiercely controlled rage. Dougal's slouch and nearly perpetual insolence. Katie's childish lack of knowledge about what will be expected of her, what she's gotten herself into, how living in an apartment out of the family home will mean new and necessary responsibility. She's too young for any of this, he knows. Too alien. Her culture of peers is too collectively foolish to give her good advice and her peers are the only ones she will ever *ask* for advice. So why don't he and Alex intercede? Instead, they're obliged to show up to help them move into what they know will be dire circumstances. Aren't he and Alex ignoring their responsibility to be elders, to be wise? Their impotence—their failure to provide insistent leadership to their progeny—and the act of moving Katie have combined to make Richard quietly furious.

"Don't these people have friends who can help them move, help them slug the furniture around? And why is the furniture so new, so expensive? How come I don't know about these purchases? Why weren't they discussed with me? And who moves December first when they could wait until the new year?"

Alex acts like she doesn't hear him.

Richard lugs boxes, cases and small furnishings from the truck he was forced to rent, to the elevator in this building.

Midway through the move, he corners his daughter in her new apartment kitchen. He is tired now, the lifting of boxes and suitcases, his quiet, unrelenting rage about her partnership with Dougal. He's in a terrible mood.

"Did you even ask your friends to help you move?" he demands to know.

"Yes," she replies with a Richter scale sigh.

"Well, what did they say?"

"They said they couldn't."

"And these are *friends*?"

"People aren't friends only if they help you move. We don't expect that, Daddy. We don't want to move *them* either."

"Jesus," Richard says. "Because that's what parents are for, right?"

Katie just sighs and storms out of the room. Soon Alex arrives with an armload and tells him to knock it off, to be more gracious, they're nearly done. Then, that said, she insists that she and Richard take the young people to dinner at a restaurant down the street now that everything has been lugged into the apartment. "We all need a break, and a reward for our efforts," says Alex. Then, after the meal, she adds, the two young people can be left to unpack.

"Shouldn't they be buying *us* dinner?" Richard replies.

"They don't have the money for that and you know it."

Richard nods. He does indeed know it. "And now they'll have rent to pay."

"They're going to get jobs."

"Sure," mutters Richard, "and pigs are going to learn to fly."

Feeling victimized, Richard nonetheless relents on dinner. What choice does he have? Ahead of Katie and Dougal lie a thousand obstacles of one kind or another. As a dutiful modern parent, Alex will expect him to help her clear every single obstacle away. Which, Richard is convinced, is what went wrong in their career as parents in the first place. Someone at Cascade called it snow plow parenting; he remembers nodding in agreement.

"Alex?" he says as his wife is turning away.

"What, Richard?"

"There are no jobs. Not for them."

"Oh, Richard."

"There are no jobs. On this one, I'm on *their* side. We, you and me and the system, have killed the decent jobs."

For a moment, Alex gazes at him in silence. Then, "Doesn't your negativity ever get tired?"

She leaves him there to sort it out on his own. On his own is exactly how he feels.

VIOLET BLAMES THE OTHER WORLD for the loss of her children. The other world, she says, was at the root of their decision not to choose Oblivion, not to know about Oblivion, not to opt for a different way of living life, such as the one Oblivion offers.

Richard has finished work on The Bulletin for the day and has left his new cabin early to meet Violet at the school. It is a fine summer's day and the children she has been teaching are outside with her, gathered in a grove of mature poplars and aspens, shaded by the leaves which endlessly applaud a delicate breeze. Richard knows many of the names of the children now, nearly two dozen in all. Violet is teaching them how to draw and measure straight lines with rulers, how to draw a conceptual cabin layout to scale, with rooms and walls, windows and doors. The older children—none of them over twelve—have been paired with younger versions of themselves, aged nine or ten, and the older ones help Violet teach, and their younger friends to learn. Violet is more than an artist; Violet can teach the rudiments of design. She has gained most of her knowledge here in Oblivion. In the other world, she says, any aptitude for art or design was blocked by the responsibility she had to the family she served. But in Oblivion she has been able to harvest the fruits of her aptitude and share it with her neighbours.

Soon, when Violet's students have completed their lesson, another teacher, or another parent, or another instructor—sometimes an elder—

takes them to another lesson where the children learn something else. And soon there will be time for play, not only among the children, but between parents and children and teachers as well. Fun, Richard has learned, is shared by everyone. Fun is an integral part of life in Oblivion.

In Oblivion, Richard has learned, raising children is not left to parents and teachers alone. The rights parents have with respect to their children are not sacrosanct in Oblivion. The responsibility for young minds and sensibilities has evolved to include everyone in the larger community. Responsibility for everyone is inherent.

Self-interest is not a virtue in Oblivion, it is not called ambition or some other euphemism. Oblivion's children learn this from an early age. Parents, teachers, elders, people at large. *All* of them are elders and set the same important example, taking responsibility for the same vital instruction. Richard is used to this fact in Oblivion. All the grown-ups here are grown-ups. Rights, freedoms and responsibilities all enjoy an equal status.

The grove, now empty of Violet's students, feels wondrous and cool; Violet and Richard remain there alone, leaning against a tree trunk where they talk about Violet's children, Emily and Tom, not about a choice *not* made, but about a choice *made*.

"Why didn't Emily and Tom emulate the gentleness and warmth of their mother instead of the bitterness of their father?" is the question Richard asks. "Did he pressure them? Was it manipulation?"

Violet thinks for a moment, clearly looking for the right words. "It's that other world," she says. "It doesn't function in the same way as this one."

Richard waits for her to continue.

"In that other world, there are homilies people repeat to one another to explain their crueler choices. 'It's a tough world out there,' they'll say. These perceptions of a world that is cruel by its nature are popular there and people use various expressions and sayings to justify the times when they're unnecessarily mean or selfish." Violet glances at him to make sure he is understanding her.

He nods.

"In that world, most of the decisions we made about life were based on the examples of *other* peoples' decisions or choices. I remember this myself. I spent much of my life being busy and making certain I had my neighbours' approval. I was a farmer's wife. Like Nathan, my husband, I had many hours of work in front of me each day. When he went to war, I had to do his job too. I worked and I slept and I looked after my children. Every day. I had time for little else. I'm not complaining, by the way. What would be gained here, now, by complaining about how hard I had to work then, or whom I had to impress?"

"Nothing," Richard says with a smile.

She nods, goes on. "I'm just trying to explain that the other world has a system that is very powerful and pervasive. It's difficult to escape. Our peers in that world would judge us, would resist any efforts we made to be independent in any authentic way. There were pressures brought to bear to correct any non-conforming approaches to life. Is this making any sense, Richard?"

He touches her leg with his leg where they sit together under the trees, to reassure her. "It's hard to imagine," he says. "But I understand what you're saying. So you had to farm a large farm, right?"

Violet grins. "Not large by *that* world's standards. There, it was small. But we farmed far more than we needed so that we could sell the rest. That's larger than a farm in Oblivion where you meet your needs and other people's needs when they present themselves, nothing more."

"And your children? Emily and Tom?"

"Yes. They learned bitterness and cruelty are relatively acceptable human qualities. All the peer pressure there, most of the norms of that society taught my children to look out for number one and amass as much wealth for themselves as they could to protect themselves from a dangerous world. Not how to make the world less dangerous."

"And Emily and Tom learned to choose that world?"

"Yes. It's very, very compelling to people who don't understand the compulsion, who don't think deeply enough to see through it. It takes great courage sometimes to make a different choice when the motivation to be conventional is so relentless, so insistent. The conventions are not only numerous in that world, but familiar. Even if something is less than ideal, people cling to its familiarity."

Richard waits for her to finish. The day is fine and brilliant. For now, the day is more than enough.

"The other world talks a lot about human nature," Violet muses after a time. "You know, what qualities are inherent to humans and just can't be helped. What we're just going to have to put up with. But it isn't a matter of human nature. Not really. Endless self-interest isn't human nature at all: it's *social* nature. Am I making any sense, Richard?"

"I think so. Is there no human nature at all?"

Briefly Violet leans her cheek on his shoulder. "Oh yes, my love. The need for and ability to love, for instance. Curiosity. The need to create. The need for tranquility and peace. Empathy and compassion." She lifts her cheek away to look at him. "I'm sure all of these and other kindnesses and wonders are human nature."

Moved by what she has said, Richard nods. He has seen all of these kind and generous characteristics in Oblivion many times, so much so that he feels their veracity beyond his ability to understand the words describing them.

"But in the other world," Violet is saying, "human nature reflects the characteristics of a narrow collective goal. Ambition, struggle, victory in war, ideology, winning, greed, peer acceptance."

"These aren't human nature?" Richard asks.

"Not really. Human nature is the qualities we would exhibit if we were alone or with one other person or a few people. Those other characteristics we nurture so that we can please and perpetuate society at large."

Richard considers what she has said for a long time. "Social nature and human nature can't co-exist?"

"Of course they can, Richard. It's a matter of which one has precedence and *how much* precedence it has. Here, in Oblivion, everyone's human nature is so fundamental that human nature is hardly mentioned at all. There is a social nature here, but it's very benign and dependent on a more gently powerful *human* nature. Here, it's working together, leaving people alone to live authentic lives, encouraging peace and harmony. That's *our* social nature."

"And back there?" Richard swallows, feeling that he will again leave this world, the one where Violet lives, to return to his other life. At this moment he longs to control his journeys back and forth between this place and the other one.

"It's the reverse," Violet replies. "Socialized nature is everything. Human nature is just the explanation offered up for bad behaviour, for acting in bad faith."

"Does it ever work out?" asks Richard.

"Of course it does," Violet replies. "It's just a matter of balance. Authentic people make authentic choices. The balance is in our authenticity. Our human nature is to be authentic. People in that other world are socialized so that everyone stays in line within the system."

Richard places his hand on her knee, gently squeezes it. "Were you always this smart?" he asks.

Violet shakes her head. "Not until I had the time to be. Here, in Oblivion, we have the time to improve our minds. Everyone does."

"Nothing holds you back."

"No. What I do with myself is entirely up to me."

"And most people improve their minds, right?"

"Not *most* people, Richard. Everyone does. We have the peace and the time to do it. It's human nature to improve your mind, to learn, to make the most generous use of your faculties. You see? It's all in what yardstick you use."

A FEW MINUTES OF ANGRY SNOW. It comes in at a slant, stinging the eyes. Then, in a moment it is gone again. The two men who meet on the sidewalk in the city's downtown, obscured by skyscrapers and noise and vehicle fumes, pay the snowfall no mind. It snows like this now and again, some reminder by Mother Nature that she, and no one else, is actually in charge. Coffee is sipped. The two men ignore most interruptions, attentive to their camaraderie, the things they talk about.

"This Dougal you complain about . . ." Derek says shortly.

Richard sighs deeply, automatically.

". . . What is it about him, specifically?"

Winter on the street, the snow that just fell already melting and getting filthy. Richard and Derek have been watching people go by, bent against a wind that suddenly relents before picking up again, keeping them off balance. It's busier today, more young people than usual passing by, large headphone sets of gleaming chrome spewing music into their ears, or cellphones held out in front of them, thumbs dancing in the cold over the tiny keyboards. A few T-shirts and shorts in minus zero temperatures. What, wonders Richard, would compel a person to choose to be cold when he or she could be warm?

"Poverty," answers Derek, though Richard hasn't asked the question. "Students living in relative poverty who can't afford warmer clothing, unless they give up something else they think is more important."

"A little like someone else I know."

Derek doesn't respond to this.

Maybe it's university reading week. Or college. Still, muses Richard. All these young people on the street, together but alone, yes, dressed stupidly against the winter, tattoos, body jewellery, goosebumps. Dougal. Even the mention of his name makes Richard judgmental.

"He's a gronk," Richard pronounces eventually.

"That's it?"

Richard glances at his friend. "Not smart. He controls my daughter. I think she's convinced, without Dougal, no one will ever love her again. He's surly and without ambition. No manners."

"The usual stuff, then," Derek says.

"Yeah. I s'pose. I wasn't perfect either at that age. But I wasn't as *im*perfect as Dougal is."

Derek seems to consider this.

"There's another issue, though," Richard adds after a time. Suddenly a car alarm goes off just up the street, interrupting him, and he waits for it to be silenced before he goes on. "It's our lives and what children sometimes do to them."

Derek waits.

"As adults, generally speaking, we give up a lot for our children. Me? I wanted to be in the newspaper business. Alex wanted children pretty much right away. I got into communications marketing to make sure we could afford to live, because Alex wanted to stay in the city. But I would have preferred struggling along somewhere in a smaller place, a small daily, a community newspaper, you know, a weekly or something."

"Sounds like it's more about Alex than it is about the kids," says Derek.

Richard nods. "A lot of it *is* about Alex. But that's a different topic. We were talking about Dougal and Katie."

"Okay."

"I don't expect kids to carry around this incredible burden because their parents make sacrifices for them. I mean, that's what we do, right? Parents. But I expect my children to care, Derek, to at least be aware that it happened, to give the smallest of damns."

Derek nods. "Yeah, I see."

"Katie has no idea that, essentially, I lived a life I didn't really like so that she could have the one she has now. And if she does know—and I'm only sort of convinced she doesn't—she simply doesn't care. All of that goes double for Drake."

"So you think your sacrifice should be acknowledged, right?"

"Yeah. Its existence should be acknowledged. Treat it like historical fact. Nothing more. But as fact."

"I see."

"And I don't mean a card on Father's Day. I mean by communicating about it, an acknowledgment, mentioning it every so often, showing an *aspect* of appreciation.

Both men are silent a time, gazing out at the street for several noisy seconds as if from their own insulated cubicle.

"Good luck with that," says Derek at last.

Richard nods. "You'd think parents would teach their children enough to get them over themselves, enough to have empathy for people, including their parents."

"Empathy is dead," Derek says with astonishing finality. "Replaced, I think, by spectacle."

Richard looks at his friend, feeling saddened by his words. "So it would appear," he mutters under his breath. "And, in my children's defense, I was one of the perpetrators. For the most part, through my work, I helped to lead people away from empathy and into the din of spectacle. I feel bad about this so often now, it hurts."

"The din of spectacle? Is hyperbole spectacle?"

"Very witty, but don't confuse me."

Derek grins. "You're saying it's how everything has to appear, the bigger, the better."

"The crazier and the more profane."

"Even the deadlier and crueler."

Richard nods, feeling deeply ashamed of himself.

"CHILDREN HERE IN OBLIVION. Do they get to choose the other world at some point, when they've grown up?"

Richard and Violet have finally given up today's hour or so in the poplar grove, after Violet's lessons, and he is walking her home to her cabin.

"You mean, if children born and living here, knew of the other world, would they be allowed to choose it?"

"Yes," says Richard. "That's what I mean, I guess. But how would they know about the other world to even be able to make a choice?"

Violet takes a long time to consider her answer.

"I don't mean children," Richard adds then to clarify. "I simply mean people in Oblivion who are not here because they chose it, but the ones that have been living here from birth. Do they ever reach a point at which they can choose and, if so, as, say, young adults, they want to choose, are they allowed to do so? Can they decide they prefer the other world? Is there a way to see it so that they can make an informed choice?"

"This would be easier, Richard, if I was an elder."

"I'm sorry, Violet. I know."

"I know this much: it *is* allowed. This is Oblivion. It's not a prison camp."

"I know that."

"No rebuke intended," murmurs Violet.

"I know that too, my love."

"I'm going to take you to an elder."

"It's time, isn't it?"

"If it is, if it's time, the elder will know." Violet squeezes his hand. "Our young adults get to visit the other world if they want to. And, if they want to, they get to choose."

"How?" asks Richard.

"When you speak to an elder," Violet replies, "when you get to ask questions, be sure to ask about gatekeepers."

"Gatekeepers?"

"Yes. Ask the elder what a gatekeeper is."

"Okay," Richard says.

VIOLET FINDS RICHARD MODESTLY FRETFUL that evening when she joins him on his porch. She has brought tea on a tray and sets it down on a small table he has found for that purpose. He is very slowly outfitting his cabin with simple furnishings. At this moment, it is clear he has been thinking and she is curious about the nature of his thoughts. But she does not ask if he is all right. He knows she knows he is all right. Of course he is all right: for now he is in Oblivion.

Which is what he talks about.

"When I'm back there, in the other world," he says at last, "am I clearly away from here?"

Violet considers his words, finds it difficult to respond.

Richard poses the question another way. "Are my absences from Oblivion long? When I'm in the other world, is it a long time here until I get back?"

"No," says Violet. "Not long."

"Days?"

She smiles. "No. Hardly even hours."

"How can that be? Time moves slowly here. If being here in Oblivion lasts a long time, wouldn't my *not* being here seem really long, even interminable?"

"I can see why you'd think so," Violet says.

"But?"

"But . . . it doesn't work that way. This is something even elders can't explain: the way time actually functions here. But then, when you think about it, the other world doesn't know how time functions either. It's just measured there . . . and it's shorter. Measuring it doesn't necessarily mean you know how it functions. Maybe time functions through each person's unique perception of it."

Richard considers this. "I can't figure it out," he says finally.

Violet sips her tea.

Richard sips his tea too.

"Maybe when I choose," Richard muses at last.

Violet doesn't say anything. Richard's choice is his own. They are both aware of this. At times like these there is refuge in silence.

RICHARD WANTS TO KNOW WHO IS IN CHARGE. "Who leads in Oblivion," he asks. "Is it the elders? Is it just *one* elder? Is it a benevolent monarch?" He grins slightly at this latter question.

On this occasion, he strolls with Violet and Kevin along the water's edge. The beach, interrupted at times by rocky outcrops, stretches seemingly forever. It softens in the distance to grays and dark browns as dusk begins to arrive. Richard holds Violet's hand, Kevin strolls barefoot in the surf beside them.

Kevin and Violet exchange glances, conferring comfortably as usual in silence about which one of them should answer his question. As he often does, Kevin defers to Violet.

"No benevolent monarch," Violet says. "Oblivion enjoys a pure democracy. Ideas here are implemented by consensus."

"Consensus?" Richard is startled.

"Pretty much. People in Oblivion exercise so much free will that there is no additional independence gained by not working for the common good. Most ideas, being directed towards the common good, end up with unanimous approval," Violet explains. "There's nothing to object to. We fall back to a position of unanimity."

Richard nods. He has been told that the other world is, in varying degrees, an oligarchy—Kevin has described it as such to him—and he has no clear sense of the truth in Kevin's assessment. He senses, though, that unanimous consensus would be impossible there.

"How does it work?" he asks at last. "I know what you're trying to tell me. But unanimous consensus still sounds impossible to achieve."

"But it's not," says Violet. "If you've chosen to be in Oblivion, a virtual unanimous consensus is precisely what you believe in. And if you've been brought up in Oblivion, it's all you've ever known."

"And no one feels a loss of personal freedom? No one feels oppressed?"

Again, Kevin and Violet exchange glances. Kevin takes over. "What's oppressive about the common good?" he says. "What does the common good prevent you from achieving? You're still free to live your life the way you want to and everyone shares the things you need to live your life in the way you've chosen."

They walk on in silence while Richard digests his son's answer.

"Dad, I remember the other world," Kevin says shortly. "The idea there was that the only way to achieve personal freedom was to try to own it all. If the system didn't permit you to own everything and keep it from everyone else, then this was deemed a loss of your freedom. That world—so far at least—hasn't figured out that there are dozens of ways to feel personal freedom without subjugating everyone else in a system that imprisons them. Do you see what I mean? A full life isn't *having* everything; it's more like *being* everything."

"Yes," says Richard.

"And, in Oblivion, we understand a fundamental truth that the other world *never* understood: that whatever you possess, possesses you. The more of everything you own, the more it owns you and the less personal freedom you actually have."

More silence.

"It's very difficult to grasp," Richard says. "I ask these questions to at least intellectually understand what Oblivion is all about, when I can't see the complete picture myself."

"I know," Kevin says.

"We understand," adds Violet.

"I think," explains Richard then, "my original question about who is in charge is about laws. Like, who enforces the laws? Who is in charge of the police?"

"I'll take this one, Kevin," Violet says. "Richard, the only laws here in Oblivion are individual and based on selflessness. Hence they're entirely benign. I have laws that motivate me personally—probably the same ones that motivated me to choose Oblivion in the first place—but my laws about me don't apply to anyone else. Other people can't break my laws because they're only *my* laws. Other people don't have to obey my personal laws even though they may have personal laws of their own that are entirely the same. We're all here in Oblivion to be gentle, kind and only self-interested enough to live tranquil, creative, rewarding lives. No one needs to police us. We're not here to amass riches, take advantage of others, to seek power, to lie, cheat or steal, to cause anyone pain. We chose Oblivion to *not* do those things. You see?"

Kevin joins in. "So there are no police. There is no crime. There's nothing beyond a basic selflessness, and that would never need policing."

Richard continues to nod in understanding. "So there's no hierarchy?"

"No," says Kevin. "We don't require it."

"Makes sense," says Richard.

"Equal opportunity and freedom here ended up a destination, not a state that we have to enforce. Freedom here is the natural way we live our lives. Dad, when you don't measure your freedom *against* someone else's idea of freedom, it's just freedom, right?"

The three of them fall silent again. Soon, without anyone suggesting it, they turn and walk together back along the beach in the direction they have come.

"*Everything just lives here,*" Kevin says, reminding his father of the familiar four words they have all come to know so well.

"Yes, I see that," Richard says.

And Violet, walking closely along beside him, takes his hand again.

IN OBLIVION, DINNER PARTIES ARE POPULAR. Richard appreciates their frequency and fraternity as much as everyone else. They are usually potluck events, usually eight to ten people. Often someone brings a musical instrument. Or there are games. Mostly, though, such gatherings are defined by rich conversation and storytelling, and Richard listens to the talk in deep fascination. He is like a man learning a new language. No problem understanding the words, but often a great deal of difficulty understanding the *concepts*. The people who come to dinner or the people who invite him and Violet to dinner are in every case familiar with Oblivion and with the world where they lived their lives *before* Oblivion. The tales they tell that bridge both worlds get complicated for Richard because, in many ways, he has become a stranger to both worlds.

Because of this, Richard spends much of his time listening and biting back questions it would be premature to ask. He knows his passport into Oblivion is choice but he is aware intellectually that his decision remains mysteriously delayed. Something soon must happen, he knows. But when and how the choice will happen, he has no idea.

It is at one such dinner, during a freewheeling discussion about the more lighthearted foibles of the other world (which Richard views with a half-hearted incredulity) that Violet comes to him and takes him into an empathetic embrace. "I'm sorry, Richard," she says. "I can see how left out of the talk you are, when it focuses on the other world."

"I'm okay," he murmurs as they break the embrace.

But Violet gazes at him, unconvinced.

There is another enthusiastic burst of laughter from around the dining room table. Richard and Violet stand close to one another in the kitchen area, hearing the laughter and the man hosting the dinner beginning to tell another story.

"I'm not being fair," Violet says, barely above a whisper.

"Fair?"

"Yes. It's clear we should at least try to get you to an elder. I should have done it before now."

"It's okay," says Richard.

"We don't like to interfere in the process of choice," Violet explains. "But when it makes someone awkward and confused, well it's time to let an elder make the judgment."

"What judgment?" asks Richard.

Nearby, a loud peal of laughter fills the cabin.

Violet ignores it. "An elder will know how best to *not* interfere with your ability to choose. The judgment will be what you should know or not know, so that your ability to choose is unimpaired by any coaching from Oblivion."

"I see."

Violet touches his hand. "I'm going to see about this right away, my love. Okay?"

"Thank you," says Richard.

Violet smiles at him in encouragement before they rejoin their hosts and the other guests.

To the people of Oblivion who, unlike Richard, remember well the other world, many of the moments of hilarity at any social gathering take place around the topics of television and the Internet. Kevin too, Richard has noticed. His son considers these elements of his past life in the other world with no small measure of dismay. The subject comes up often when he and his father walk around the village or stroll down the beach or take a breather from a run through the trails on the ridge. Not everyone in Oblivion remembers television, Kevin explains. Even less remember the Internet, which, in the other world, is still relatively new to mainstream society. "Don't forget, Dad," Kevin has said, "Violet chose Oblivion before the other world *had* television or the Internet."

"She doesn't know what they were like. But you do, right?"

"Yes, I do." Kevin frowns. "I don't miss them."

Richard can only nod. There is much to be confused about and he can only listen with patience.

"I'm glad we don't have television here in Oblivion. I'm *ecstatic* that we don't have the Internet."

"Why would people invent something there that's bad?"

Kevin nods. "It's not bad on purpose exactly," he replies. " Television was supposed to be an educational tool, a way to ensure that humanity could learn efficiently. The Internet was designed for essentially the same. Improved and fast communication so that everyone could *learn*. A kind of informational commons, a free meeting place for everyone. But both ended up commercial enterprises, a means of reaching large masses of people with ads. So what could have broadened human horizons instead homogenized people's tastes and attitudes. The Internet even became a means to anonymously bully people, to invade people's privacy, to make them victims or more compliant consumers, to manipulate facts, even to breed intolerance and hate. Terrible, terrible inventions, always in your hand and in your head. Keeping you awake and on edge. Keeping you comparing."

Kevin's face is flushed and he is breathless. Richard puts a hand on his shoulder. "But you're here now, Son. It's all behind you."

Kevin nods. "Thank God, for that."

They gaze at one another.

"I'm not sure I should tell you this, Dad, but back there, beyond your work, you don't have much interest in the Internet or television or technology. I remember this myself."

Richard grins. "Like father, like son?"

"We knew what was going on, Dad. We didn't like it much."

AN ELDER IN OBLIVION is someone who made the choice to be here a long, long time ago, Richard has been told. On the day that he is introduced to his first elder, he is greatly taken aback therefore that the woman is not a fossil, that she looks instead barely older than he does. Life is long in Oblivion. Richard has noticed this even without remembering that life in the other world is much shorter. He can *feel* that life is longer here. *Sense* it intuitively. He has been told by both Kevin and Violet that life is long in Oblivion because, theoretically, there is nothing angry or hateful about someone's life here to significantly shorten it. The woman standing before him, whom he hopes can answer his questions, is evidence of this fact.

The elder, Clara Hutchinson, smiles and shakes his hand. She has a pinched, sardonic face, her gaze is calm and thoughtful. "It's not that I'm smarter than anyone else," she explains, verifying what Violet has already told him. "It's because I've been forgotten for so long by the other world. You could say then that I've got a lot of experience, at being here in Oblivion and at being completely forgotten back *there*."

As usual, Richard is disoriented when this world and the other one pass each other by, forever missing each other by inches. Sometimes he wishes his two lives *would* collide. He knows the collision would give him the necessary contrast to choose. He nods his head to show Clara Hutchinson that he understands what she said, even if he cannot experience her meaning.

"Being forgotten isn't cumulative, though, is it?" he blurts out.

They all smile at one another, him and Violet and Clara, because the question is obtuse.

"No," says Clara at last. "It's not cumulative. Back there, the forgetting is complete right from the beginning. Here, though, in Oblivion, the forgetting *seems* to accumulate back *there*. But the cumulative sense of it is merely an illusion. Because you have been here *and* there. You see?"

Richard nods. But he doesn't actually get it. He continues waiting to get it.

"But I'm an elder because the time period of the world that I chose to be forgotten in was a long, long time ago." She glances at Violet. "Nearly one hundred years before you, dear." She turns to Richard. "Which, I'm afraid, won't mean much to *you* under the present circumstances."

"You mean because I'm here *and* there?"

"That's exactly what I mean," Clara Hutchinson says.

Again Richard nods. And he considers: it is one thing to live a long time in Oblivion, but they are actually talking about how short life apparently is in the other world. To him, this is the implication.

"We may have much to talk about, Richard," the elder says. "Or we might not. I don't know yet. Care to join me for a walk around my garden while we find out?"

IN JANUARY, RICHARD NABS A JOB INTERVIEW with Calliope Resources, a company with extractive holdings in oil, natural gas and coal. The interview is with the company president, Frank Prentice. Like his previous employment, the position is vice-president of communications marketing. Richard has only one day to prepare for the interview. He tells Alex about it right away, as soon as the appointment is made. He must text her to do so—it has been two nights since she joined him at home for dinner. She has been eating with Katie and Dougal with increasing frequency. The two young people are painting their apartment and Alex is lending a hand. Richard tends to view the young people as playing house, and Alex, regressing back to her own younger days, at least in Richard's mind, seems to be playing too. He has no wish to be part of this distraction with his wife and his daughter. It would seem Alex has no wish to join *him* at home as well. He believes she is avoiding him until he gets another job, which will release her from her fears about the family's security. Richard hasn't confirmed this with her; he suspects, were he to ask, that she would simply suggest he needs the vast space at home to concentrate on his efforts to find work. Drake has resumed his long absences from home as well and Richard is too forlorn and preoccupied with his own personal dilemmas to do anything about it, although Drake calls for permission to miss dinner, as they had previously agreed a month or so ago.

So the job interview news comes at a good time. "Terrific," Alex's return text about the news says. "*wonderful fingers xed hope your ready*"

Suddenly deflated and not really knowing why, perhaps by her cautionary response, perhaps the lack of punctuation mirroring much of his life and its communications these days, Richard responds with "Everything

OK."

The next morning he tells Derek about the upcoming interview too. They shiver together on the street. Winter has smothered Richard's heart. This morning, especially, winter squeezes him in its arms, an almost murderous hug. Derek is still homeless. Whatever it is that drives the people who pass them by on this street seems to drive them by even more pointlessly in January, now that the celebration, the promotion, the noise and clamour, the artificial inebriation of Christmas are over for another year. All these cold changes chill Richard to the bone. It feels quietly pointless to be alive on days like this. Sighs, his and those of others that he overhears, are deep and hopeless.

"You don't sound very excited," observes Derek from his cardboard place mat on the sidewalk. "It's been months since you even had a sniff at an interview."

"I guess excitement would be premature," Richard remarks with a shrug.

In truth, Richard is conflicted by his first interview in months. He's not sure he wants to re-enter the work environment he knew back at Cascade Enterprises. He does not miss the culture of high-powered executive work, nor the rush of adrenalin it is purported to create and require. During the four months of his unemployment, he has had time to examine his working career and he has begun to enjoy elements of this opportunity to not work to question the relevance of what he did at Cascade Enterprises and why he persisted, even while he knew what he accomplished was irrelevant to him. And he still toys with the notion that he and Derek could use his severance to set up some kind of business away from the city, rescuing both of them from this hopeless street corner. Derek keeps turning him down but his friend's refusal doesn't stop Richard's imagination from exploring the idea.

But save for Derek, who sits on the cold sidewalk not far away, these are thoughts he keeps to himself. Alex's anger, fear and disappointment that he has no job remain ceaseless. She shows him no love and no patience. She is often not home, working at the library part-time, then gone with Katie and Dougal. Richard finds no appeal in the silence between himself, his son and his wife when the three of them do manage to convene at the dinner table where Alex is present mostly to reconnect with her son. The entire family, including Katie and the ever-repugnant Dougal, faked it over Christmas, gritting their teeth and feigning gratitude and affection for the uninspired gifts and ceremony. Since then, though, no one has had the heart to be part of a family or even maintain the pretense.

To Richard, the members of his family are engrossed in only the issues that affect or interest *them*. Katie is preoccupied with playing house with Dougal. Alex is preoccupied with Katie. Drake is preoccupied by whatever it is he is doing with his friends from high school. Richard too is preoccupied, separate from his family. He knows he, himself, is focused only on what is wrong with his life and the inertia he endures about doing anything about it. Sometimes Richard wonders how he and the members of his family function, with so much pressure from one another to do what they *should* instead of what they *can*.

Richard has mentioned all of these troubling developments to Derek. Derek understands them. Derek even understands how the disintegration of his friend's family and marriage exacerbates the personal ambivalence Richard feels about securing another position in communications marketing. Richard has said he wants to start over, taking an abrupt turn in life, going somewhere different to do something different. He wants his future to make more personal sense than his past, yet an abrupt transformation seems impossible because of the tremendous resistance from his family.

"If I get a job, it won't be because *I* want the job or the working milieu," he says. "It will be because *they* want me to get the job so that I can resume the breadwinning purpose I had before Cascade fired me."

"'They'?" clarifies Derek. "You mean Alex, Katie and Drake, right?"

"And the forces that motivate them too—peers, society, this culture. It's not that the family wants to be demanding, to be mean or cruel. It's that the milieu is so overwhelming not one of them can conceive of a life significantly different from the one they live right now."

"Interesting," says Derek, mulling this view over.

Richard nods. "So when I contemplate going back to the kind of work in the milieu I knew before, I know it's not because I want to do it, but because I feel I *should*."

"Not an uncommon dilemma for men and women in our world," Derek says.

"I suppose not." Richard sighs. "Suppose I get the position at Calliope Resources. I'm pretty sure it will be as meaningless and pointless a work week as the one I used to know at Cascade Enterprises."

"Maybe so," says Derek.

"And Calliope Resources is an extractive resource company. Privately, Derek, I think it's time the planet left all of that shit—oil, gas, coal—in the ground. All this fracking and drilling and pipelining . . . Jesus."

"Sounds like the Calliope job would compromise your beliefs, my friend," says Derek.

"But no one will care about that. My family will be happy with me because I'm doing what I should to keep my salary coming in, never mind the bending of my principles. Bottom line? I'll be living my life entirely for them and for reasons I don't personally accept. To me, it's a way of being used, Derek. They don't love me for who I am, but because they need me to function in a certain way. You see what I mean?"

"I do, my friend," says Derek.

"When people ask—you know, at a party or something—what you do for a living, they're really asking you what they can use you as."

"A barbed way of putting it, Richie, but often true."

Richard gazes at his friend and feels a not uncommon tug of affection. "You've got to be the worst paid psychiatrist in this city," he says after a moment.

Derek grins broadly. "But it's important work nonetheless," he says, gesturing at the street. "My office could use an upgrade, but . . ." And he shrugs.

This time, when they turn to watch the street go by, it is with wry amusement. It is cold and ugly here on the street but, in philosophical terms, Richard knows he and Derek often find periods of levity they can use to sustain their faith that things are going to get better. Analysis is analysis. Humour is humour. Even here on the street with winter coming down uglier and uglier.

WITHOUT KNOWING IT EXACTLY, DEREK IS RIGHT about his office on the old city street. By contrast, the Calliope Resources president Frank Prentice's office has a bathroom and shower, a large well-stocked bar, a desk as big as an aircraft carrier platform, and a vast wall of awards, as well as photographs of various celebrities and conservative politicians, posed with Prentice like smiling trophies of gigantic fish. The office has a sofa and a love seat separated by a large table. Both loveseat and sofa look out over a wintry panorama of the city's skyline. The office boasts a pool table with a rack of pool cues hung on a nearby wall. There is an exercise bike in the corner but Richard notices the bike is unplugged, that the electric cord is coiled on the floor below the outlet.

No surprise then that Prentice is stocky and roughly shaped. His face is pock-marked and pudgy. Money has been used to improve his looks—he wears glasses that are fashionable and expensive and an equally expensive suit, made to measure, Richard assumes—but the various components of

Prentice's body are so out of sync with themselves, not even a suit of this quality can look better than just okay on his strangely chiselled body. His manner is rough and abrasive too. It's a style that he exudes from the very beginning. He is on the telephone when Richard is ushered in. He gestures impatiently towards the love seat.

"I want the project finalized by Friday," Prentice is saying in a gruff voice. "I mean Friday, okay? And Ryan? No fucking excuses, okay?" And he hangs up.

Prentice takes a moment to gaze hatefully at the telephone, then rises, pasting his version of a welcoming smile in place as he approaches.

Richard rises from the loveseat and the two men shake hands.

"How long's it been?" Prentice wants to know.

"How long?"

"Since Amanda Drew canned your ass."

"Oh. About four months, I guess."

"Tough out there in the job market."

"Yes," says Richard.

"But you got a million, right?"

"Nearly," Richard says.

"What's it like working for Amanda Drew?"

"Fine," says Richard.

"Everyone I know wants to fuck her." A bit of a smile shows up to alleviate the crudeness perhaps, but Richard isn't certain. Then, "It comes up a lot." Now Prentice laughs outright. "No pun intended. If I hire you, people will wonder if you were one of the lucky ones. We'll all be envying you."

"I guess," Richard mutters barely audibly, deeply embarrassed to be in the vicinity of Prentice's comment. He feels ambushed by the way Prentice has somehow made him ashamed of himself. He suffers no temptation to laugh along with Prentice, and no temptation to comment further.

Prentice presses his advantage by finding Richard's discomfort funny and laughing even more heartily. "Okay," the company president says after the long, uncomfortable moment passes. "Let's see what you know about Calliope Resources . . ."

They get down to business.

Eventually Richard stops wondering if his refusal to lie about or deny sleeping with Amanda has lost him this chance at the job.

LATER, WHEN HE TELLS ALEX ABOUT THE INTERVIEW, there is much he doesn't report. He does not tell her how odious he found Frank Prentice to be, the man's remarks about Amanda Drew, his endless mantra about being a self-made man, Prentice's pride in the dirty politics he plays in the fossil fuels industry. "We own the government in Ottawa," he bragged. "We intend to keep it that way."

"Of course," said Richard, all he could come up with to serve as some kind of reply.

"You're on board with all of that, right?" Prentice finally asked outright. "The politics?"

"Yes," Richard replied, feeling he should appear to want the job while not knowing precisely what "all of that" would actually represent.

He used his imagination, though. He knew about oil companies, coal, natural gas, extractivism. If he thought his position at Cascade Enterprises was defined by spin, the spin would pale by comparison to the misinformation he would be disgorging for Calliope Resources. And the proximity to various politicians would be disquieting. Richard would know himself to be even further away from the journalism—and its commitment to truth and balance—which had been his chosen career when he was young and appreciated such ideals. Offered this job, taking it . . . would his allergy come back? Would he break out in a worse rash than the one that had helped get him fired at Cascade?

He skips relating many anecdotes to his wife—and certainly his conclusions and apprehensions—when he reports to her on the interview. But he mentions they are to join Prentice and his family at dinner on the weekend, both husband and wife. Prentice has insisted.

"Really?" Alex says, breaking into a broad, relieved grin. "You must have the job, Richard. That must mean you have the job."

"Prentice said that was when the real interview process begins, when you and I meet his family at his home."

"It must be a family-oriented business, more than most," Alex remarks.

Richard says nothing to this. His sense of Frank Prentice is precisely the opposite of family oriented, at least on first impression, and he can find no way of saying so to his wife without seeming petulant or doubtful, and risking her ire.

But Alex is already planning her approach to what will be a positive first impression. "I'd better make sure I have exactly the right thing to wear."

Richard isn't surprised at all by what now preoccupies her. "I know you don't think it should matter, Richard," she has said, "but one of my jobs is to see that you get ahead. When *you* succeed, we *all* succeed."

"I WANT TO ASK YOU ABOUT GATEKEEPERS," Richard says now that he and Clara Hutchinson are alone.

Clara is a farmer. They stroll around a small garden where she grows vegetables and herbs. In the distance, free range chickens peck at treats in the yard. A rooster struts his stuff among the brood. There are worn pathways on each side of the garden patch and Richard wonders if many others like him have come here to circle this small section of aromatic herbs with Clara, pacing slowly over the warm grass, wanting to learn from her about this world and what it means to live here. In the distance, each time they round one of the garden corners, Richard can see Violet on a chair on Clara's porch, where she is waiting for him, and he delights each time she is embraced inside his gaze. He loves her endlessly and, at all times, easily. He anticipates seeing her this way each time he and the elder circle her garden.

Clara is a long time answering his gatekeeper question. Richard realizes instinctively that the proper protocol with an elder is to wait for her to speak before saying anything else.

"One thing you should know first," she says finally. She is short and gazes up at him after her remarks.

"Yes?"

"You haven't chosen, Richard. Until you do, I'm limited in what I can tell you. Any questions I answer cannot serve to influence your choice in any way. We are not here to disparage the other world or sell you in any way on this one."

"That makes sense," Richard says.

They stroll further in silence.

"Gatekeepers," Clara says at last.

"Yes."

"On the surface of it, gatekeepers are a little like you," the elder says. "They're like you in the way that they spend time in both worlds. But with one major difference: they are knowledgeable about both worlds at the same time, not just one or the other, one at a time, wherever they happen to be, the way *you* forget each world when you're not there, because you haven't chosen. Do you see the difference?"

"I think so," Richard replies. "But does this mean the gatekeepers haven't chosen?"

"No," answers Clara. "A few of us choose to be gatekeepers, in the way you chose to operate *The Bulletin*. They have their reason for their choice—and it *is* a choice—and their choice to be a gatekeeper is respected.

Gatekeepers occur from time to time and we know they're essential. It's something they deeply want to do. We don't understand it necessarily, but we know how important they are."

Richard glances at the tiny woman beside him. "Are elders gatekeepers? Are you a gatekeeper?"

"Oh no," she says. "On both counts. My reference to 'us' meant all the people of Oblivion."

"I see," says Richard. "This business of being in both worlds, does that mean I might be a gatekeeper?"

Clara ponders this question long and hard. "It's always possible, I suppose," she says at last. They round a turn at the edge of the garden and she watches Richard's gaze seek out Violet on her porch in the distance. "But somehow I doubt it," she adds. "I'm told you see your function as a publisher of the truth. Hence *The Bulletin*. That's you. You're not a gatekeeper."

Richard shrugs and smiles, concealing, he hopes, a significant relief. Clara's remarks signify he still has a choice ahead of him, a choice he hopes to make.

"Gatekeepers know about both worlds. They give neither world up. But they know about both worlds the way I do," Clara says. "The way Violet does. Gatekeepers, though, are motivated differently than those of us who choose. They open gates and, in a very innocuous way, bring potential choosers inside. And, if it arises, they let other people out of Oblivion. Books, information, these come through gates between Oblivion and the other world. Gatekeepers are different than us. They serve this world and the other one by happily being gatekeepers."

"As a calling, then?" asks Richard.

"Yes. A terrific word for it. A 'calling.'"

"I'm definitely not a gatekeeper then, am I?" Richard murmurs more or less to himself.

"I don't think so," Clara replies. "You'd be the one to know. I think you'd know something like that."

Richard nods. "It's just this business of going back and forth . . ."

"I'm told you have a son here who has chosen Oblivion," the elder says then.

"Yes. Kevin. But I don't remember him from there, from that other world."

"Of course you don't," Clara says. "It's a rare circumstance, you and your son. It doesn't happen often that two people from the same family come to live in Oblivion."

Richard nods. He has heard this same opinion from others.

"Violet tells me you understand the difference between children born here and children born in the other world, how it can happen and how it cannot."

"Yes."

"She says you want to know if young people here know about the other world, if they can choose it the way people choose Oblivion. In reverse, if you will."

"Yes."

"That's where gatekeepers come in; it's one of their functions. Young people born in Oblivion are taken by gatekeepers on a tour of the other world. To show them what it's like."

"How long do they stay?"

"Long enough to see its reality clearly. The time they spend there is measured in Oblivion time. Clarity can take longer than expected sometimes. Oblivion is in no hurry. Oblivion reveres patience."

Richard continues to nod. He feels something he would describe as tender amazement. "So they can choose clearly," he says thoughtfully, something plaintive caught in his throat. It strikes him that it is a wonderful world that encourages in everyone the right to choose where and how to live his or her life.

"Yes," replies Clara. "You have to choose Oblivion. You can't be here by default."

"I gathered that."

"The gatekeepers provide Oblivion's young people with the tools to choose the other world if they want to."

"And do any of them choose the other world?" Richard wants to know.

"No one has yet, I'm told," Clara reports without inflection. "Maybe someday. Maybe not."

"But at least they have the choice."

"Yes. So far, all of them have chosen Oblivion . . ."

". . . Which is the only way *into* Oblivion. Choosing it," finishes Richard.

"You learn quickly," Clara says.

"Thank you," he replies.

And they keep walking in the rectangle on the path surrounding Clara's garden of herbs.

"Are there children born here who never want to consider the other world, who, despite hearing stories about it, are happy staying here?"

"Of course," says Clara.

"And it's allowed?"

Clara nods. "Of course. If they don't want to see the other world, they don't have to. Sometimes, through books, contact with people here, and the stories people tell, that's enough to convince them to stay here."

"And I suppose, if someone from here chose the other world, they would remember both, wouldn't they?"

"I don't know, Richard. To my knowledge no one has ever chosen the other world after they've lived in this one. I can't answer the question; I have no idea. It would be speculation on my part."

Richard nods. "Still, I wonder if they would remember Oblivion there."

"In dreams perhaps," Clara says with a shrug. "Maybe only in dreams."

More walking.

"There's something else I've wondered," Richard asks shortly.

"Yes?"

"How large is Oblivion?"

"Geographically?"

"Yes."

Clara considers this question with a frown. "I'm no expert, but there are a few things I can tell you. This community, where you live and work when you're here, is only one of many. I don't know how many there are exactly. Some people in Oblivion travel great distances and they would have a better idea than I do. Travel in Oblivion is different. Travel here is on foot mostly or by boat. We have horses, carriages, wagons. People will give you a ride when you need one. The bicycle is the most popular way of travelling on wheels in Oblivion. In the other world, I'm told they fly and drive motorized vehicles."

"Fly? You mean like a bird?"

"Yes. Airplanes. Hundreds of people at a time in an airplane and they cross the oceans in a matter of hours. I haven't seen this myself. Just photographs and stories I've been told. I chose Oblivion before airplanes, Richard."

In a practical sense, Richard is capable of imagining this, but the concept is nonetheless mystifying. "And we don't have this flying ability elsewhere in Oblivion?"

"No."

"Why not?"

"Many of the wondrous things in the other world were invented primarily for war and profit. Oblivion doesn't have war and profit, so it doesn't have war's or profit's inventions. We don't miss them. We're not in a hurry. Certainly we don't appreciate anything here that perpetuates a system dedicated to war and profit. People here have chosen not to live with these conditions. That's why they're here. Me too. I've been here long enough to see war and profit as life without dignity, never mind the cruelty and death they create." Clara glances at him a moment. "You know about war, don't you?"

Richard nods. "Violet told me."

"In a nutshell, Richard, some things, then, don't need to be invented. We only invent products that meet basic needs here and these are freely exchanged."

"Of course," Richard replies after a moment.

"But to get back to your original question, there are many hundreds of towns and villages in Oblivion and, when you travel, as some people here do, you will see them. The residents of these towns are like us. They will welcome you. And they exist in a state of shared plenty as we do. I'm told they are of many nationalities and cultures, and many languages are spoken. But they are the same as us. We are all welcome to live and associate in each other's culture. Like us, they live in peace and tranquility."

"It would take me a long time to see all of Oblivion," Richard muses aloud.

"It would," agrees the elder. "But then, if you had the time, wouldn't you do it, if you wanted to?"

"I guess I would. It's a gift, isn't it? Having the luxury of so much time."

"I hope I haven't said too much," Clara says in some alarm. "I was trying to be honest, not persuasive."

"Thank you," Richard says.

They continue to walk around her garden, around and around, orbiting the humble rectangle containing the various herbs she grows. Richard begins to recognize some of them. Chives, basil, oregano. Knowledge garnered in Oblivion, he wonders, or back there in the other place he lives?

"What about higher education? I've seen the school. But what about more sophisticated subjects? Violet is an artist. Where do people learn what they don't learn in the community schools?"

"Ah," says Clara, as if she has anticipated this question. "People have the time and the curiosity in Oblivion to learn how to do things. Or . . . that's something Violet can show you. Why don't you have Violet take you to the library. All the libraries in Oblivion are outstanding, I'm told. The one here, in this area, is the only one I've seen. It's wonderful."

The walk continues. Clara Hutchison seems to have endless patience.

"I sense you have another question," she says eventually.

"I'm not sure you'd be willing to answer it."

"Ask it and we'll see."

"When will I choose?"

"When you're ready, Richard. I know that sounds vague and unhelpful. But it's true."

"I want to choose, Clara. I want to choose Oblivion."

"I believe what you say, Richard." And she squeezes his hand.

"Thank you."

"But you choose when you're ready, not when you want to."

The distinction between *being ready* and *wanting to* is too subtle for Richard. He glances in Violet's direction, where she still waits for him on Clara's porch. He feels love for her and, with it, impatience with himself. He cannot imagine losing her to a choice he apparently does not yet know how to make.

Clara follows his gaze. "You have to be ready, Richard," she says. "That's when you choose. When you're ready. And not before. I can't tell you when that will be."

WHILE THERE ARE BOOKS ABOUT OBLIVION in the village library, written and published by the people of Oblivion, there are many, many more books set in the other world, conceived there and written there. Thousands of them, Richard can see. The day he and Violet go to the library for the first time, Richard turns to her, a not unexpected question in his eyes.

"So that we don't forget things about the other world," Violet explains. "And so that people who only have ever lived in Oblivion know what took place in the other world, what people thought. The stories they told. The knowledge they had."

Richard nods.

"Our library is Oblivion's university," Violet tells him. "It's here that professors who have chosen Oblivion work and teach. They do their research here and they teach in small groups here, humanities, history, philosophy, science. There's no tuition. You have the opportunity to learn to the utmost of your capacity. It's up to you. I learned to paint here. I have a friend, Chloe—you know Chloe—who is studying biology. There are three of them, students, I mean, and they study under a renowned biologist."

"You said the library is the university?"

"Yes."

"And every community in Oblivion has one?"

"As far as I know," Violet replies.

"But you can use the library on your own, without a teacher, right?"

"Yes. In other words, it's for education as well as for reference," Violet adds. "There's the element of written history, of course. The library is there so that we keep up with what's wrong—or getting right—in the other world and what people write there when they think they have an idea that can fix what's broken." Violet touches his arm. "It reminds me how wonderful Oblivion is too."

"I'll bet," Richard says, although he grows preoccupied by a new idea at this moment.

"What?" asks Violet, noticing his expression.

"Will it help me make a choice if I read about the other world?"

Violet shakes her head. "It's not the nature of the other world, or knowledge of it, that's at the root of your choice. It's you, Richard. It's you all by yourself that will choose."

"Okay," Richard says. He needs Violet to know again what worsens his impatience. "I love you, Violet," he adds. "Everything in my heart loves you. I don't understand my delay."

"I know," says Violet.

"But if I were to come here and study the other world, would it help me to know, even though I haven't chosen?"

"I don't know," says Violet.

"I might even find some reference to me back there, something about me *there* that I can know *here*."

Violet takes him into an embrace. She kisses him lightly. They gaze at one another a moment.

"You don't think it would work," Richard concludes.

"It'd just be some kind of partial back door into the times when you are here in Oblivion," she says.

"It wouldn't be permanent."

"No. You have to choose Oblivion. You can't study your way in. You can't sneak up on the choice, ambush it."

"So you keep saying."

"Because it's true, Richard."

They have begun to move along the endless rows of books. Here, among so many, Violet has found one she was seeking. She checks it out and they stroll outdoors and stand in the sunshine a moment before beginning

229

their walk towards the school where Violet will teach this afternoon.

"So many books, thousands and thousands of them," Richard remarks.

"And so many librarians," Violet says. "Oblivion has so many people who love books and want to work in the library."

"I have one more question, though," Richard says.

"What's that?"

"All these books from the other world get here through gatekeepers. Do the gatekeepers select which books to bring to Oblivion?"

"They bring them all. No exceptions. At least one copy of each."

"There must be a lot of gatekeepers."

"Dozens and dozens, I'm told," Violet replies.

"It sounds like a huge sacrifice for a person to make, being a gatekeeper."

Violet nods. "They have their reasons. I can only imagine what those reasons might be. Gatekeepers, I'm told, don't share their motivations."

WHEN PEOPLE DIE IN OBLIVION, Richard has learned, there is a major celebration of their lives. Death in Oblivion is extremely infrequent but it happens nonetheless.

Now and then there are serious falls, from cliffs, against rocks, even from rooftops. There are accidents, tree limbs fall in storms and, on rare occasions, a bear or some large predator takes a life. People drown in storms. There have been others fatally struck by lightning. If it is a serious illness that takes someone's life it is usually the result of a genetic defect brought to Oblivion from the other world when that person chose to come here. Richard has been told there are no plagues in Oblivion, no epidemics. Nature here exists in a clear state; it does not carry murderous diseases. Murderous diseases, Violet has told him, have their proliferation in society's structure in the other world, in its inventions, in its endless poverty, in its abuse of its environment.

Normally, then, there is an extraordinary longevity to life in Oblivion. Under usual circumstances, people have a long time to learn how to develop a vast array of abilities and achieve a wide variety of modest accomplishments. Kevin has also told him that the nature of a person's world is mostly what allows them a long life or condemns them to a short one. "Back there," he says with a sweep of his arm that embraces his past, "it's all stress and struggle. Here, I'm constantly replenished, rejuvenated by freedom and tranquility."

"Can you give me specifics?" Richard has asked.

"Yes. Death in the other world is *caused by* the other world—pollution, violence, stress, anxiety, despair, vice, hatred, war, abuse, bullying, greed and a myriad of other reasons—causes that do not exist in Oblivion."

Other people Richard has met here in Oblivion make much of this contrast. They explain there is no suicide here. A person who would choose Oblivion, choosing to be forgotten in the other world and resisting forever its endless judgments, is not the kind of person who would choose suicide in Oblivion. Suicides in the other world take place when someone has left it too late to make a choice and sees no other way out than death, Richard has been told. Or as a means to conclude a painful period of dying. Kevin has told him suicide can be a skewed idea of retribution against a world that has abused someone in various ways, an act of desperate atonement. Choosing suicide to be remembered or for redemption only takes place in the other world. "I had friends back there who mentioned suicide now and then, at school. They wanted someone to be hurt by it. They wanted someone to know they had been wronged. I told them it was stupid. In my case, they listened. All the people I knew listened to me."

"That's good," says Richard. "That's wonderful."

"The punishment for the people in that other world," Kevin remarks one day with a trace of sadness in his voice, "is having to live in that other world, to suffer its various abuses. It's not *all* bad, of course. But peace and tranquility in a world of plenty?" He shakes his head. "Not a chance back there. A world of plenty is only for a few people who feel entitled to it."

When, now and then, people die in Oblivion, they are cremated. Their lives are celebrated by various small and large gatherings for up to a week after their death. If people know the stories about the lives they lived before they came to choose Oblivion, some of these are told during the celebrations too. Of course the dead are remembered in Oblivion until eventually they are forgotten. In the other world, they are already entirely forgotten, as if they never lived. There is no memory to forget.

This part—the part about being forgotten—still confuses Richard. Clarity eludes him. He has only Kevin or Violet to explain things to him, and what Clara Hutchinson told him that day in her garden. But their words continue to reside only at the edges of his understanding.

KEVIN GIVES HIS FATHER A LONG LIST of items that do not exist in Oblivion, yet remain a significant motivation in the other world.

"Crime," he says one day.

Richard gazes at him uncomprehendingly.

"The other world has all kinds of crime."

Richard does not know what crime is when he is here in Oblivion.

"Murder. Stealing. Taking things from other people. Doing them harm. There's no greed in Oblivion, no need to make someone suffer in any way. That's what I mean about there being no crime. You see, there's no motive for it. People who choose Oblivion would never feel a motive to commit crime. If they had the motive for any kind of crime, well, they'd stay in the other world where they could commit it. They wouldn't choose Oblivion. We live in Oblivion in a state of plenty. There's just no need for crime."

Richard nods. Kevin's explanation makes sense but here he cannot imagine a world that would have crime.

"There are no churches, no shrines, no monasteries, no temples," says Kevin. "There is a sort of religion, though."

"Religion?"

"Spiritual life."

Richard shrugs, shakes his head to convey that he does not know what Kevin means.

"A sense—even a *powerful* sense—that our lives have a purpose we can't see or understand, that there is a unifying force of which we humans are a part."

Richard nods. "I've sensed it here," he says. "But it's difficult to understand."

"Because it's private," Kevin explains. "In Oblivion, if you talk about it, it's just conversation. It's still private and personal. There's no need to convert adherents or followers to your spiritual view. You're the only one who needs to be happy with your spiritual view. If you needed followers or a church or a religious movement with doctrine or dogma, you'd stay in the other world where they think they need these things. If you were after power through organized religion, you wouldn't choose Oblivion where you can peacefully enjoy your own spiritual life. All you really need for a spiritual life is yourself and the freedom to live it. You see, Dad?"

"I think I do," Richard replies.

"As for community, Oblivion already has that outside the context of organized relation. Community isn't based on a personal matter such as spirituality. There's no need for a church based on community."

"I see," his father says.

Kevin also talks frequently about something he calls "spectacle."

It is a warm day where they have been swimming at the beach. They have dried themselves and spread their towels. Now they lie back and gaze at the sky. They are richly calm. *Everything just lives here*, Richard remembers as he soaks up the tranquility of the sun.

"The other world," Kevin muses, "during the time that I lived there . . ." Up on his elbows to gaze at his father's reaction to his words . . . "and your times too, that world was preoccupied by spectacle."

"Spectacle," Richard murmurs again. Richard remembers spectacle being mentioned before.

"Yes. Our various entertainments, games, parties, gatherings, events, even our sexual activities became spectacles. Nothing like the games, entertainment, social gatherings, and even lovemaking that happen here, but more involved, and more outlandish. The distasteful got to be *more* distasteful, the violent *more* violent, the provocative *more* provocative, the contemptible *more* contemptible. The more society's individual senses were stimulated, the duller those senses became and the more frequently the need for provocative stimulation increased. Like drugs and an addiction, I guess. To get the same kick, you had to find a stronger dose of stimulation. Back there, Dad, everyone was bored or frightened, and not much else. Society— mostly the people who control it and profit by it in particular—kept increasing the dose of distraction with more and more spectacle. It kept society occupied and distracted and there was a fortune to be made in selling it."

"Why isn't there any spectacle here?" Richard asks his son after a few moments' thought.

Kevin ponders how best to respond. "Well," he says at last, "you know already there's no greed or lust for power here."

Richard nods.

"That's one of the reasons. No one here is trying to amass wealth or influence."

"Yes."

"But there are other reasons. First of all, when people choose Oblivion, they choose it because they are authentic, self-possessed people. They're not tied to some idea of themselves that suits the society in which they live. In Oblivion you get to be who you are, not who your society thinks you should be. We've discussed this before, Dad. People here don't peer into the fabric of this society in search of the definition of themselves or their actions, to know who they are. They already know. Is this making any sense?"

"Yes," says Richard. "I'm satisfied with myself here. There's no idea out there for me to try to assimilate."

"That's it, Dad."

Richard gazes out over the water. *Everything just lives here.*

"Spectacle, then, back there," adds Kevin, "is a larger, more distracting way to peer into the social collective's idea of what you should be doing and whom you should be emulating while you're doing it."

"No spectacle here in Oblivion," says Richard.

"No spectacle here, except for maybe this beautiful day."

Father and son are silent for a time.

"Maybe *you* should be an elder, Kevin," Richard says sometime later.

Kevin merely smiles and doesn't say anything more.

Richard puts a hand on his son's shoulder, pleased his progeny enjoys the compliment.

THERE ARE HOSPITALS AND DOCTORS IN OBLIVION. They treat illnesses and injuries, only some of which are serious. Doctors and nurses are paid for these activities the same way everyone else in Oblivion is paid for *their* activities: with food and rest and clothing and shelter and anything else they might need. For this, doctors do not try to work miracles. Life is long in Oblivion, and doctors do not have to labour in most cases to try to make it significantly longer. Medicine in Oblivion is almost entirely focused on repairing damaged bodies, the result of an accident. "Oblivion is like an isolated primitive culture," Kevin explains. "There are no serious viruses here."

"How do you keep serious viruses out?" Richard wants to know.

"We suspect," Kevin says, "that people in the other world, carrying a dangerous virus, aren't capable of choosing Oblivion while they have a virus. We suspect they contract the virus by embracing the environment where the virus is created. It's a choice—coming here, I mean—that would be almost impossible to make if a person wasn't healthy."

"Because of the immense power in the choice, the courage it would take?"

"Pretty much," says Kevin. "Or else, the choice itself abolishes communicable disease, the choice being more than merely intellectual or emotional. Obviously it's a physical choice as well. Your body is here, Dad, right now, nearby, right next to me. It's not a stretch to assume that the physical choice to live in Oblivion would cure you of a communicable disease. In other words, you not only get to choose to come here, you get to choose to come here healthy, from a communicable disease point of view. You don't bring any epidemics with you."

Richard is aware in every way that there is nothing wrong with his health. Here, in conversation with his son, he cannot imagine what it would be like to be catching a cold.

KEVIN JOINS HIS FATHER FOR BREAKFAST one morning. They eat on Richard's porch. Violet has dropped by to say good morning but has soon departed for the school. Richard watches her leave in mild dismay, a little disappointed that she has left so soon.

"It's okay, Dad," Kevin says, a playful smile on his lips. "Violet knows why I'm here."

They've had a full breakfast—eggs, ham, a fresh tomato fried up in the pan with the ham. Toast. Fresh homemade marmalade a dedicated *Bulletin* reader has given Richard.

The day is going to be sunny and gentle but, for the time being, it is partially cloudy. Richard has learned there are seasons here in Oblivion. Violet has told him. He simply doesn't know them yet, what they are like, how short, how long, how intense. He senses memories of the seasons in the other world, but mostly he cannot remember them. Today, then, could be spring, summer, fall, even winter. He doesn't know for sure.

"I was hoping I could show you something today," says Kevin. "What I get up to here, how I keep busy. What I do creatively with my time, I mean."

"Sure," says Richard, unexpectedly pleased. "That would be great."

"And I want you to meet a couple of friends, my partners."

"Sounds good."

Kevin rises. "We're down at the beach, on the cove, at the outlet."

"I know where it is," says Richard. "Where the creek comes out."

They make their way down the steps of Richard's porch and head down the road towards the sound of the ocean and the beach.

"I found out what I want to do," explains Kevin as they walk.

"Your vocation, you mean?"

Kevin nods. "You do *The Bulletin*. I'm building canoes."

"What kind of canoes?"

"Various sizes. You'll see. With sails, without sails. Various types. For fishing, for pleasure. For excursions along the shore, short excursions, long journeys. For two people. Ten people. Whatever is needed or wanted."

"And you have partners, you said?"

"Yes."

"That's great," says Richard.

They walk in silence for a few minutes before Kevin remarks, "You and I have canoed together before, Dad. Back there in the other world."

"I see. I wish I could remember it."

"Me too."

"Soon, I hope."

"Soon what?"

"Soon I'll remember it, I hope."

"Me too," repeats Kevin. "Camping. I loved it. We went wilderness camping a few times. We canoed into the woods."

Richard nods. He can recall a sense of the event but it is barely discernible in his memory.

They walk. The shoreline approaches.

"That's what gave me the motivation here," says Kevin now. A gesture at the gently rolling waves in this diminishing distance. "And there's all this shore. So much nature. I'm not surprised I would have an aptitude for building some kind of boat."

"I'll say," says Richard.

"And then I met Linus and Danny."

"Your partners."

Kevin nods. "And the cultural circle was complete. We've talked about it. We come from three different cultures in the other world. Different canoe cultures. When we build canoes together, we blend the knowledge of the various cultures. It's really quite amazing."

They are on the beach now and have veered away from the village. A few hundred yards ahead there is an outlet where the creek finds the larger sea. Richard realizes the building on the other side is their destination.

"When was all this accomplished?" Richard asks his son. He can now discern how much work has gone into the building. He estimates that the warehouse is ten times the size of his cabin, perhaps even larger.

Kevin doesn't answer at first.

"You and your friends, your partners . . ."

". . . Linus and Danny . . ."

". . . You did this yourselves?"

"Yeah. With help from other people, though, you know people with a certain expertise. Electricians, carpenters. You know, people helped in the way they do here."

"But when, Kevin?"

They are close to the building now and father and son come to a halt to deal with the important question.

"In the past few weeks, I guess," Kevin says then.

"You guess?"

"Yeah. Time here is weird, Dad. You know that. Ultimately we don't keep track of it. We lose the will to want to."

Richard nods.

"So it's hard to answer your question in terms of time periods that you'd understand."

Richard says nothing to this.

"Time here doesn't measure itself the way it's measured in the other world. And we don't measure it either."

"But there are days," Richard counters with mild exasperation. "There are nights too."

"Sure," replies Kevin. "But we don't count them. There's tomorrow, of course, but beginning with the day after tomorrow, measuring time here gradually comes to a halt. There's no next week or next month, or next year."

Richard considers his son's words a moment. "So, in terms of Oblivion time, I have no idea how long I've been coming here and then going back."

"No."

"And back there?"

Kevin shrugs. "Back there only misses you while you're here for a few minutes at most."

"You don't know how long you've been in Oblivion, do you?" Richard asks.

"Not in a measured sense. And I don't care, Dad. What difference do measured days, weeks, months, years mean?"

Richard is aware of a powerful emotional ambivalence at this moment. Oblivion feels as wrong as it is right just now. Half of his nature is jealous of Kevin's life here, half of it is a bit ashamed of it.

When he glances at his son, torn in this way, he finds Kevin smiling at him. "You have to endure this kind of existential crisis," Kevin says gently. "Until you choose."

"You?"

Kevin nods. "I remember it."

"It doesn't feel good," Richard says.

"No. I remember, Dad."

They stand there a moment or two longer.

"Want to meet Linus and Danny?" Kevin asks.

Richard nods. "Yes, I do," he says.

LINUS IS BLACK AND TALL AND MUSCULAR, slightly older than Kevin, which doesn't mean much in Oblivion, especially to Richard who doesn't remember here in this world what five decades means in that other one. Danny, it turns out, is Mohawk, the oldest of the three, at least that is how he appears with a bit of gray in his dark hair.

There is a large canoe, an outrigger, on large concave sawhorses here in the warehouse. In the background is a wall of tools, chisels, hammers, saws, everything neatly hung on nails and pegs. Richard stands there a moment, impressed. If the layout is any indication, Kevin and his partners are accomplished at what they are doing.

"Whaddyuh think, Dad?" says Kevin.

"Beautiful," his father says. "The boat looks . . ."

". . . I know," interrupts Kevin. "Polynesian, North American, African, all at the same time."

"I guess that's it," says Richard, taking Kevin's word for it, the cultures unremembered by him at this moment. "The main thing is that it's beautiful, no doubt about it."

"Not done yet," Kevin says. "It'll have a small mast, a sail. You can sail or paddle depending on the weather conditions."

The four of them stroll around the boat a couple of times. They pass a rudder, a tiny cabin, a place to store gear.

"Whose design?" Richard asks.

It's Linus who replies. "All three of us," he says. "At least three different approaches were brought to this project. Maybe even more. We haven't had the time to go back and research the history. We'd rather build boats than figure out the smaller details of their origins. But we know culture influences boatbuilding the way it does every other art form."

"Beautiful," Richard remarks again, understanding Linus's point of view.

"Maybe, when it's done, you can go out in it with us," Kevin says. "After we've tested it out."

Richard glances at Kevin's friends, to make sure.

"Absolutely," they say nearly in unison.

"You're happy here?" Richard asks Kevin's two partners when he is leaving. "In Oblivion, I mean?"

Both of them nod and gesture at the outrigger nearby. "Look what we get to build," says Danny.

"It's beautiful work, you guys," Richard says.

All three builders respond with a smile.

DEREK GIVES HUMANITY FIFTY YEARS. MAX! "I'm kind of disgusted with everything today," the homeless man says.

Richard gapes at him a moment. "Just so I'm clear," he says at last. "You mean *extinction?*"

Derek nods. "I mean extinction."

"How? The environment?"

The homeless man nods again. "The environment and our own unscrupulousness. A rapidly deteriorating environment, vicious, even catastrophic storms and natural disturbances, and the ensuing ruthlessness of humanity's self-interest."

"I'm not following you," Richard says peevishly. "You sound like a lawyer. Give it to me in layman's terms."

"Rising sea levels, weather extremes, food, water, and shelter shortages, tornadoes, hurricanes, typhoons, blizzards, ice storms . . . ." He stops to take a breath. "Increased crime, hatred, political autocracy, genocide, religious warfare, economic collapse. It'll all fall apart and everyone will die. And then there's all those nuclear weapons that are lying around waiting for some maniac to use them. People forget about *those* these days, but they're still out there. Nuclear weapons can still destroy the planet many times over. Imagine those rockets and bombs in careless or unscrupulous hands." Derek shivers, which helps him to make his point.

Richard is tempted to snort with disdain over the nearly hysterical exaggeration in his friend's opinion, but Derek is usually deadly serious about topics such as these. This morning he's on a rant.

Light snow is falling here on the street, but barely. It's cold. There are sooty and littered snowbanks in the city, although they are not very high. The setting on their street corner near Cascade Enterprises and Starbucks seems to be almost pristine underneath the gentle snowflakes, except for people hurrying by and cars honking their horns, as if perpetually annoyed in spite of winter's attempt to be aesthetically pleasing.

"People won't let it happen," Richard says at last. "There are problems ahead but the ship will be righted in the end, before the debacle you're talking about. Common sense will prevail."

"Nope," says Derek flatly. "Not this time. That's what everyone wants to think, but it isn't so." He gestures at the throng of passersby talking on cells, texting, scurrying here and there, lugging purchases, clearly oblivious. "Are any of these people righting the ship? Do any of them connect the dots?"

Richard admits the sample passing along the street this morning isn't inspiring, but they're a very small group. "But we have leaders, scientists, people with power."

Derek is ready for him. "Not enough people are listening to scientists. Or being *allowed* to listen to scientists. And too many of the others are in it for themselves, either economically or politically."

Richard shakes his head. "If the rich and the powerful knew they were doomed, they'd put on the brakes right now, right?"

"Shit," says Derek. "The rich and the powerful don't think beyond themselves either. That's what wealth is for, isn't it? Thinking you're invulnerable? Thinking the rules, Mother Nature's and otherwise, don't apply to you?"

"You mean they can wall themselves in, avoid the cataclysm? Is that what you're saying?"

"That's precisely what I'm saying."

"That's crazy," Richard says. "I don't mean you, in this case. I mean *them*. That would be crazy."

"Yeah," says Derek from his piece of cardboard on the cold sidewalk.

"Crazy. You're forgetting that allied oil interests sold oil to Hitler in World War Two so that Rommel could keep fighting in North Africa. For the sake of doing business, that's giving the enemy the means to shoot at and kill your own kids."

Dozens more people pass along the street. Richard notices how oblivious they are to the homeless man and the friend who has not given up on him, standing nearby.

"Crazy is an understatement," Derek says at that point.

"I suppose outer space is always an option," Richard says after a time.

"You mean as a destination for the rich?"

"I guess so."

"If so," Derek replies. "Shame on them and the horse they rode in on. Every day I wander down here to this street corner with the rich on my back. It's why I'm here. So people can see what a broken back looks like, how a back can be broken by someone's greed. Maybe they'll look at me and recognize why they have a sore back, what they have to carry around day after weary day."

Richard gazes around a moment. The snow continues to fall lazily, perhaps a little thicker, mercifully silent against the racket of the traffic and human congestion.

"Yeah, I know what you're thinking. I'm the one without a job, without a home. Some would say I'm the one riding the system. The rich say they carry the shiftless lazy *us* on *their* backs," says Derek. "The reverse is true, Richie. Corporate bailouts. Tax breaks and loopholes. Offshore accounts. *We* carry *them*. Have done so ever since they were kings and princes, ever since they were slavers."

Richard contemplates this but says nothing. Then, "You want another Starbucks?"

Derek considers the invitation. "Better not," he says at last. "The caffeine. I'm cranky enough as it is."

THE MAN RICHARD SEES IN THE DISTANCE one day looks like Derek. And, just for a moment, he remembers Derek, his friend who was a lawyer when both of them were young. And just for a second, he catches a glimpse of the Derek in his more recent memory, the one he almost—but not quite—knows is a homeless man on an urban corner of the other world back there where life is so much different.

On this day, in Oblivion, it is drizzling. Richard is on the beach. It's a colder rain than usual, slanting towards him in a breeze pummelling the ocean, which offers up breakers that crash on the shore.

"Derek?" Richard muses aloud. He moves forward a step.

But the man who resembles a distant memory of Derek, tall but unclear in the distance, turns towards the woods with long, hurried strides and disappears into the trees.

For a long time, Richard stands on the rain-swept beach. Cold. Wet. Wondering if the man he saw was actually there at all.

The constant going back and forth, the chronic lack of memory from one world to the other, his apparent unwillingness to choose. That man in the distance—if perhaps it was Derek—might have had some answers about what he should do to make up his mind.

RICHARD IS APPREHENSIVE AS HE DRIVES HIS AUDI into Frank Prentice's driveway. It is not an unfamiliar apprehension—he has felt it numerous times over the years demarcating his working life—but he cannot remember feeling this kind of dread so deeply. It strikes him how much he does not want to be here. He does not want to sell his labour to the despicable despot who lives in the modern castle nearby. He does not want to play this game, with Prentice, even with Alex, who sits beside him in a state of apprehension all her own. When did everything come to this? Why must he shortly climb on a block in Prentice's home to have his teeth checked, the state of his muscle tone examined, the compliance of his attitude confirmed, the sublimation of his free will assured? He tells himself his thoughts are merely metaphorical but deep inside his soul he knows it's the truth—that tonight is the second of two meetings that add up to surrender to a life of work and consumerism on behalf of the family he is supposed to support.

Prentice's home is extremely large, occupying several acres of rolling landscape. In the distance the Braddocks can make out a pond, but winter has grayed it and tufts of disheartened grasses poke through what remains of the late winter snow. The house itself is a layered collection of segments, as if confused in some way between being a house or a sprawling condo or apartment building. Richard is reminded of a bowl of jelly formed into cubes, the kind of dish served for dessert in diners he frequented in his university days. These particular cubes, constructed of glass, stone and mortar in no particular pattern, are a haphazard mess—there are enough of them to convey wealth, but the effect is so incoherent it ultimately reveals nothing more than a lack of architectural taste. Yet clearly an architect has had a hand in the house's design. The dichotomy is fascinating: to Richard the home offends the landscape on which it has been built, (a little like the abrasive character of Prentice himself) and Richard sits in the blazing floodlights, feeling irritable and hopeless.

"Are you okay?" Alex asks after a moment or two, after he has pulled to a stop and remains motionless behind the wheel.

Richard knows he has sighed deeply. When he sighs it troubles Alex, usually annoying her. She interprets his sighs as criticisms of *her* or of a world about which they now fail to agree, the same one to which she now doggedly clings. "I'm fine," he says quickly. "The house. It's ugly."

Alex says nothing to this. "What do you think it's worth?" she asks instead.

"I have no idea." Then, to appease, her, "A few million, of course."

A moment passes.

"Well," says Richard at last. "Let's get it over with."

This time it is Alex who sighs as they get out of the car. He has conveyed his terrible attitude and Alex will feel threatened for a part of the evening until things settle down. Still, Richard is a little surprised that they are not getting along in this setting; in the past, a kind of professional solidarity has generally kept the peace between them, moderating their impatience. But this evening, Richard senses he and his wife are both exhausted by the prospects of going through the evening's demands, albeit in dissimilar ways. To admit it, though, would only exhaust them further. Life, in quandaries such as these, in a state of disingenuousness like this, is a fine mess indeed.

When Prentice answers the door he is alone, but for a glass of whisky in his right hand. "Scotch," he says when Richard glances at the drink and its rattling ice cubes.

"Hard to argue with that," Richard says, already steeled for a night of expressing obsequious reassurance. "My wife, Alex," he adds. "Frank Prentice, Honey."

They shake hands. Alex has worn a snug sweater to make the most of her ample bosom. Prentice's gaze pounces on this fact for a moment too long, before turning towards a room his guests cannot see.

"Gloria? Where are you?" he shouts. "Our guests are here." His voice explodes in the great hall.

Richard manages to avoid being visibly startled.

But Gloria arrives as if rocket-propelled, carrying a goblet of wine of her own. Richard concludes right away that she is already tipsy.

"My wife, Gloria," Prentice says, handing her his glass, the ice cubes still tinkling.

More "how do you do?s."

Trophy wife, thinks Richard without expression. Tall, blonde, slim, pretty, striking figure. He knows Alex is wondering if she's had cosmetic work done.

Prentice, unencumbered by his drink, hangs their coats in a gigantic closet nearby.

"Everyone else, the kids and their entourages, are in the family room," Prentice says, placing one hand each on the small of the backs of both women to steer them where he wants them to go.

Richard follows behind. Oh great, a crowd. Then, again . . . Digging for his sense of humour, he imagines everyone walking ahead of him naked from behind. He feels pleasantly irreverent to fancy nude buttocks illuminating the way to his destination, gleaming and hairless and jiggling to the beat.

PRENTICE HAS FOUR CHILDREN, TWO OF EACH. They range in age from eighteen to twenty-five. Each has brought a girlfriend or boyfriend. None of the children are Gloria's, Prentice is quick to point out early in the proceedings. If Gloria has children as a trophy wife, she apparently keeps them elsewhere, where they can be neither seen nor heard. As for Prentice's progeny, they are flat and predictable. Familiarity with the nature of their lives together, the riches and the copious amounts of liquor, Richard decides, combine to make everything in their lives basically tolerable for the Prentice clan, or so it seems to him.

"The kids won't be joining us for dinner, they're all going out," Prentice explains at one point. "But I wanted you to meet them."

"Thank you," Alex says from her place on the loveseat beside her husband, although Richard knows she is more gratified for the implication in Prentice's words that he will likely be offered the job with Prentice's company than she is by Prentice's offspring. Alex has remarked many times that she loves and enjoys *her* children. Everybody else's are just pains in the ass.

Conversation at this point is all about the young people, school and careers, celebrities, the fun they had at exclusive parties they enjoyed the previous fall when they attended the international film festival. They name drop celebrities and talk about the selfies that they snared. Like his own children and their friends, Prentice's family is entirely at home in this new millennium's technological cult. Each of them, at some point during the conversation, drifts away to text someone or chase information on the Internet through an app of some kind, before nodding or smiling at someone to acknowledge something they did not actually hear or see. One of the young people seems to be playing a game on his cell phone—every now and then he grimaces and then apologetically smiles at the screen as if the grimace has offended it. Yet, just when Richard is becoming comfortable with their lack of interest, one of them addresses him with a remark and he feels strange again, aware that he is from a different tribe than these odd millennial beings who behave so disingenuously towards him. It strikes him that encountering and trying to communicate with a lost tribe in an equatorial jungle would be less difficult, less awkward. At least a primitive tribe wouldn't be trying to multi-task.

Soon, though, as if the final buzzer has sounded at a sporting event, the young people get up and abruptly depart. The family room, spacious now, is left to the two adult couples. A pall descends on the room, a silence that walks in naked. Richard is clearly aware of how much he hates this evening. He wants to glance at his watch because the slow passage of time will reinforce how much he suffers. But to do so would be worse than death, if witnessed. His watch remains ignored on his wrist.

Prentice has put his hand on his wife's knee. He pinches it slightly. "Gloria, do you think you could rustle up some cheese and crackers or something. I don't know about Richard and Alex, but I'm starving."

"Sure, Honey," Gloria says, rising.

All of them watch Gloria leave the room. Richard confirms that Gloria has already had a lot to drink. Her gait out of the room seems to swim in on itself, as if eddying around a cluster of beachside stones. Richard wonders for whose benefit the exaggerated wiggle is conceived.

"So how long have you guys been married?" Prentice wants to know.

"Going on twenty-five years," Richard replies.

"Twenty-two," corrects Alex gently.

"Not bored yet?" Prentice smiles at his own joke but they all know he isn't joking.

"No," reply the Braddocks in almost perfect unison.

"Gloria's my third wife," their host explains in the way that he might report a hangnail.

Richard nods and smiles. Yup, Gloria is the classic definition of a trophy wife. The tan. The tall, slim build. The perfect ass. The rest of it. Of course she is.

"Great with my kids," adds Prentice. "Terrific in bed."

Again Richard nods, his smile more difficult to replicate this time.

"Marriage is funny," Prentice says. "We overestimate it. We try to make it bigger than it needs to be. No offense to you two in saying so, I mean twenty-two years is good, but marriage, you know, it's not the edifice people try to make it out to be."

"It takes work, all right," admits Alex.

Richard glances at her briefly, feeling a trifle betrayed by her words.

"You have to experiment," says Prentice. "Try things on for size. Demystify the thing, marriage, I mean, take its clothes off, parade it around naked, so to speak. Marriage shouldn't frighten us. It shouldn't be frightened *by* us either."

Richard nods despite the obtuseness he finds in Prentice's words.

But Gloria is back with a large tray of hors d'oevres, which she sets down on the coffee table between them. Richard is relieved she has intruded on Prentice's line of conjecture and its implied sexual imagery. The tray contains crackers of various kinds, a couple of plates of cheese, some trimmed vegetables someone—or Gloria—prepared in advance. Gloria explains the dips.

"Try this one," she says, gesturing. "Lime and avocado. You wouldn't believe where I got the recipe."

"Tell us where you got the recipe," her husband says, familiar with a story that has been told before, giving his permission to its telling once again.

Gloria grins. "Off the side of a tractor trailer we were passing on the highway one day. It think it was President's Choice. I looked up—Frank is such a crazy fast driver—and I had time to see lime and avocado dip as we whizzed by. Then I looked it up on-line. So here it is."

"Amazing," says Alex in just the perfect way, taking a shard of green pepper and dipping it into the tractor trailer recipe in an enthusiastic way.

Richard tries some too.

"Oh, Gloria, it *is* good," says Alex.

"Delicious," Richard adds.

"Of course, you have to add other stuff, other items, to make it your own," says Gloria.

"They can't put the entire fucking recipe on the side of a truck, now can they?" snorts Prentice, addressing this to all of them.

Gloria flushes, a trifle wounded.

And so it goes in this way, they nibble and chat, nibble and chat. Sometimes it is all four of them. Sometimes the women talk to the women and the men to the men. But they discuss the usual topics. Fashion. Money. The market. Money. Politics. Money. Pop culture. Money.

Then, a time later, after a second and third cocktail, a female voice with a fairly pronounced accent tells them from the doorway that dinner is now ready. Prentice encourages them to follow him to the dining room right away.

RICHARD HAS NEVER SEEN SUCH A LARGE DINING ROOM in a private home. They are not served, but the meal has been set up in buffet fashion along a table at the head of the room a few feet from a large dining table. Four place settings have been set at one end of the table, which otherwise could hold twenty people or so.

"Do you entertain a lot?" Alex asks Gloria as they approach the buffet.

"I'd say so," their hostess replies. "Business mostly. Frank's children and their friends. Not much fancy stuff. Frank's a meat and potatoes guy. No spicy stuff. No *brown* food."

Richard winces. Each time he does not challenge a slur he feels drawn into the bigotry of it, as if he has subscribed to it all along. He cannot challenge Gloria's slur; he is a commoner held prisoner by the tyranny of the royal court.

"My kids all have entourages," Prentice is saying behind him, clearly proud of the fact. "My place is their place. That would include the culinary spread."

As one, Richard and Alex say, "Of course."

And Richard ruminates over parasites because his world is filled with them.

They continue in two short lines along the buffet table. Italian food mostly. Two pasta dishes, a rice. A seafood lasagna. Chicken. Meatballs. Salads. At the end of the table, in a perfect dome, Richard recognizes a Zucatto they will have for dessert. Prentice loads his plate with enthusiasm. Although the food looks pleasing, Richard uses more care. Alex, he knows, is watching him, measuring his servings for appropriateness. Too much and he'll look unemployed, virtually homeless. Too little and he'll insult his hosts.

The two women, as expected, pick at the food like birds.

"What about you, Gloria?" Richard asks. "Do you have children of your own?"

"No," says Gloria, not looking up from a salad she is serving herself.

Compelled to by the ensuing silence, Richard glances at Alex and she is transmitting one of her looks. He recognizes it and translates: Don't ask questions, let *them* ask the questions. Alex could be right. His question and Gloria's terse reply have initiated a silence.

"Gloria's a terrific mother to my children," Prentice says behind him, filling the gap.

"They're wonderful kids," adds Gloria.

"That's great," Richard says, hoping his words are recovery enough to satisfy Alex's fears.

They move to the table with their plates and sit down.

As they begin to eat, Prentice begins the not unexpected speech about being a self-made man. Richard continues to be astounded by the number of times he has heard the self-made man speech. Its cliches and fundamental bombast. The speech drones on like an electric saw through its various necessary components—the sweat of my brow, the dangers of too much specialized education, how the smart are actually stupid and lacking focus ("Too much university, not enough high school," Prentice pronounces at one point, grinning broadly at his own wit), how one has to be strong and dispassionate to succeed, resisting the forces of society that drive over-regulation and laziness, that "defy the natural purity of the free market." He repeats that line twice, clearly in awe of it—"the natural purity of the free market."

Dutifully, through all of this, Richard nods and expresses other forms of apparent agreement. He feels disingenuous, mostly because he is betraying himself more than Prentice by his silence, by his acts of agreeableness.

"People like you and me, Richard," Prentice maintains, "made the world what it is today. We're at the root of all of its success. We drive the wheels of progress. The slackers and liberals forget all that. They forget that everything they have was provided by our initiative, our investment, our financial risk. Where would they be without us? Nowhere, that's where. Nothing would have been invented."

Thank god for the food, Richard reflects, noticing how much Prentice drinks. Prentice is an ugly man—the way too much liquor relaxes, even causes the folds of his face to droop, only makes it worse.

Prentice serves himself seconds from the buffet. The others moan that they need room for dessert.

Richard watches Prentice eat and talk. A kind of patient disgust he has never noticed so strongly before makes him feel terribly sad. He feels like he holds himself in a vicious bear hug in case, should he let go, he will break apart.

AT SOME POINT AFTER DINNER AND DESSERT Frank Prentice and his wife continue drinking and Alex, at a slower pace, continues drinking, while Richard sips at Perrier. Richard begins to grow uncomfortable about Frank Prentice's agenda. Prentice, to Richard's dismay, has offered to let them spend the night if Richard gets too drunk to drive (an offer Alex declined because they haven't brought any overnight supplies). "Gloria and me, well, we like to sleep in the nude, if you know what I mean," says Frank.

Richard glances at Gloria and notes she does not blush or feign any disapproval. He switches his gaze to Alex, wondering if she feels as uncomfortable as he does, but his wife resists the opportunity to meet his glance.

They've been talking about movies. More drinks are served. "Gloria and I have different tastes," says Prentice. "The guy-woman thing."

Richard can only nod.

"Frank sleeps through romance," says Gloria without drollness.

"But not through sex," says Prentice.

Gloria gives him the required naughty wink.

The Braddocks laugh dutifully.

"Who feels like a swim?"

Richard and Alex hesitate. They have no bathing suits.

"There's an indoor pool, sauna. The works," says Prentice.

"We have lots of swim wear," Gloria adds, "just for situations like this."

"If you're the kind who needs it," puts in her husband with a snort. "Either way, it'll shake out the cobwebs. If I don't stop drinking for a bit I won't be good for much of anything."

Richard's discomfort grows. Could he ever work for or *with* a man he finds so unsavoury?

Alex is nodding her head at her hostess, conveying she could do with a swim and some time in the sauna.

Prentice is all over her decision to go along. "Come on, Richard. Let's go change and give the women a chance to get ready."

They leave everything in the dining room behind them. As soon as they are gone, Richard knows, staff will show up to clean up the mess, discreetly and on cue.

THE ODOR OF CHLORINE ASSAILS RICHARD'S NOSTRILS. The echo that is pool water inside a cavernous room confronts him. Richard treads barefoot through this setting on his way to a sauna near a small hot tub. While Prentice checks the dials in the sauna, Richard takes a moment at the large windows looking out over Frank Prentice's immaculate and large back yard. Spring has not sprung in the slightest—it's the second half of March and too early in the year for that. The land is brown and leafless, looking nearly post-apocalyptic in the sparse moonlight outside, now that most of the snow has melted.

Prentice joins him at the window. "The women will be along soon," he says, as if impatient, as if Richard should be impatient too.

And Richard senses at this moment that he knows what is coming. He feels a rush of strange, commingling emotions that arrive in a flurry of babbling argument, trying for a moment to outshout one another. Trepidation, anger, frustration, sadness. These voices screech at him like a tone-deaf choir.

"You and Alex," Prentice says. "What's your arrangement?"

Richard decides he must go with this to wherever it goes. "Arrangement?" he echoes.

"Your marriage. Do you do the open thing or the conventional?"

"The conventional." In the cavernous room Richard thinks he sounds like a soldier responding to a superior officer. He imagines himself saying *conventional, Sir.* Even in his imagination, he doesn't like the sound of it.

Prentice begins to lead him towards the sauna. "Your choice? Alex's? Both of you? Or have you never talked about it?"

"Both of us," says Richard, following Prentice into the sauna. The heat, the humidity slap his flesh. "Both of us," Richard says again to Prentice's back.

"You've talked about it?"

"Not recently. It hasn't come up." In fact, it hasn't come up for decades, Richard knows. As far as he remembers now, it may never have been discussed during their entire marriage, not even in conjecture about friends or as some kind of prank. But he's not going to let Frank Prentice in on that.

"Gloria and me," says Prentice. "We're open."

"Well," replies Richard, knowing he must reply. "We're all different people."

The men sit down on the sauna benches. They begin their perspiring.

"We know other people like us," Prentice says. "The open idea, I mean. Sometimes we get together."

"Like a club?" Richard's mouth is dry. He knows some kind of pitch is coming.

"No. Not so formal."

Richard just says, "Oh."

"Personally, I always find it more fun the first time," Prentice says.

"The first time?"

"With new people."

"Oh."

"I like it to be a first time a lot." Prentice laughs as if what he has just said was very amusing for both of them.

"You mean a new couple?"

"Yeah. It's the variety thing, I guess," Prentice says. "But sanctioned. Not cheating."

They fall silent.

Richard gives the silence a moment to endure, then, "Employees too?"

The door opens then and the two women, Gloria and Alex, slip inside, wrapped in towels. Richard very nearly jumps, as if in guilt. He is angry at this. What does *he* have to be guilty about? He glances at Alex, trying to read her expression, her understanding of what is going on at this moment, but he can find nothing in her eyes to interpret. The two women merely smile, like servers greeting guests in a restaurant. At this moment, Richard realizes his current life needs Stepford wives. He doesn't, but his life does. He feels ashamed of his life. How can his life require a vacuity that he does not want or respect?

Prentice is looking at the women, imagining perhaps, maybe comparing them.

"Employees too?" Richard asks again.

His question gets Prentice's attention. "Yes," says Prentice brusquely. "Why would they object?"

"Because they're committed to the conventional approach," says Richard. "Because that's what they prefer, I guess."

Richard gazes at Prentice to make certain he has been understood. Prentice gazes back at him.

Alex can feel the tension, but it's Gloria who breaks the silence. "Honestly," she says. "Are you two going to talk business all night?"

"No, honey," Prentice says. "When you girls are ready, I think it's time for a dip. And then I'm afraid we're going to call it a night."

Alex glances at her husband and he knows she senses something. "Yes," says Richard. "A wonderful dinner but I'm afraid it's getting late."

They swim in silence. For a few moments the water is cold. Then they get used to it. The water. Not the silence. Everything is awkward from that point on, right to the very end.

IT'S LATE WEEKEND TRAFFIC ANYWAY. Richard finds his way through it in silence, glad for the distraction. Beyond the fatigued goodbyes at the door, nothing much has been said since the swim in the pool.

"Okay, what happened?" Alex asks at last, when Richard has cleared the worst of the traffic and they are nearly home.

"In the sauna?"

"Yes. I felt a tension. What happened? Was something said? Did you do something wrong? What were you talking about?"

"Marriage," replies Richard, the one word he will for now provide to answer all of her questions. "Marriage," he says again with an almost giddy aridity.

THE DETAILS DON'T REALLY COME OUT until they get home. Richard can't find a pleasant way to explain anything while he is driving and he is afraid that Alex will be bitterly disappointed that he won't get the job at Calliope Resources. In fact, she may question how he knows this, regardless of what he tells her, but her disappointment will not let her understand what happened. And his feelings all night about Prentice? He'd best stay away from that—she'll think the human failing is his, that he judged a man so harshly he judged himself right out of a job.

Once home, at least they don't go immediately to the bedroom. If something bad is going to happen, Richard would like it to take place somewhere else, the family room, the living room, even the kitchen. So it is that they end up in the living room.

"Nightcap?" Richard asks.

Alex shakes her head. The days of pleasant post mortems on the heels of a social event, with one final drink before bed, are now years gone by. Richard realizes this fact powerfully at this moment, remembering how he would find himself a scotch with some ice back then, soon listening to the tinkle of the cubes as he and Alex laughed and talked. But tonight he would have to drink alone and he doesn't want to at this point. So he sits down on the love seat beside her. It's going to be a meeting.

"Are you trying to keep me in suspense? If you are, I wish you'd stop."

"No," says Richard. "I just don't know where to begin."

"This sounds serious." Alex takes a deep and noisy sigh. "He's not going to give you the job, is he?"

"No. Probably not."

"You mean you don't know?"

"Not officially. He didn't say anything."

"For god's sake, Richard, be clear! You're just confusing me. I don't know what *happened*. What you're *talking* about."

"Okay, Alex. Okay. Give me a minute. It's kind of delicate."

They sit in a burred, prickly silence, like children who now realize they are lost in a small woods.

"He's not going to offer me the job," reports Richard at last. "He hasn't said so, but I know he's not going to do it."

"Oh, Richard, how do you know that?"

"Because I was there when it happened."

Alex's eyes are wide with disappointment, with alarm. "Something in the sauna, right?"

Richard nods. "He wanted to wife swap. I said we didn't do that."

Alex's dismay intensifies. "He *said* that?"

Richard continues to nod. "Not in those words, exactly, not that boldly, but that's what he was talking about. He and Gloria have an open marriage and they sleep with other couples who have open marriages. He asked about us. I said we had a conventional marriage, in short we didn't sleep with other people's husbands and wives. I know it was over after that. If you want the job, you do what Frank Prentice wants. I declined in this instance, that's all. He won't hire someone who declines *anything*."

A long silence.

"Alex?"

"Hush," she says. "I'm thinking."

Richard waits a moment. Then, "About what?" he asks.

"Maybe you're just reading too much into what he said or what he didn't say," Alex offers at last.

"I'm afraid not," Richard replies.

"You need that job, Richard."

"Not enough to agree to terms like that."

Alex studies her hands. They are trembling. Richard sees it too.

"You could have played along a bit, Richard."

He is staggered by her words. "You mean flirt with him and the idea?"

"No," says Alex. Then, "Maybe. I'm just saying you didn't have to be so definitive about it, so abrupt. You must have been abrupt. I could feel the tension in the sauna, when Gloria and I walked in."

"Never mind if I was abrupt, which I wasn't, by the way. I *was* clear, straightforward. That's not abrupt. It's just straightforward. His job posting said nothing about swapping wives with him as part of the qualifications, Alex."

"Of course not—I'm not stupid!"

Richard sighs. "I *know* you're not stupid."

"You need that job, Richard."

"No, I don't. Not if it involves swapping wives, even on a temporary basis."

"Are you absolutely sure that's what he meant?" A new frantic tone has entered Alex's voice. He can feel her panic ratcheting up.

"Positive," says Richard. "All of it going back to the invitation to spend the night. You remember that, how we declined because we hadn't brought any overnight things with us?"

Alex merely nods.

"I know what I heard, Alex. I know what he was saying."

"You mean like a foursome?"

"I don't know. I didn't get any idea it was a foursome. Maybe if the conversation had gone further—you know, you and I open to being open—then maybe it would have gotten to that. Jeezus, Alex, I don't need a job bad enough for any of this. I don't know why we're examining the obvious so much."

"But you *do* need a job."

Annoyed, Richard gets up and moves away from the love seat a few steps. "What are you saying, Alex?" he says after a moment.

"I'm saying you need a job."

"Are you implying I should have gone along with him?"

"You mean, *if* that was what he meant?"

"Jesus, Alex. There is no fucking 'if', okay?"

"You don't know that. You don't know that for certain."

"Yes, I do. I was there. He and his wife get bored, he said. They sleep around, with other people, out in the open. He wanted to know if that's what we did too. I said no."

Alex says nothing.

He waits.

"You need that job," Alex murmurs eventually. Her voice has a pronounced tremor in it now.

"What are you saying, Alex? Stop dancing around things."

"Just that you need that fucking job. You have *no* job."

"Are you saying we should have swapped sexual favours with Frank and Gloria Prentice?"

"C'mon, Richard, that's not the point."

Richard is furious. "Is that what you're saying?"

"What?"

"That I should have offered you to Frank Prentice and tried to sleep with Gloria? Is that what you're saying? Because I need the job?"

Alex hesitates. "Of course not," she murmurs at last. "That's not what I'm saying at all."

At that moment, to his dismay, Richard does not entirely believe her. He retreats to silence.

"It's just that you need that job."

"Not enough to whore around for it."

"Jesus, Richard. That's such a stupidly over the top thing to say."

"No, it's not."

"Yes, it is. No one, especially me, has ever asked you to whore around for a job."

"Frank Prentice did."

Alex leaps up from the loveseat, growing ever more enraged. "We don't *know* that," she screams.

Richard's voice is calm. "Yes, we do," he replies.

"Are you fucking crazy?" Alex screams. She's pacing now gesticulating frantically, shrieking at him. "You don't have a job and you don't *want* one. We're in terribly fragile circumstances. We could lose everything."

"We still have the better part of two years for me to find work, Alex."

This only enrages her further. She positions herself in front of him so that she can back away from him in fear. "Stop it, stop it, stop it!" she screams.

"Alex, everything is okay. This makes no sense."

"Don't come near me. I want you to stop talking and you won't stop talking." Her voice is an agonized shriek. She backs away as if he has advanced on her, as if he might reach out and strike her.

But he has not moved. One arm reaches out for her, to bring her into his arms. His voice is calm and low. "It's okay, Alex. We don't need Frank Prentice."

She screams her response. "Stop talking about it! Stop bullying me with this! I want you to stop talking and you won't stop talking!" She turns and hurries out of the room.

In a moment, he hears the bedroom door slam shut.

He makes the effort. Fatigued, having no words that will end this altercation or make everything all right, he treads down the hallway and touches the handle of the bedroom door. The door is locked. Gently, he knocks. "Alex?"

"Stop it!" she screams on the other side. "Leave me alone. Shut up and leave me alone!"

He stands there for a few moments, feeling bruised and shaken. Then he goes back to the living room.

NOW RICHARD POURS HIMSELF THE SCOTCH he didn't have earlier. It is good scotch, but he goes to the kitchen to find ice. He listens to it rattle around in his glass—he uses one of the good crystal glasses he got for Christmas—and gazes at its silky movement through the diamond-like edge of the glass. He is strangely calm. He is sad. The scotch does not entice him as something he should down. He sits in their living room in the dark and sips at the drink. It is the middle of the night. It is the middle of his life. It is the middle of the place where all his choices come together, the ones he has already made and the ones that still seem to wait in the wings.

For a long time, he doesn't think anything very much, although he can't quite shake the image of Alex's ferocious rage. As usual, after fights such as this one, his heart pounds. Underneath everything, he knows, she suffers an equally ferocious fear. Recognizing this, he does not know what he can do. If she would let him, he would take her away from all of this. He would take her away to a smaller city perhaps, where a million dollars is still a lot of money, maybe a place that needs a newspaper reporter. But they've talked about it dozens of times. She will not go. No one, Alex has said, reads a newspaper any more.

He drinks with his thoughts. Eventually he drains the glass. He is suddenly slightly drunk. He returns to the closed bedroom door one more time and, without knocking, in a hushed and gentle voice, asks Alex if she is all right. When there is no answer, he returns to the living room, curls up on the couch and soon falls asleep, not knowing what else to do with the rest of the night. His heart pounds. It is a very long time before he gets any sleep.

TWO DAYS OF DRIFT. Richard wakes up, covered by a blanket. The couch is leather and groans in feeble objection as he turns over on his back, blinking to get his bearings. Alex pads through on her way to the kitchen, neither speaking nor glancing at him. Her face is pale, lack of sleep perhaps, or her residence in what is now the sad phase of her diminishing anger.

"Alex?"

She stops in her tracks, sighs, and gazes straight ahead, refusing to look at him.

"Thanks for the blanket," Richard says.

She glances at the blanket, then at him, clearly mystified by his words. Then she continues on to the kitchen, leaving him to realize he must have retrieved the blanket himself in the middle of the night, although he does not yet remember doing so. The buzz of the scotch perhaps. Or his emotional and physical fatigue.

Alex comes back. "I'm expected at Katie's. I don't know when I'll be back."

"We should talk," Richard says.

But his wife barely nods. She cannot look at him. Why, he wonders, can *he* look at *her*? She goes. He hears her in the front hall for a moment or two, putting on her coat, finding her car keys in her purse. Then he hears the door close behind her.

Richard remains where he is on the couch for quite some time, listening to the groaning leather and wondering what to do and concluding he and his wife are at an impasse. Mostly he feels numb about this. He also still feels shocked by Alex's rage. Richard has always been able to control himself—he doesn't understand rage. He resists understanding it because he believes that understanding it will tempt him to tolerate it, in others, in himself.

He misses Derek when he goes downtown. Finding no Derek where Derek usually is, even this is deeply disturbing. What the hell? Is Derek all right? He looks up and down the street, spins, then searches again, several times.

No Derek. He might have talked about things with Derek. It might have been a comfort.

TWO DAYS OF DRIFT. Dinner out somewhere. A burger and fries. Another scotch, poured over ice on principle, then left barely touched because it tasted funny. Like his tongue is too skinny to find the flavour. He watches a movie, a British murder mystery on Netflix. He sleeps in his own bed that night. For ten hours.

No Derek again when he goes downtown the next day. It smells like spring again. Soiled somehow, the way it did last year when his life was so much different, when he still worked at Cascade Enterprises, before he became the man he appears to be now, whomever that is.

And where the hell is Derek? Derek should know what's going on. Derek should find a way to let his friend know that he is safe.

TWO DAYS OF DRIFT. When he gets up the next day, Richard feels new energy. He digs out his running gear. A run, he suspects, will get him started again, will give him the drive to figure things out, to take action, deal with some kind of resolution—him and Alex, the future, what they are going to do—regardless of what that resolution might be.

Where the hell is Derek? Is Derek all right? Has he moved on without notice, without telling his friend where he was going?

Jesus, where the hell is Derek?

And where am I? wonders Richard. Where the hell have I gone?

After all my angst about making a choice, I can't remember the choice when I made it. I don't remember the moment it happened. I just know I made it and the choice was now behind me—Richard Braddock, just sayin', to Kevin and Violet one day when they are walking along the beach.

LATER

ON THE DAY RICHARD WILL MOVE to Oblivion permanently, he will choose to do so during a run around his neighborhood. At first, everything along the various streets will look the same as it always does when he passes in sneakers and shorts and t-shirt. He will run by stretches of asphalt, hedges trimmed and not quite trimmed, curbs, concrete, trees, flower gardens, garages—like twin or even triplet warts on the fronts of split level homes—and a few daring human beings outside tinkering among all this early, still nearly dormant, tidy nature with a lawn mower or rake or a weed whacker. He will be aware of his breathing, its sound loud and sighing. Not panting. No, sighing. This is how it will sound to him. He will smell spring, muddy, winter debris still giving off its stale aroma. The scene will be so *familiar* to him as he jogs through it, as it passes him on either side. It will seem tediously banal. He will not be aware at first that he is making a choice. He will not consider, for even one second, that he is giving anything up. He will feel no sense of loss. He will not contemplate or feel or believe that anything is slipping away from him, that something is being taken away, that there will be something left behind for him to grieve the loss of. He will be aware, though, as he runs, as his sneakers crunch on the gravel of the walkway and then slap the asphalt suburban streets, that he has been wishing certain things in his life were better, not just for him but for everyone he knows, even, in the end, most astonishingly still, for so many people he doesn't know and will *never* know, the world's beings that he cares about in the humanistic abstract, that he hopes will somehow survive all that assails them, depletes them, diminishes them, trivializes them.

He will be wishing all of these certain, better things on streets that are so, yes, *familiar*, just moments before he sees them differently. His surroundings will shift shape under the weight of his wishing and their familiarity will begin to disintegrate until everything in his suburb is increasingly harsh to him. He will run along the streets towards the high school wishing things were different. He will realize that his act of wishing will, itself, be *familiar* too.

The first of these wishes will be specific: wishing Alex was still in love with him, wishing Alex had wanted to make love with him in the past year or so, wishing Alex would stop fearing what doesn't require fear, wishing Katie hadn't run away from school to live with someone like Dougal, wishing Drake was a son who knew how to be friends with him, and wishing he knew how to be friends with Drake. Wishing he had a job that made him happy. Wishing he had a job at all, and that *he* was the only person his job was intended to satisfy. Wishing the world's various modern technologies, hundreds of them, thousands—so noisy, so distracting, so astonishingly without substance for the most part, so pagan in the way they are worshipped, so dangerous and cruel where their intended uses are extreme—would shut up, fall into silence, move on and leave him alone, or at least become the hammers they need to be to drive the nails that need to be driven, finding some other purpose than merely the generation of profit, some other purpose than pretending to be the technological wand of some religious myth, cell phones and tablets and hair removal devices, computers and electric carving knives, and coffee makers and digital this and digital that, and robots and machines, all of it taking the restraint of its hand off his arm so that he can fall free of the system's fist.

Then will come general wishes, things he would choose if only he had a choice, these arriving in his thoughts in a rush of clarity, as he runs in his neighborhood, needing everything to be different. General wishes, the choices he could make. As he will run, he will find himself wanting a world where there is enough for everyone, where people accept the shared wonder a state of plenty provides, where the prevailing atmosphere is tranquility, a calm so prevalent, so all-encompassing, that there is no war, only peace, where love for all and everything resides in a natural stasis, and the world goes on forever in peaceful harmony. A place where no one has a reason to lie or manipulate. A place that has no greed, no lust for power or authority or control, where envy and contempt are foolish and unnecessary, a waste of human emotion, something to feel with embarrassment instead of inevitability or pride.

One more thing, though, as Richard will run that day. He will think of Drake, his son—at least he will think at first it is Drake, his son. Except it won't be Drake—Drake isn't a runner, no, Drake will probably be playing a shooter game in a basement somewhere with friends. Yet, running, Richard will turn and nearly glimpse his son jogging along beside him, a twin, someone who looks like Drake, who will ponder the phrase with him that he has heard so frequently in the last twelve months of his life: *Everything just lives here.*

Kevin? Will Kevin be his name?

Everything just lives here.

And, at that moment, wondering who Kevin is and then beginning to remember him, even here in the suburbs of this world he is about to depart, Richard will move to Oblivion. As soon as he leaves, back in his city suburb, Richard will be forgotten and the people who forget him will live their lives, from beginning to end, with no knowledge of his existence. Richard will be one of those people the world leaves behind. Richard will be in the place where the world releases the people that it forgets. Richard will be in Oblivion.

But the choice will be Richard's choice, finally made while he is running around a neighbourhood that will, at just the right second, never know that he existed. And he will remember what has forgotten him, the things that he left behind bobbing in the wake of his choice.

HE WILL MAKE LOVE WITH VIOLET at some point not long afterwards. They will be happy and refreshed after making so much love in his cabin together. Richard will make coffee and they will go outside to the porch to drink it. Richard will not yet be used to living in Oblivion exclusively and he will have to adjust to being able to remember too what he needs or cares to remember about the other world where he used to live. Ever increasingly, he will know both worlds in his memory. This one, Oblivion, and the other one back there, where he was a different man. Here, secure in his love for Violet and secure in Violet's love for him, he will be able to sort out the tangles that are as yet unresolved in him. About this place and that place, and the protracted, bumpy road of choice that lies between them.

"What about Alex?" he will ask a couple of times at first.

"Alex won't remember you. You'll remember *her*, though. That life, the one lived *then*."

"And Drake and Katie?"

"You'll remember them. They won't remember *you*. This is Oblivion," Violet adds patiently, "the place where people from the other world exist unremembered."

"Of course," Richard will say. "Of course. I'll be hoping that my children are okay. And they won't know or care that I'm hoping. Right?"

Violet will smile and nod and tuck her head against his shoulder a moment. "That's what we do here in Oblivion," she will say. "We live our lives here hoping everyone back there is okay in the world where we used to live. Over time, it gets much easier to realize that our connection with them is no longer necessary and what we remember about them is only something *we* remember."

"Your children too, Violet."

"Yes. My children too."

Richard will ponder this, aware of the conundrum of being forgotten in the other world as both easy and difficult to understand.

"It shows the importance of choice, Richard," Violet will say. "How we need to live our lives. It's vital to live our lives without shackles, without the bondage of fear. Do you think so?"

"I do," Richard will reply. "I definitely do."

RICHARD WILL PREPARE *THE BULLETIN* MOST DAYS, publishing it once a week and leaving it in various locations in the village where he lives, where residents can pick it up and find out what is going on. Like just about everyone else in Oblivion, he will find time to work with Oblivion's children. He will regularly jog with Kevin and remember when Kevin was one of his three children while here, in Oblivion, he is the only child Richard can ever have.

They will not talk about this much, even though Richard will know that Kevin remembers when he had a twin brother and a sister with a troublesome boyfriend named Dougal. It will be like a story they tell, a legend they can share and enjoy, in a way a mutual invention. Gradually, thinking back on

Alex and Katie and Drake will inspire no regret, no imagined or actual fondness, not really, no wishing of any kind now, for what it could have been back then or what it can be now. Beyond hoping the family that they once knew can survive the peccadilloes and cruelties of their world—the family whose components weren't well known at all, when love was more an idea that one compared to an ideal—most of the time Kevin and his father will find it easier and easier to just forget.

And there will be so much to do in Oblivion because the doing has so much simple purpose: the next meal, making love, enjoying friends, learning hundreds and even thousands of new abilities and pieces of knowledge, having so much more available privacy than the other world would permit, enjoying a free will unquestioned or unencumbered by the other world's collective judgment of what free will should be and whom should be allowed to have it.

"Life is full when there is plenty," Richard will tell his son one day, not for the first time and not for the last, although it amuses Richard to know that Kevin probably knew this before *he* did. The child is father to the man, he said once, probably quoting someone.

Kevin will nod in agreement anyway—Richard is his father, after all, and Oblivion, where one stays much younger than in the other world, appreciates the wisdom of its elders. And there's always that slight and tender zealotry one feels after one chooses, for a brief time anyway, which is forgiven by everyone in Oblivion because it soon evaporates.

KEVIN WILL OFFER ONE OF HIS BOATS to his father and Violet because Richard and Violet have decided to go on a journey to see more of Oblivion. In the end, though, Richard will decline. Instead he will suggest that Kevin travel with them for a day or two to the next community some distance along the shore. Kevin can then take the outrigger back and leave his father and Violet to continue on foot or by bicycle.

They will set out using a sail and will head in a direction that might be east, towards a rich sense of freedom Richard now understands. Sun sparkling on the sea. They will steer the boat and rest on the small deck and water will ripple around them. And they will talk at times about life in Oblivion and about memories of the other world which is so different from this one that each of them chose some time ago.

After a couple of days, Kevin will drop them on the shore and wish them happy trails. There will be embraces all around. No one will ask when Richard and Violet intend to return because Richard and Violet do not know. They will return when they return.

Kevin will depart. Richard will watch his progress along the shoreline for a few minutes before he and Violet pick up their knapsacks and head into the nearby village to find something to eat. There will be lots of food to spare. This is Oblivion—there is always what everyone needs and more of the same besides.

RICHARD AND VIOLET WILL OFTEN TAKE TRIPS along the roads and trails and waterways of Oblivion. By then Richard will have a journalist friend, Angus, who looks after *The Bulletin* while they are away. The lovers will walk to a variety of villages in Oblivion, or they will ride bicycles or be picked up by wagons, meeting new people there, others who've made a choice to live in this place. On one trip, they will walk to a village nestled at the foot of a small range of mountains. Here too they will meet and be welcomed by new people who have chosen.

Richard and Violet will decide to take this walk to other locations in Oblivion whenever they get the mutual urge. They will enjoy travelling this way, finding pleasure in meeting a wide diversity of people. It will become an important part of how they live their lives in Oblivion. And they will have stories to tell about their travels here and about some of the things that happened to them when they lived in the other world, when they recall how limited there their choices actually were.

Their lives will seem unmeasured because they live without fear. Buddha, of course. One single aphorism that bridged both worlds even before Richard chose. But it will be the breadth of the present tense that makes Richard's life so long, the past a microchip, the future barely any kind of chip at all.

EVENTUALLY RICHARD WILL NOT RECALL with any regularity the world where he used to live. He will not think about the lies he used to hear and tell, the myths to which he felt compelled to adhere, the skewed idea of what plenty is: namely too many people with nothing at all, a small few with unimaginable plenty to spare. Instead of remembering the other world with any kind of frequency, Richard will love the plenty and abundance he knows in Oblivion, including the plenty that *time* provides, and he will love the way life goes and goes *on*, its love and tranquility and calm. Things will happen and things will not happen. But there will always be mirrorless love and the time to exist inside it.

ON ONE OCCASION WHEN THEY HAVE BEEN AWAY, Richard and Violet will return to discover that Kevin has met Brooke. She will already have become his companion in Oblivion by the time they return from their travels to the mountains and back. Kevin will be very happy with this new young woman and, sometime later—no one keeps track of time much in Oblivion, even during pregnancies—he and Brooke will have children. In the interim, like his friends Danny and Linus, Brooke will help him design and build boats, something she has always wanted to do and for which she possesses much skill.

Richard will be happy to be a grandfather, much more so than he would have been in the other world. And Violet with him. They will be youthful grandparents, but elders to their grandchildren just the same.

Everything just lives here, they will say, teaching Kevin's children why they—as parents and grandparents—made the wonderful choice that they did. Indeed, *everything just lives here* in Oblivion, but when people say so sometimes, perhaps remembering the first time they ever heard the four words together, they use no emphasis in speaking them, not because all the words are equal, but because, in Oblivion, there are no chants, there is no speaking out in ceremonial unison. In Oblivion no one is the same as anyone else—but everyone is similar because they are *not* the same.

OFTEN GATEKEEPERS LIKE DEREK bring back news from the other world, the way they bring back books and other information for the libraries of Oblivion. News such as this finds its place inside the catalogue of memories the residents of Oblivion already possess. People who have chosen Oblivion feel no responsibility for what goes on in the other world, the changes and developments that take place there, the way matters too often tend to worsen. They have no time to agonize over the way, to a person in Oblivion, the other world just seems to get crazier, more insane over money, power, war, and fear, and the endless, frantic search for something unnecessary to buy.

Derek, asked by his old friend, Richard, will admit that the comprehensive miasma of evil and stupidity, of endless human fear, is worsening.

"Anything specific?" Richard will ask his friend, the way they once did on the city street where they gathered each morning for coffee. "You know, stuff we would have mentioned with a Starbucks in our hand in the old days."

Derek will smile a bit at the near euphemism of Richard's words, "the old days." He will shrug. "More war. They're developing robots as weapons."

"We would have discussed the morality of that," Richard will say. "The lack of morality, I mean. You and me on the street corner. We would have shared a rant."

Derek will nod. He doesn't seem to stay long in Oblivion. Gatekeepers are back and forth, back and forth. Or so it seems to Richard. Richard will never know exactly. Derek will never explain exactly. It's not a state secret. It's just that *everything just lives here* and the questions about how it takes place don't end up very important somehow. *Everything just lives here.* There's no "why" to a statement like that. Or why some people choose to be gatekeepers and others make no such choice.

Soon Derek will say so long and be gone until the next brief time when they encounter one another again.

"So long, Derek," Richard will reply.

And Derek will depart.

Later, Violet, knowing he and Derek have been and continue to be close friends, will ask him what Derek said. Richard will tell her. They will sit silently together for several minutes in sad wonder over the choices being made in the other world that are so opposite to what *they* chose.

"What happens to us," Richard will ask, "if they destroy themselves?"

"I think most of us anticipate some of them will choose differently," Violet will reply.

"Choose Oblivion, you mean?"

"Yes. Choose this over that."

"But what if they don't get a chance?"

"I don't know," Violet will say after a moment's consideration. "*Everything just lives here.*"

SOMETIMES DEREK WILL JOIN HIM in a walk along the beach, when he is back in Oblivion. They will talk like they once did on the street corner near the other world's busy Starbucks. Except the conversation will be different. The necessary change in Richard, the result of the choice he made, will make life itself feel structured by open spaces of ideas that are, themselves, conclusions. Richard's life will feel *concluded* here in Oblivion even though it continues for a very long time in a state of rich tranquility and beauty. It will feel *grown up* to him; this maturity is the way in which it will feel *concluded*. Like he's arrived somewhere important even while the journey isn't over.

"What's going to happen to the people in the other world?" Richard will ask while he and Derek walk along the beach.

"I don't know," Derek will reply calmly. "It's hard for me to say."

Thoughtfully Richard nods.

"It's a matter of choice," Derek will say. "You know that."

"I do indeed."

"You know something, Richard?"

"What?"

"It's the not choosing that kills you. The not choosing is where you fail. Back there, I mean. It's the *not making a choice* that ends and ruins lives. It's the sitting around and letting the world's life happen to you instead of letting your life happen to *it*."

Richard will nod because he knows this already.

The two men will continue to walk the beach until whatever grim sadness in what they have talked about has eased. Then they will discuss easier, even wonderful possibilities instead. They will get together from time to time when Derek is not busy being one of Oblivion's many gatekeepers. They will be old friends within a new friendship. They will have a short past together and a future they do not consider much or ever worry about, past and future separated by a very long present that may or may not be endless.

Both of them will know, after this day, that their sad discussions are primarily over. They will hardly ever speak in sadness again.

STILL, DEREK WILL FIND HIM one morning in particular. They will have learned the end of regret by this time and Richard will ever increasingly begin to take for granted the wonder in the choice that he made. They will sit together by the sea, looking out over the water. It will always be pleasant when Derek comes to Oblivion, which is why he will often look Richard up.

"The people who you used to work with. . ."

"Yes. At Cascade Enterprises."

". . . They go by on their way to Starbucks."

Richard will nod, remembering some of the people from Cascade Enterprises.

"They don't remember you."

"No," Richard will say after a moment, grinning broadly at the understatement in Derek's words. "I don't imagine that they do."

ABOUT THE AUTHOR

Barry Grills is a former chair of The Writers' Union of Canada and the Book and Periodical Council. His short stories have appeared in various literary magazines and anthologies over the years, including Best Canadian Stories. His critically acclaimed memoir, *Every Wolf's Howl* won an Alberta Book Award for its publisher, Freehand Books. His first Fluid Grouse Enterprises book, *Roadkill,* was a finalist in both the Next Generation Indie Book Awards and the Whistler Independent Book Awards. He is also the author of three musical biographies on the lives and careers of Anne Murray, Alanis Morissette and Celine Dion. His work on an updated version of Dion's life, co-authored with Jim Brown, was the source for a CBC television movie. He currently lives and works in North Bay, Ontario, Canada.